Leedles and the Golden Tree

Alex McGilvery

Leedles and the Golden Tree
Alex McGilvery

Copyright Alex McGilvery 2021

ISBN: 978-1-989092-57-6

CHAPTER ONE

The magic ate at Leedles from the inside as if she'd swallowed an ant's nest. All she'd done was whisper a tiny chant to clean the smell of manure from her dress before she went in to wait on customers for her Uncle Urt.

The stable smelled of roses. Reeked more likely, the horses tossed their heads and snorted their displeasure. Leedles fled before the magic escaped. Her Uncle's irritation came close to breaking the Peace of their village.

Not like her parents, no one had ever been like them. Everyone in the village reminded her on a daily basis, as if her family's shame would serve to tame Leedles. All it accomplished was to fuel her desire to escape.

"Leedles," Uncle Urt stepped out the door and wrinkled his nose. "What is that smell?" He stepped forward and raised his fist as if only the thinnest of threads held him back from striking her. "You've been at it again. Smith forbid you from using magic. You have no discipline, no control."

"I just didn't want to stink all night."

Urt growled wordlessly and tore at his hair.

"The farmers know what a stable smells like, they don't care as long as you get them the beer they order. Now, you just smell like a tramp. Twenty-two years, and you still haven't a lick of sense."

His tavern didn't look like much, not much bigger than the houses on either side, only completely open on the main floor, with the kitchen tacked onto the back. Urt yanked open door into the public room and pushed her through, slamming it behind them.

"Don't be so hard on the kid," Karl leaned back on the rickety chair. As the only newcomer in Leedles' lifetime he hadn't earned his way onto the solid benches.

"Do you want to drink, or give me advice?" Urt glared at him, and Karl picked up his mug and made a show of drinking deeply. The rest of the patrons went back to their babble of conversations.

Leedles put on her apron and picked up a tray of mugs. She didn't wait for the men to ask for a refill. Anyone whose mug sat empty got a full one slapped down in front of them. They watched her move through the room. The Peace Tree knew she was no beauty, pale beside the earthen brown of the men. Her mother's fault: the betrayer and stranger. The men didn't condemn her father. Sure, they exiled him, and found his bones in the woods that spring, but they understood.

All night Leedles wove between tables avoiding the lustful or disgusted eyes of the customers. Only Karl, who couldn't know any better as a resident of the Peace only fifteen years, didn't eye her with anything more than pity.

"Go to bed." Uncle Urt closed and barred the door behind the last drunken farmer.

Leedles dragged herself up the steps to the hallways off which her uncle and aunt had their rooms. Their son snored from his room. He'd be up early to make the fire and start the bread. Unless he slept in again.

Leedles slipped through the doorway into her room. Moonlight from the tiny window illuminated the bed. She hung her dress, still wafting rose perfume, on a hook, then folded her shift, and placed it carefully on the stool. With the ants still eating at her, she couldn't abide cloth against her skin.

The cruel light only highlighted her ugliness. She refused to look at herself. The polished steel which functioned as a mirror faced the wall.

Something had changed. Rom's snores had stopped. What if he tried to enter her room again? He'd said he'd opened the wrong door by accident and hadn't known his mistake until he'd laid down on top of her.

Leedles fumbled the wedge out from under the bed and pushed it as far under the door as she could manage. Maybe she should whisper a lock on the door. Only last time, she'd locked every door in the inn, and those on the houses to either side.

She sat in the bed and watched the moonlight slide slowly across the wall. The magic buzzed and coaxed her, but it was a betrayer.

***

Banging woke Leedles.

"Girl, blast it. Get out of bed. Rom's sick and can't do the fire."

Hungover more like it. Beer didn't satisfy whatever drove Rom to drink. He swilled distilled liquor with his friends. Though, truthfully, she had a good idea of what drove him. The same thing driving her – the unalterable boredom of their existence. Sure, the Peace kept them safe, and kept them from murdering each other like the outsiders, but it was dull.

The shift scratched her skin like rough bark. The dress's smell made her gag. How had they put up with it all night? The only thing keeping her from leaping out the window, besides it being too small now, was the refusal to be the next one in her family to break the Peace.

Downstairs, she scraped the ashes out of the stove and fireplace, then set the fire in the stove and laid the wood out ready for the spark in the fireplace. Her aunt had already started the bread.

"I need butter," Aunt Livvy didn't turn from where she chopped carrots for tonight's stew. Leedles could walk naked through the kitchen and her aunt would speak to the air of modesty. She'd never forgiven Leedles' mother for making her brother break the Peace with such bloody abandon. No one knew why he hadn't killed his infant daughter too.

Livvy was one who wished he had.

So was Leedles.

Since she lived, she must be punished for her mother's sin.

Jon would have fresh butter, but only until others came and bought it from him. Leedles swept up the coins set on the counter and ran out the door.

Cold wind blew down from the mountains surrounding Peace on all sides. It rustled leaves on bushes and set flowers to bobbing. Shutters creaked and banged. Leedles once loved days like this. Imagining the wind coming from far away, bringing fantastical stories.

Like everything else, the wind came, but it didn't leave. Nothing left, nobody left. Leedles fought tears away from her eyes. The wind ruffled her dress, mocking her sadness. Always, the magic, stinging inside her, then emptiness.

"Sorry," Jon turned back to stir the tub which would eventually produce cheese. "Dame Coll bought the last."

Aunt Livvy would lecture the air the rest of the morning about tardiness and how the lack of butter would ruin them. It seemed that any setback would ruin them. Leedles couldn't figure how they were still in business.

She wandered through the village, letting the wind blow her where it willed. Something skittered across the cobbles in front of her. A leaf, golden like her hair. Only one tree it could have come from.

The Peace Tree, the golden tree, the tree that never, ever in any story anyone told, shed so much as a single leaf.

They'd find a way to blame her. Leedles chased the leaf through the village. None of the others paid any attention to it, though they frowned or stared after her. Dem licked his lips as she passed. *Ugh.*

The golden leaf slipped through the hedge which surrounded the park where the Tree stood. No noisy children played in these solemn grounds. Only adults, once a year pledging themselves anew to the Peace, disturbed the park. Leedles among them the last four years, wondering what the Peace was for.

Moss grew in the shade. Her feet bounced on it, making her walk like she was drunk. The leaf had vanished.

The Peace Tree stood, unmoved by the wind. The entire village would blow away before any gale disturbed the Tree. If the village blamed her for her parents, she blamed the tree.

More magic, or less would have been her parents' salvation. Violence still ugly, but not sacrilege. Breaking the Peace awful, but not so horrible it made her otherwise perfect father murder her mother with the slaughtering knife, then stand over her until the villagers came, took him away to the gate, and pushed him out of their lives.

Only then had someone thought to rescue the crying babe, still encrusted with gore. In the spring, they would find her father's bones swinging from a tree. Twice cursed, the infant had been thrust into the hands of her Aunt Livvy.

"I don't want you." The only words her aunt ever directed at her.

"I hate you," Leedles threw the words at the Tree, but the wind snatched them out of her mouth. She ran to the Tree to hit it. If she'd had an ax, she'd cut the Tree down, shed its golden sap, crush the village beneath its immense trunk. Let the world hear it crash.

Without intending to, Leedles found herself climbing the tree. The wind blew her against the bark as if it held her safe against falling. Screaming wordlessly, Leedles climbed until her hands bled and her limbs ached.

Her head lifted above the canopy of leaves, and the view shocked her into silence. Fields circled the village, but they were a thin space between the village wall and the forest. Dark green, waving in the wind like a reflection of the clouds, it stretched all the way to the mountains, high and blue in the distance.

"Why?" Leedles screamed. "Why am I alive when everyone wishes I were dead?" She wrenched at the branch in her hand, not caring it held her in place.

The branch snapped.

Leedles plummeted down through the leaves. She had a moment to realize she'd been wrong. All those years wishing her father had killed her too. She'd been wrong.

She wanted to live.

Then she hit the ground and darkness swallowed her whole.

:Go east, across the water. Plant the seed, make a wish.:

CHAPTER TWO

Leedles woke on an unyielding surface. Light came in through a tiny window high in the wall. Rough stones sucked heat from her, but at least she was dry.

She'd heard about this place from Rom's stories of his drunken antics. Created as a place for those who have imbibed more than they should to rest until sanity returns and they are able to keep the Peace.

She lay on the bench and sighed.

"No use making a fuss," he'd said. "All that does is make them keep you in there longer."

She'd wanted to live while she fell, but lying on the hard wood, she couldn't see the point. Nothing had changed. Her life would continue to be a constant reminder to her and the people around her that the peace had been broken. The only time in all the history recorded in the city hall. Some still worried the Peace had vanished and all they had was what they lived.

The patch of light traveled across the wall. The door opened and a tray with food was placed on the floor. The patch moved further as the food grew cold. Leedles couldn't summon enough energy to move. The chill from the stone wall made her shiver, but she lay twitching, eyes leaking tears she didn't bother wiping away. Let them fill the cell and drown her.

The door opened again, and the tray was removed. The patch faded into darkness no less deep than what coiled inside her.

Sometime in the night, Leedles stopped shivering, waking from a fitful sleep to discover a blanket wrapped around her. She ran a hand across the scratchy wool.

Who cared enough to keep her warm? The remainder of the night Leedles spent puzzling at the question. No nearer an answer when the patch reappeared on the wall, she sat up and wrapped the blanket around her like a cloak. Over the course of the night it had become the most precious thing in her world.

The door opened and Karl stepped in carrying a tray.

"Come on now," He sounded like he was trying to coax a puppy. Karl set the tray on the bench beside her. "You need to eat something."

"What does it matter?" Leedles hung her head. "I'll spend the rest of my life here." Tears dripped on the wool and beaded there. A thought struck her. "Did you leave the blanket?" She clutched it tighter as if he might take it away again.

"I couldn't stand to see you shivering like that. It ain't healthy. I've guarded my share of jails in my time. You leave the prisoners cold; they get sick."

"Do they die?" Leedles tried to make her fingers let go of the rough wool.

"Sometimes, not often, mostly they just wish they could die." He adjusted the blanket around her. "Please eat. You're going to need your strength."

"For what?"

"There will be a trial. The mayor's looking up how to run it proper."

Leedles shrugged, but she picked up the slice of bread and butter and nibbled at it.

Karl stayed in the cell with her until she finished. He didn't look impatient, or like he had a better place he could be. She wished she could be like him and be in a place until she needed to be somewhere else.

When she'd cleared the tray, he led her down the hall to a privy, then put her back in the room.

"Do you need anything?"

Leedles shook her head, then huddled under the blanket soaking in, not only its warmth, but the notion Karl cared enough to give it to her. He looked older than Uncle Urt, but in better shape. His hair needed a cut and grey hairs outnumbered the black. He hadn't shaved and grey speckled his face.

If he asked her, she'd marry him tomorrow. He wouldn't ask.

The boys wheedled and promised things like marriage, but she'd learned quickly they lied. Uncle Urt made her drink bitter tea every month since she'd come home with her dress in tatters at fifteen years. He'd never said anything about it, only frowned if she talked too long with a customer.

Dem with his leer was the only one who still undressed her with his eyes. For all the others, she'd become just another piece of furniture at the inn.

Leedles counted time by how far the patch of light moved between Karl's visits. His brief words comforted her, warming her like the blanket. After three days in the cell, Karl brought her a dress from her closet and a pitcher of water with a basin.

"Clean up as best you can." He waved at the water. "It ain't hot, but it ain't too cold either. Get dressed. They'll wait."

As soon as the door closed behind him, Leedles stripped her dress and shift off and used them to scrub water across her skin. The cool water made her skin tingle, almost like the touch of magic within her. The fresh dress caressed her. Odd without her shift beneath it. She wrapped the blanket like a cloak around her and knocked on the door.

"Come on, then." Karl touch her elbow, his touch electrifying her through the thick wool.

Sunlight made her eyes water. Karl led her to a chair in the centre of the square outside the city building. She sat in it, huddled under the blanket. The mayor, the smith, and another man she didn't know well sat at a table. The mayor and smith frowned, the other man looked bored. The largest crowd of people Leedles had seen apart from the annual pledge to the Tree gathered in a circle around them. People pointed at her.

"Leedles," the mayor said, and the muttering from the crowd hushed. "You were found in the park under the Tree with a branch of the tree broken off beside you."

He laid a gentle hand on the branch which lay along the length of the table. "What were you doing there?"

Leedles huddled down further on her chair. She couldn't speak in front of all these people.

Karl knelt beside her.

"You have to explain yourself, or they'll convict you anyway. Pretend you're talking just to me."

Leedles blinked water from her eyes and looked into Karl's warm brown eyes.

"I was angry at the Tree," she said in whisper, "I can't remember why, it didn't make sense. The wind blew from the mountains and helped me climb the tree, right to the top. From there I could see how small my world was. So much out there I'll never see. I screamed at the tree and shook the branches. I guess one broke and I fell."

"You fell all the way from the top of the Tree, and had no injuries?" The smith's frown deepened. "You must have used magic to save yourself. You know you are forbidden to use magic."

"Never stopped her," her Aunt's voice floated from the crowd.

"I don't feel like I do when I use magic. Maybe the Tree felt sorry for me."

"You think the Tree has feelings like a person?" the bored man leaned forward.

"Why not? Why else would we pledge our Peace to it every year?"

"You said you were angry at the Tree, why?" The mayor tilted his head as if he were truly interested in the answer.

"It didn't make sense," Leedles looked down at the blanket wrapped around her. The threads wove together, some thicker, some smaller. She peeked up at the mayor.

"Well?" He steepled his fingers and peered at her over them. Whenever he did that at the inn, he'd complain about her slowness.

"It was about the Peace, and my parents, and Jon running out of butter." She struggled to put the words together, each one fighting not to be spoken. Then she lifted her chin, if he wanted to know her anger, she'd tell him. "But mostly the Peace."

"Why would you be angry about the Peace?" the mayor's fingers pushed harder together.

"Because the Peace is killing me."

The gasp from the crowd echoed in the square. The mayor leaned over to speak to the smith and the other man.

"Leedles, you've broken the Peace by damaging the Tree. By your own admission you don't want to keep the Peace. So, you will be exiled. The guard will take you to the gate and see you out of the village." The mayor started to stand.

"Your honour," Karl stepped forward, "if I may speak?"

The mayor sat and waved his hand.

"Go on then, but keep it short, I have things to do."

"Then I will go straight to the heart of it. Exile is as good as death. I've heard the stories about her father. Do you want her death on your conscience too?"

"What do you propose?" The smith crossed his arms in front of him. "Keep her in that cell for the rest of her life? Are you going to guard her?"

"I can guide her out of the valley, then she can live or die in the world without it being on your head."

"Leedles," The smith glared at her, his eyes as hot as his forge. "What do you say about it?"

"I want to take this blanket with me." She clutched it tighter about her, the only thing keeping her from falling into pieces on the cobbles.

The mayor rolled his eyes.

"Very well, we can spare a blanket." He stood up and walked away from the table. The smith followed, then the other man shrugged and walked away into the crowd.

"Come along, now." Karl touched her shoulder.

Leedles tried to stand, but her legs failed. Karl caught her, then carried her as easily as he might a child back to the cell where he laid her gently on the bench.

"Wait here while I gather what is needed."

The patch of light faded as she waited, then brightened on the opposite wall before Karl opened the door. He frowned when he saw she hadn't moved from where he'd put her.

"First things first." He led her to the privy, then sat her at a table and made her eat a big meal.

Leedles didn't want to eat, but for this man she would stuff herself until she burst.

When she'd done, Karl walked her out the door to where the smith waited.

"We decided, in case you think you are being rewarded, to send you with a reminder of your failure." He held up the branch. Someone had cleaned it up to make a staff. The bottom, where there had been shattered wood, was capped with steel. Three quarters up the staff a chain dangled from a steel band. The top of the staff split off into a tiny branch. An acorn dangled from the twig. At the other end of the chain hung two half circles of steel. The smith took her left hand and squeezed the half circles together around her wrist.

Magic hummed to her as the smith whispered to the steel.

"There, no magic will remove this binding. Carry a part of the Peace you despise with you. The band will not chafe." The smith turned and walked away.

"I have a pack for you, put your blanket in it." Karl handed her a sack with a couple of straps hanging from it.

Leedles fumbled to roll the blanket with her left hand impeded by the staff. Karl didn't help, but he didn't tap his foot impatiently either. The blanket fit in on top of her clothes and what looked like bread and cheese, wrapped in cloth. She pulled the strings on the top of the pack tight and tied them.

"We'll undo the buckles on the left side, so you don't have to fuss with that staff." Karl held up the pack, and she put her right arm through the strap. He showed her how to adjust the length for comfort, then made her do up the strap on the left side.

Karl's pack bulked more than twice the size of hers, but he lifted it easily and settled it into place. At his waist hung the most enormous blade she'd ever seen.

"It's a sword, I suppose I should have got rid of it when I got here but couldn't bear to part with it. It's been a while; I hope I can remember how to use it. There's no Peace out there."

Leedles shrugged her pack into a more comfortable spot, then walked toward the gate.

CHAPTER THREE

No burden lifted from Leedles' shoulders when they passed through the gate, nor from her heart. Instead dust clogged her nose and the straps of her pack dug uncomfortably into her. Something in the pack poked at her ribs each step she took. Oddly, the staff quickly became part of her, helping her balance and aiding in finding footing in the rutted path they traveled.

Leedles didn't care. She was walking away from Peace, from her past, from all the problems which haunted her twenty-two years. The look on Karl's face and the sword at his side suggested she had traded them for a new set.

Karl. She ruminated about him as they walked. She'd gone through crushes when she was younger. This didn't feel like that. Then she'd been both giddy and tongue-tied, terrified of making a mistake, or of missing out. Walking beside him, she basked in a gentle warmth.

He cared enough about her to give her a blanket when she shivered in the stone cell, enough to offer to guide her out of the valley. His actions in one way or another saved her life.

Leedles didn't know what to make of him, he didn't need her, didn't ask anything of her. Perhaps it would change when they camped for the night. She'd share her blanket with him in an instant if he asked.

They left the fields before the sun rose to its highest point. The path petered out soon after, but Karl strode into the thick brush as if there was still a path to follow.

The staff took on a new role, pushing branches out of the way, helping her to jump over rivulets or keep her steady on a mossy log over a swampy bit.

The ground sloped up and got drier. Light ahead shone through the tree trunks. When they stepped out into the clearing, Leedles stopped walking to look around in wonder. The grass looked to be waist high on her and filled with colourful flowers. Butterflies flitted about. A brief puff of air cooled her cheeks.

"Quite something, isn't it?" Karl pointed across the meadow. "There's a rock over that side we can have our lunch. Whenever you're ready."

Leedles pulled in her delight and prepared to follow him through the grass, but Karl didn't move. He'd meant exactly what he'd said. When she was ready, they'd continue. She looked around again and focused on details. A bee crawling around on a spiky yellow flower. A black and orange butterfly flittering about a white flower. Tiny blue butterflies flocked over another white flower. When they'd first stopped, she didn't pay attention to the noise. The meadow rang with birdsong, and other calls her village ears couldn't identify. Perfumes wafted on fitful breezes, taking over from the musty scent of the forest. Across the clearing an animal stepped gingerly out into the sun followed by a tiny copy, only spotted.

"Deer," Karl whispered. "Skittish things."

The larger one's head flew up and looked in their direction, then they bounded out of the sunlight.

Leedles let her breath out with a soft cry. She could stand here forever.

Karl put his hand on her shoulder. Heat traveled through it into her stomach. Maybe she wasn't as far from childish crushes as she thought.

"Forgotten how it can take you the first time." He lifted his hand and Leedles bit back another cry. She lifted her pack into a better position, then nodded at Karl.

The wonder of hiking through waist high grass quickly vanished, buried beneath the annoyance of saw edged leaves scraping her shins, and bugs crawling everywhere on her. Broken stems poked up into the soles of her feet.

The rock heaved out of the field, heavy and dark. A bit of moss grew in cracks, but otherwise the life teeming around them left it untouched.

Karl climbed onto the rock, then took Leedles' hand and hoisted her up beside him. She faced into his chest. The hair there had turned grey too.

What would it feel like? She wrapped her arms around him and started sobbing. Desire pushed aside by a flood of emotion she couldn't name or control, she cried into his shirt until it hung sodden off his shoulder. His arms wrapped around her holding her safe and steady.

The flood receded, leaving her empty and light-headed. When she let go of him Karl helped her to sit and take off her pack. Then he sat beside her, she leaned against him and he put his arm around her and squeezed.

"Had a daughter, might have looked like you."

"Had?" She leaned her head on his shoulder.

"Died, back before I came here." He let go of her and she reluctantly sat up. "Ready for some lunch?"

Her stomach growled and Leedles laughed.

"My stomach is."

Karl opened his pack and dug out bread, cheese and dried sausage. He pulled out a shirt, then casually took the wet one off. Grey hair covered his chest and back like fur.

"Used to call me Bear, on account of the fur."

"Who?"

"My mates, fought together for years. Was with them longer than with my wife."

He put on the new shirt, and started cutting up food with a belt knife as if the conversation had never happened.

Leedles opened her pack and explored what Karl had brought for her. A shift, and underwear. Pants, she peered at him from the corner of her eyes, she'd never worn pants. A shirt folded beneath the pants, softer than her finest dress. Before she could change her mind, she stood up and pulled the pants on beneath her dress, then with her back to Karl took off her dress to put on the miraculously soft shirt. She couldn't get the left sleeve over the staff.

"Please, help." Leedles stood with the shirt in her hand. Heat climbed up her face and into her scalp. Karl came over and threaded the shirt over the staff and helped her pulled it down past her breast bands as if he helped women dress every day.

"Cotton from the south, brought it home for Cassie. Couldn't bear to leave it behind."

Leedles rolled up the sleeves to her elbows and had to hold up her pants to keep them from falling off. Karl cut her a length of rope and showed her how to tie it to hold them up.

She turned back to the pack, at the bottom lay a pair of boots. Leather with a design tooled on them, a lining as soft as her shirt, sturdy sole to protect the bottom of her feet. Leedles pulled them on sighing as they caressed her feet.

"How'd they fit?" Karl put down his knife and examined her feet. "Not bad, have to teach you to knit socks." He pulled a ball from his pack and handed it to her. "Put them on, then try the boots again."

The socks made her itch, but the boots fit like a second skin on her feet.

"Thank you," Leedles knelt to hug Karl. Tears ran down his face, and she wanted to ask and ask and ask. She hugged him in silence under the golden sun until he sighed. She kissed his cheek and sat beside him, admiring her boots, feeling like a new person.

Karl handed her bread, cheese and sausage, the best food she could remember eating. When they'd finished, he cleaned his knife with a cloth and returned it to his belt. He helped her repack her clothes and the bit of food she carried.

"Everyone carries food," Karl said, "in case we get separated. If we do get parted, sit down where you are and wait for me to find you. Nothing worse than two people wandering about looking for each other."

He hopped down then caught Leedles when she jumped. He gave her a squeeze and set her on her feet.

"Them boots will take getting used to. If your feet hurt too much, take the boots off and give 'em a rest. The more you wear 'em, the better, you'll need them for the pass."

Leedles danced a bit on the grass. She'd worn leather slippers in winter when the snow covered the ground, but the boots hugged her feet like Karl's arms around her. She nodded and grinned widely.

Karl stepped into the grass and led the way back under the trees.

As the sun lowered in the sky the temperature dropped. Not enough for her to get cold, but she rolled the sleeves down.

Leedles' feet started to ache just as she tripped over a root. She might have caught herself, only the staff caught a branch. She fell hard on the forest floor. Something tugged at her shirt and it ripped. Whatever tore the shirt scraped at her ribs, making her gasp with pain. The pain of tearing her shirt warred with the pain in her ribs. Her eyes filled with tears, and Leedles pushed them back ruthlessly.

Karl help her to her feet, then examined the damage to her shirt and skin with equal intensity.

"Let's go a bit further, then I'll show you how to sew that up."

"My shirt, or my skin?" Leedles took an experimental breath. Not too bad.

Karl grinned, the first time she'd seen him smile. He changed in that instant, warming her being, making her want to crawl under the blankets with him and explore the fur covering him. He turned and walked on, a bit slower, and the fire receded. Leedles followed, watching the ground carefully.

He stopped in a small clearing and laid down his pack.

"I'll get firewood if you'll put some rocks in a circle. He put his hands a little less than shoulder width apart.

Leedles found rocks under the moss and roots. A large rock sloped a bit, but still looked to be the best place to make her circle. She made the circle, fitting the rocks together carefully.

"Good job," Karl dropped a pile of sticks beside the rocks. The sticks made a small hut on the sloped rock. He stuffed something from a pouch under them, then struck the back of his knife against a stone from another pouch. Sparks flew off, one of them caught and quickly the flames climbed the sticks. As it crackled he fed larger pieces in until he nodded and sat back.

"There's a creek a bit over this way." He pointed into the dark. "You can wash up a bit, then I'll take care of that scratch for you."

"Please come with me?" Leedles shivered looking into the black. The forest wasn't nearly as friendly with the sun down.

"Ok, but I'm not scrubbing your back. Get your dress out of your pack. I'll sew up the shirt after you've bathed." They walked in the dark, Leedles took Karl's hand with her right hand. He gave her hand a squeeze and held on. They entered a tiny clearing with just a little more light than under the trees.

She wriggled out of the shirt and let her pants drop. The underwear and breast band itched with sweat, and probably seeds and bugs too. She pulled them off. The water in the creek felt as cold as winter snow, but she splashed every part of her with water, a bit awkward with the staff. Then she sluiced her underwear and breast bands through the water, kneading them on the rocks, soap would be better, but it would do.

Her dress stuck to her wet skin, but still felt better than underclothes she'd worn for days. Karl picked up her wet things, slung her shirt and pants over his shoulder and held out his hand for her.

As she gripped his hand, Leedles admitted to herself she loved this man, she would to her dying day. She had no idea what she'd do about it.

CHAPTER FOUR

Leedles shivered in the night air. Sleepily she pulled her blanket tighter around herself. Something solid kept her back warm. She rolled over and snuggled up against the warmth and fell back to sleep.

The birds woke her before the light. She lay cuddled up against Karl under their blankets, the hair on his skin soft under her hand. Leedles stayed there, up against Karl's back until his breathing shifted and she reluctantly pulled her hand away and sat up.

"Morning," Karl sat up and stretched.

"I'll get the fire going again." Leedles crawled out from her blanket and set small twigs against the last remaining coals from last night's fire. Her dress had dried stiff against her. She pulled it off and reached for her breast bands. Their cold made her gasp, but they warmed up quickly. Her underwear went under the blanket to take the chill off before she wriggled into them.

Dressing with the staff attached to her wrist was going to be a nuisance. The dress fit loosely enough it went over the end of the staff and puddled on the ground easily enough, but the shirt had been awkward even with Karl's help.

He sat dressed on the ground with the shirt in his lap, threading a needle.

"Wait a bit," Leedles sat beside him. The chill air reminded her she was next to naked. "I need to be able to get dressed without help. It's not that I don't appreciate your help." She took the shirt and turned it around in her hands. Only one way she could see to make it work. "Can you open up the seam on the left side? I could pull it over my right arm, then bind it somehow on my left."

Karl pulled out his belt knife and started cutting stitches while Leedles used the staff to pull her pants over to her. She wriggled into them, rolled up her dress, then her blanket and packed them away. They'd have cheese and bread for breakfast.

By the time she'd done, Karl had the shirt ripped open along the left side. It pulled on easily over her right arm, but gaped on the left side. She felt more naked than she had sitting in her underclothes in the morning air. Karl put the needle and thread away and pulled out a long strip of cloth.

"Bandage." He wound the bandage around her wrist and arm, trapping the end beneath, then tugged her shirt closed before winding it a few times around her chest and stomach. Tucking the end under the bandage finished the job. He stepped back and looked at her.

"You may start a new fashion." He smiled at her, then set to cutting slices for their meal.

Leedles lost count of the days they walked toward the mountain. Karl casually pointed out things they could eat, and collected berries, mushrooms and plants to supplement the food they carried.

"I'd hunt small game," Karl said after a rabbit hopped across their path, "but it would take too much time, we'd eat more than we'd save. Animals aren't as stupid as they look."

Leedles didn't know what to make of Karl. Sleeping cuddled together for warmth, waking and dressing in the cold morning air, and he still treated her with friendship, and not a bit of passion.

She must be uglier than she thought.

The trees where they walked now stood farther apart with little brush under them. The biggest risk was low branches.

"Why did you rescue me?" The question took Leedles by surprise. She hadn't intended on asking him anything, trying to match his unflappable demeanour.

Karl kept walking until she thought with relief, he hadn't heard her.

"You remind me of Cassie." He lifted a branch out of her way. "Every time I came home, she looked a little more lost. Like she didn't live in the same world as I did. I brought her gifts and tried to talk to her, but..." He shrugged, then adjusted his pack. "I'm not much for talking. Her mother blamed me, I did too. Something ate her up from the inside. Last time I went home, the house had burned to the ground. Neighbours told me Cassie had found a knife and carved up her arm. Bled to death before her mother found her. Priest wouldn't bury her, so her mother laid Cassie in her bed then burnt the house down. Don't know where she went after that." He held another branch for Leedles, his tears glinted in the sunlight.

She threw herself against him and held him as tight as she could, hoping her arms might give him as much warmth as she received from his.

He stood for a long time, still as a tree before he wrapped his arms around her and kissed her on the top of the head.

"I wandered after that, ended up here somehow. Only to watch another girl be eaten from the inside. I couldn't let it happen."

"It's magic that consumes me," Leedles said into his chest. "Like liquor to my brother. They forbid me from using it, because I can't control it." She took his hand and started walking again. Leading him up hill but having no other notion of where she went. Karl followed her.

"I'd do little things, and sometimes they worked, mostly they didn't, but the magic tingled inside me. The more I used, the more it demanded of me. I changed, couldn't work much, couldn't do anything much. If I stopped for a while, the tingling would vanish and leave a hole in its place."

"Magic out of control is dangerous." Karl followed her under a branch. The trees grew smaller and further apart now.

"It didn't feel dangerous, it was like the strongest wind, almost lifting me up and carrying me away. But it did things I didn't intend, like when I magicked a broom to sweep out the storeroom. When my Uncle came to check on me, he found a hole twenty feet deep and the broom still sweeping.

"The smith stopped it. He's the only one in town who can use magic properly. He tried to teach me, but nothing he said made sense. All about stilling myself and reaching deep for the source of magic. It's all around me begging me to shape it into something, anything. One time I tried to call a breeze to dry the sheets faster. A wind came and blew them away over the wall and lasted for two days.

"That was when he forbid me to use magic. But I couldn't stop, it's there waiting for me." She drew her hand through the air, and it whispered to her. The weight of the staff on her wrist made her sigh and grip the wood again.

"There are wizards in the Queen's City, if anyone can teach you to control the magic, it will be them."

"Will you take me there?"

Karl pulled her past the last of the trees. Bare rock rose high into the air where the mountains blocked out the sky.

"We need to get over that first."

CHAPTER FIVE

Leedles picked through the forest collecting dead wood while Karl set up camp. The mountain loomed over her, cutting the blue sky off. She didn't believe they could get over it, but she trusted Karl.

When her arms held as much as they could, Leedles returned to find Karl pulling food out of both packs. It didn't make much of a pile.

"Out of practice." He picked up a rock and hefted it in his hand. "See if I've still got it." Karl handed her the pouches with the flint and the tinder, then vanished into the woods.

The tiny sticks, what Karl called kindling stacked easily enough. She poked the tinder into the gap under the kindling. The flint fit comfortably in her hand. All the fires at the inn had been started from coals banked the night before. Karl made it look easy.

The magic flowed about her hand whispering she could use it to light the fire. It taunted her, dared her to use it. She hadn't done anything with the magic since falling from the Peace Tree. A hole opened in her and demanded to be filled. Only magic would fill it. Leedles clenched her fist and pushed the magic away. She could light the fire, and probably burn the entire forest in the process. The hole refused to go away. The magic begged.

The only way was to light the fire with the flint. Prove she didn't need the magic.

Leedles didn't have anything steel to strike to create a spark, except for the shackle on her wrist and the matching one on the staff. The chain gave her only a foot or two's slack, enough to let her use her left hand for some things. She held the flint in her right hand and struck the manacle on her left wrist.

A twinge of pain accompanied the paltry sparks. None landed on the tinder. Each strike caused more pain, but she got better sparks as she figured out the best angle.

"I'm only trying to light the fire!" She shook the staff, then angrily hammered the flint against the shackle. Pain shot up her arm into her head, and the world spun dangerously around her. One of the sparks landed in the tinder. Leedles fought the spinning and blew gently on the spark until it burst into flame, then fed it larger sticks until the fire crackled and danced in the circle.

Her wrist burned as if she'd put it in the fire. Blisters formed around the shackle. Cradling her arm, Leedles curled up on the ground and whimpered. The breeze scraped at the burn; the magic sneered at her.

Hands picked her up and pulled at her arm, then cold water splashed on it. Leedles screamed, then gasped as the pain receded enough for her to take in her position. Karl held her close and poured water from his leather bottle onto the burn. When the bottle was empty, he pulled his pack over and dug into it, pulling out a small box.

"Sorry, going to hurt like hell." Karl tightened his hold and held her arm still. With his other hand, he flipped the box open, then scooped out a gob of foul smelling ointment. When the ointment touched the burn, she screamed. Leedles' throat hurt, but she couldn't hold in the pain. When it got worse, she gave up and let blackness take her.

***

She woke wrapped in her blanket held like a small child by Karl. Sizzling came from behind her along with the scent of cooking meat. Her stomach growled and Karl looked down at her, his face just inches from hers. Her right arm snaked behind his neck and pulled him down.

Her experience of kissing had been limited to quick stolen pecks on the lips, and one night of slobbering and bruising kisses while Dem had laid on top of her taking what he wanted from her.

Her lips registered the texture of his, the taste of his breath was on her tongue, a very different fire coursed through her making her tighten her grip. Then he pulled back.

"I can't, would be too much like being with Cassie." Tears glistened in his eyes.

Leedles curled up against him and cried until the heat in her veins died and she fell asleep.

The ache in her stomach woke her. Night had fallen, but Karl still cradled her in his arms.

"Ready for something to eat?" He gently set her on the ground, then pulled the roasted rabbit off the rocks and cut a piece for her.

The rabbit was a pile of bones before Leedles noticed her arm didn't hurt. It didn't feel much of anything, like she'd been lying on it too long. Karl had wrapped it with bandages.

"Thank you." Leedles poked gingerly at the bandages. The burn ached, but nothing more. "What was that stuff?"

"Come from a plant far south. Learned about it fighting down in the desert. Done until we get to the city." He turned red and looked away from her into the fire.

Leedles took his hand and opened her mouth, then closed it again. She tried to put the words she needed to say in order.

"I never knew my father, he murdered my mother, then hung himself in the forest when I was a baby."

"Heard the stories."

"Uncle Urt raised me, my Aunt wanted nothing to do with me, and he didn't try very hard to be a father to me. I was more like a dog he'd been stuck with but didn't want.

"For a long time, I believed the only way to escape was to marry." The ghost of something she thought she'd put away forever found its way into her voice. "No one wanted to marry me, they'd take other things, but never give me anything back." Breathing had never been so hard. She focused on air moving in and out of her lungs until she had breath for words again. "Uncle Urt thought I slept around with the boys, but I didn't, after..."

Leedles pushed back the memory, imagined it in the fire, burning away. "Well, I gave up on being loved. Gave up on being anything but the ugly, cursed child of peacebreakers. This blanket," She stroked the wool, familiar as her own skin under her fingers. "This was the first time I can remember when someone cared whether I lived or died."

Karl made an inarticulate sound and his hand trembled in hers.

"When you led me out of the village, I knew I loved you. I drank in everything about you. The way you walked; or could stand still as if you'd stand forever. The feel of your hair under my fingers, the touch of your hand. When you didn't respond, it was okay. I couldn't expect you to love someone as ugly and cursed as me." Tears sprang from her eyes, and she had to force the words past the lump in her throat. "When you held me, I never felt so safe, you looked down, and I wanted..." Sobs burst out of her. She curled up in a ball trying to hold her heart together. Shards of pain stabbed out of her gut, her heart, her head. Her legs muffled her howling.

Karl held her hand but didn't move. Like he'd turned to stone. The only person who ever cared, didn't.

Then he picked her up and held her again, his sobs dissonant against her wails. The fire grew low as they sat together.

"I failed Cassie," Karl's ragged voice broke the silence. "Knew something was wrong, but I had to go fight, was all I understood. When I learned how she died, my heart broke. Didn't care if I lived or died for a long time. Wandered around until I found this valley, found peace. Let her go. Then you..." He hugged her tight. "Then I saw you, another Cassie, only inches from death. Tried to talk to your Uncle. Told me to mind my own business. When they put you in that cell, I had to do something, or it'd be Cassie all over again. So I took care of you, then asked to guide you so I knew you'd be okay. Saw you falling for me, but you don't want an old worn out soldier like me. Didn't say anything, told myself you'd be fine, t'would pass."

He shuddered.

Cassie squirmed around in his arms until she could see his face. He might have aged years in the time the fire burned. Her hand stroked his face.

"I wish I was your daughter, then your heart wouldn't be broken." She dropped her head against his shoulder. "I used to dream about having a father like the other kids. Someone who'd pull out my splinters and tell me stories."

She thought Karl had fallen asleep, he sat still and silent so long. The warmth of his arms and chest eased the ache in her soul.

"I could be your father." The words came as the slightest whisper.

"I'd like that," she whispered back.

CHAPTER SIX

Morning brought frost on the ground, but Leedles had learned to keep her clothes under the blanket with her. She dressed quickly and looked around for Karl. He wasn't there, but his knife lay on the rocks by the fire along with the flint and tinder.

The fire burned brightly, warming her face.

"Morning." Karl dropped a load of sticks beside the fire, then put a skinned rabbit on the rocks to cook.

"I thought we were crossing the mountain today."

"Need to carry firewood with us. None up there. Will take two days to get through the pass."

Leedles examined her heart while they waited for the rabbit to cook. The pain of the night before hadn't vanished, but it had shifted into something she could live with. Her body ached for something she couldn't put a name to, but there was also a bright shining contentment. Karl cared. Not the way she'd imagined, but he cared. She'd never been a daughter before. How should she act?

She still hadn't figured it out when Karl handed her some rabbit.

"Will want as much energy as possible. The path is hard and cold."

The rabbit tasted better than anything she'd eaten, even better than their first lunch on the rock. She'd cried then too. Maybe being a daughter was as simple as letting him comfort her.

But she had to stop the crying, it was too hard on them both.

When Leedles started to stuff her things in her bag, Karl stopped her from rolling up the blanket. Her pack lay flat with only her shift and dress in it.

"Take a bundle of sticks," Karl handed her a length of rope.

The bundle hung lopsided from her pack when she'd finished, but it wasn't half the size of Karl's bundle.

"Put your pack down a moment." Karl picked up her blanket and folded it to make a triangle. He put it around her shoulders so a point fell down her back, and the other two on her front. He tied it on with another bit of rope, then did the same to his blanket.

He helped her hoist the pack up again, then they started up the side of the mountain. Leedles had thought she'd got used to walking through the forest, but now each step meant lifting her body. Like climbing an endless flight of stairs, but without the secure footing.

The staff helped her climb, her arm ached, but otherwise felt fine under the bandages. Karl used a rough stick.

Her legs ached before the sun was halfway up the sky. Karl sat on a rock and pulled out his water bottle making her drink before he took his water. He stood and led the way up the mountain again. Leedles bit back a groan and followed him.

The sun had fallen to near the horizon before they reached a valley which extended level deep into the mountain.

"Further we go today, the easier tomorrow will be."

Leedles settled the pack on her back and nodded.

They didn't have to walk up hill, but the valley tortured them in a new way. Loose rock formed the level ground. Each step, they had to test their footing. The staff helped, but Leedles stumbled and almost fell more than once before they arrived at a tiny rivulet running through a sandy bed.

Karl lit the fire as Leedles laid out the last of their food. They ate in silence, then climbed under the blankets. Like every night before, they lay back to back, sharing the warmth of their bodies. She reached back with her right hand and found Karl's hand. He squeezed her hand gently, and she fell asleep with a contented smile on her face.

***

Leedles woke up shivering in the night, but refused to roll over to snuggle closer to Karl. She had her mind made up, but her body still refused to listen. The cold air slipped under the edges of the blankets, making her colder. The more she shivered the colder she got. The moon's white light only made her feel more chilled.

Magic moved about her, offering her warmth, if she only trusted herself. Leedles focused on what she needed, something to give heat. A fire would use up their wood, Karl had refused to burn more than half the load they'd carried up the mountain.

The shivering was as bad as when she lay in the cell. Maybe if rocks could steal heat, they could throw it as well. Not too much, she didn't want to cook either. The stone fireplace at the inn got warm enough Uncle Urt would set customers' cloaks near it to dry them. About that warm.

Controlling the magic so tightly made her head ache. It fought her, wanting to erupt into white hot flames. Leedles picked a rock a few feet away from her, bigger than the rest. She let the magic trickle through her fingers, whispering instructions.

"Heat the rock, just that rock, no more."

It flowed into the rock, mumbling and complaining, at the last instant it flared up. Leedles squeezed the flow off, but not before the rock split in two. A faint red glow came from the interior. She'd done it. Used magic without it running wild. The familiar tingle lay beneath the agony of cold and shaking muscles. Heat from the rock eased the pain, soon she drowsed while staring at her handiwork.

:So you can learn.:

CHAPTER SEVEN

Leedles giggled as Karl walked around the rock, feeling the heat it radiated.

"How long will it last?" He looked at her with something different in his eyes, she hoped it was respect.

"I don't know, I didn't think to put a time limit on it."

"I've worked with a few wizards, I don't know any who could do something like this for any length of time, maybe the ones in the city? Who knows, they're stingy with their secrets." He shrugged and picked up his pack. "Don't tell too many people about this, some don't take kindly to wizards."

Leedles tried to stop it, but her face fell. She picked up her pack and swung it into place, fastening the left side strap by reflex.

"How about you?" She adjusted her pack. "What do you think of wizards?"

"Most of the ones I've met were arrogant twits who barely acknowledged the rest of us were human." Karl put his hand on her shoulder and looked into her eyes. "You aren't like that, won't become like that. I'm proud of you, but a bit scared too, to be honest. Some won't like the power you have and will try to take it or destroy it."

"Okay." Leedles put her hand on his. "Let's get out of this place." She stepped out in the direction they walked the day before.

The sun hung low in the sky by the time they reached the edge of the valley. The tingling had become the sensation of ants crawling inside her, but Leedles set it aside. She wouldn't use magic again, not until she knew more about what she was doing.

They camped in a hollow halfway down to the treeline.

"Walking downhill is worse than climbing." Leedles rubbed at her calves.

"It is, but tomorrow I'll find something to eat."

They went to sleep early, Leedles's stomach a hole in her gut.

She dreamed about food, and the magic whispered it could bring them something to eat. Pushing the dreams and the whispers away, Leedles went back to sleep.

Two days after they entered the trees, they found a road. Not much of a road, but easier walking. Karl headed off to the east and Leedles matched him step for step. She liked walking beside him instead of looking at his back.

They wound around the sides of valleys, high enough up Leedles could look down on soaring eagles. Her calf muscles insisted they still walked mostly downhill.

"We're maybe a day, maybe two away from a village, smaller than Peace, not as pleasant. Follow my lead, and we'll build up our supplies before heading east again."

"What are they like, these people?"

"They're people, some good, some not, most too busy to worry about it. Violence is going to be a problem, but I'll deal with it." He smiled and patted her shoulder, you'll be fine."

Next morning Leedles woke up not sure if she was excited or terrified. The fluttering in her stomach didn't help. They ate berries for breakfast, then shouldered their packs and walked on. At least they didn't need to carry firewood now.

At midday, they walked through a valley. The heat made the road waver in front of them. Leedles daydreamed about how she might make something to cool them off.

The first she knew of the people on the road was Karl putting his hand in front of her.

"Let me handle it." Karl stood with his arms crossed conspicuously showing the sword hanging from his belt.

The men sauntered forward holding long staffs. Occasionally one would spin the staff in a manner Leedles expected was supposed to be intimidating.

"Hello, Grandpa, we're just collecting the toll for using this road."

"There are no tolls on the Queen's roads." Karl's voice grated like stone. It made her take a step back and she stood behind him. The men should have run away in fear.

"This isn't a Queen's road, not anymore. Keep arguing and you'll pay double."

"I've been walking roads since before you were born." Karl didn't move from his stance though both men were within striking distance.

"Well, that's kind of the point, isn't it? You're old, do you really think you can take both of us?" The speaker, slightly taller than his companion, flicked his staff within a hair's breadth of Karl's head. The older man didn't flinch. The speaker raised an eyebrow at his fellow, who'd walked a bit further and now stood between Karl and Leedles. He couldn't be much older than her.

He lunged at her, and she squeaked and jumped back. Karl looked back and the one in front attacked. His staff caught Karl in the belly, folding him over, then rapped his right shoulder.

The one in front of Leedles grinned unpleasantly and stepped toward her. Leedles grabbed a handful of magic and threw it at him. He stepped back a half step, then began to advance again.

The wind roared down the mountain and struck the men, sending them tumbling over the edge of the road. She ran over to see them running downhill making wild leaps from rock to rock. The road under her shook, the roar of the wind became the sound of the mountain sliding toward them.

"Oops," Leedles said.

:Fool!:

She tried to run to Karl, but the staff twisted in her hand and dragged her to the edge of the road. Magic twisted and screamed as the staff slammed down on the road. Then the first rocks were upon them. Leedles resigned herself to death, but the rocks flowed to the side. She tried to scream or turn away, but magic rooted her in place.

The slide went on and on. Even with the magic barrier, Leedles didn't know how she still lived. She couldn't turn her head to see if Karl was safe. The tingle of magic became the familiar ants crawling, then needles sticking out through her skin.

The last rock tumbled past and Leedles could move again, she dropped to her knees and keened in agony.

"We must move, now." Karl lifted her up. "The rocks won't be stable yet. More could fall."

Leedles tried to make her legs work, but each time she stood, they failed.

"Hold on then." He swung her onto his back, then began climbing the huge drift of rocks blocking the road. Boulders shifted and settled, but he kept his footing. An hour later he stepped off the slide onto the road.

"What happened?" He stood her on the road in front of him.

"I was scared, they were going to murder us. You said you'd protect me, but you didn't." Leedles clenched her fists and tried to stop screaming at Karl. "You just stood there and did nothing!"

Karl's shoulders slumped and he walked to the side of the road.

"Couldn't draw my sword." Leedles could barely hear him. "After all this time. I've never lost a fight, I was fastest, strongest, most ruthless. Then I let two beardless youth beat on me and put both of us at risk." He undid the belt holding his sword and held the weapon staring at it. "Should have let you go long ago." He pitched the sword over the edge, and it disappeared into the brush on the hill.

"Let's go." Karl turned and walked away down the road. "We have a ways to walk before we get to town."

Leedles forced her legs into action. Each motion sent agony through her, but it didn't hurt as much as the defeated slump in Karl's shoulders. She walked as fast as she could and still could barely keep up. Her staff struck the road so hard it vibrated. The vibrations traveled down her arm and spread through her body. The agony of the magic fell back to ants crawling, then tingling, then nothing.

:Just this once.:

What did that mean? Why did she think that? Maybe she'd heard other thoughts which didn't belong to her. The Tree told her to go east and plant the acorn which still bobbed on its twig at the top of her staff.

"Are you talking to me?" She looked at the staff and shook it. Stupid, it might have come from the Tree, but still, it was only wood. Leedles shook her head and ran after Karl.

They walked into town, side by side. Leedles' palm on the staff slipped, and she wiped her other hand on her blanket. What would it be like? Stories of the outside were warnings of unremitting violence. Would the people attack them? Leedles breathed deeply and wiped her palms again. Karl didn't look worried; she'd just wait and find out.

Karl hadn't spoken since throwing his sword away. He looked diminished, older. He turned into a building facing the street and sat in a corner. Leedles slid in on his right side and tried to set her staff so it wasn't in the way.

A man came over and frowned at Karl.

"Don't allow slaves in Dunstown. Don't hold with that."

"Not a slave," Karl's words rasped harshly in the room. Others raised their heads and looked over at them. "My daughter."

"But the chain..."

"Religious thing." Karl tossed coins on the table. "Need supper and a room."

"That's mighty old money you're throwing about." The man picked up a coin and peered at it. "This is the old Queen."

"I'm an old man," Karl reached out to take back the coins. "Are they good or not?"

"They'll spend." The other man swept up a few coins and pushed the rest toward Karl. "The girl will come with stew."

Stew turned out to be mostly vegetables in thin gravy, but the bread was good. Leedles made her portion vanish quickly. The girl brought another bowl and a slice of bread.

"You want more, you pay." She picked up the empty bowl and left them.

"I'm sorry I yelled at you," Leedles put her hand on Karl's. It twitched like he thought to pull away, but didn't. "Do daughters fight with their fathers?"

Karl snorted and patted her hand with his other hand.

"Cassie and I had our spats, mostly about me leaving for another war. She had a mind of her own. One time she took a notion to learn the sword and come with me. Asked me day and night to teach her. I knew what war was like, no place for a kid. So she picks up my sword one day and starts swinging at an old stump. Her legs were in more danger than the stump." He took a bite of stew and shook his head. "Couldn't stand it after watching her a bit. Had to fix her grip, then her feet, by the end of the day we were hammering at each other with sticks, her screaming like a banshee and me laughing so hard I could hardly stand. Even her mother cracked a smile.

"When I left that time, told her to practice hard, and next time she'd be good enough to come along. Cassie was determined but lacked stamina. Figured she'd lose interest."

"What happened when you went home?"

"Found a burned-out house and a dead daughter. Maybe if I'd brought her with me, she'd still be alive.'

"If she was fighting magic, it wouldn't have mattered where she was." Leedles sighed and leaned back. "It would be nice if the world was fair."

The tavern door slammed open and the two men from the road staggered in. They sat on stools by the bar.

"Give us a drink," the taller one said.

"Do you have money to pay?" the owner went to stand beside the barman. The barman didn't look like he needed support, his head brushed the beams above him, and his fists were the size of Leedles' head. "You've run out your credit here, and everywhere else too, Cordin. Go back to where you come from."

"They don't like us much there," the other man from the road said.

"Don't like you here, neither. Coin or you get out."

The one called Cordin looked like he was going to argue longer, but his companion pulled him to his feet. Cordin opened his mouth to argue, but locked eyes with Leedles, he went white as a ghost and dragged the other man almost at a run.

CHAPTER EIGHT

The room was no more comfortable than her room at Uncle Urt's inn, but it wasn't any worse. Leedles settled her bag and went to find the owner to talk about baths and laundry.

"I'll put water on to heat," the girl who'd brought them stew said. "Cost you a penny."

"A penny if you have soap." Leedles stuck out her chin.

The girl shrugged and put her hand out.

"My father will pay, he's in the tavern yet."

"Won't heat the water till he pays."

"I'll be in my room." Leedles went and changed into her shift, the bath was at the end of the hall. She'd wash her clothes after she was clean. A knock on the door let her know the water was ready.

Leedles closed and barred the door to the room and dropped her pile of hers and Karl's clothes to wash later. Water steamed in the tub made of half of a gigantic barrel. Lines strung about the room would give her a place to hang the laundry.

Sitting in the hot water made Leedles sigh with pleasure. She soaked for a while before reaching for the soap. The girl had put it on a chair just out of reach of the tub.

"This what you're looking for?" Cordin handed her the soap.

"What are you doing here?" Leedles sunk down until just her head was out of the water.

The man who'd tried to rob them on the road grinned at her "You're the wizard, you tell me." Cordin pulled the chair over and sat on it. "In case you're thinking of blowing me out the window, or turning me into a toad, my mate Tad, is hanging about the square near where the Queen's guard works. On a normal day, we aren't on speaking terms with the guard, but today we'll make an exception."

"That doesn't explain what you're doing here."

"Right, here I am blathering on, and you want to get to business. Here's how it's going to work. You make us some magical objects or spells or whatever you do, and we won't let the Queen know a rogue wizard is about closing down the roads."

"I don't know how to make magical things."

"I expect you're going to learn then, wizard, or there will be trouble." Cordin stood and bowed to her. "I'd love to stay and watch, but Tad will be getting to wondering what happened to his mate." He slipped out the window.

Leedles jumped out of the tub to close the window. She locked it too, but didn't think it would do much good if he wanted to come back. The bath didn't feel as inviting, but she scrubbed herself pink with the soap and washed her hair, knocking her head with the staff more than once.

She worked out a system to do the laundry which didn't add any more bruises to her collection, and hung everything up to dry. They might be musty, but they'd be clean.

The hallway was clear when she peeked out, so she dashed back to her room in her shift.

In the room, Leedles sat on the bed and ran over her options. She didn't know enough to tell if Cordin was lying. He probably was, at least about some things. She couldn't ask Karl about it, he'd want to go and talk to them, with neither his sword nor his confidence, that wouldn't go well; couldn't ask anyone else without revealing herself. Violence was one thing; this slippery blackmail was different.

She needed to figure out how to do what Cordin wanted.

When she'd made the rock warm, her focus had been so tight it hurt, but she kept the magic within the limits she set. Thus, first she had to define the limits, so it didn't get out of control. It had taken a long time, and her head ached from the concentration. She needed time to work without interruption. That bit of rebellion at the end worried her, finishing off her work without losing control was key.

Karl flung the door open and staggered into the room reeking of ale.

"Out, don't need no floozy, not that kind of man."

"Karl, it's me, Leedles." Leedles reached toward him, but he slapped her hand away.

"Don't care what you name is." He pointed dramatically toward the door.

"Daddy, you said I could stay with you."

"Cassie?" Karl looked around. "You OK, girl?"

"I'm fine, but I want to sleep in a real bed tonight."

"I'll sleep on the floor, keep you safe." He fell to the floor between the bed and the door.

Leedles watched him until her eyes wouldn't stay open, then lay down to sleep.

***

A woodpecker banged on the outside of the inn. Leedles woke and stretched. The clean clothes had been neatly stacked on the chair. Karl was nowhere to be seen.

Leedles dressed in her pants and shirt, then packed her dress, shift and blanket away in her bag. Karl's bag sat in the corner, so she left hers there and went down to breakfast.

"Your father is an early riser," the innkeeper said. "He's out cutting wood for the day. My daughter, Sella, will show you about town, everyone knows her, and knows better than to cause trouble with me. If you stay close, you'll have no problem."

"C'mon." Sella urged Leedles to walk faster. "I'm already late." Leedles half ran to keep up with her. They reached the square and Sella ran ahead and threw herself into a young man's arms. They kissed passionately, ignoring the people who had to walk around them.

"This is Needles, or something like that, don't ask about the stick, it's religious." Sella rolled her eyes. "I'm supposed to show her around."

"I've got to get to the forge, the smith told me he'd dismiss me if I was late again."

Sella pouted, but after another kiss, the young man ran at full speed out of the square.

"Isn't he darling?" Sella said, "And a smith's apprentice too, just think of his muscles." She winked at Leedles.

Leedles had stood on the fringes while girls in Peace had talked about boys. She couldn't see the point. None of them would choose for themselves who'd they marry. Maybe it was different here.

"I need to talk to someone about my shirt." Leedles waved at the bandages holding the shirt on.

"Ooo, clothes, Mistress Fall will be just opening. I can check on my new dress." Sella took off at a mad pace again while Leedles wove through the crowd trying to keep up. It didn't help that everyone who saw here stopped dead in their tracks to stare at her.

Sella was knocking on a door and bouncing on her toes when Leedles caught up to her.

"Why is everyone staring at me?" She asked, immediately regretting the whine in her voice. "Am I really that ugly?"

Sella turned away from the door to examine Leedles.

"Not ugly, but you won't be turning any noble heads neither. Diff is what you are, the whole barbarian thing. Do you have any fur? I adore fur."

"Good morning, Sella," the woman who opened the door blinked at them. "You're earlier than usual, I take it your young man will be on time for a change." She stepped back. "No use letting the flies in."

A treasure trove of fabric filled every corner of the house. Colours, patterns, and textures Leedles had never imagined.

"She needs clothes, her name's Deedles or something."

"Does she speak for herself? Go put on water for tea, then we'll look at your dress."

Sella walked through to the back, while Mistress Fall circled Leedles, touching the fabric of her clothes, examining the stitching.

"My name's Leedles." She held herself still.

"Sella's not good with names, at least not girl's names." Mistress Fall finished her circuit.

"I'm guessing from the shirt you can't take that stick off. Your solution is ingenious, but a bit unwieldy. Could do larger sleeves, maybe have the wrap attached to the shirt. Hmmm, I like a challenge."

"Water's on," Sella returned to the room. "She's got a blanket she wears like a coat, saw it last night. Came in with some old guy, said he was her father."

"We have no reason to doubt it," Mistress Fall pointed to a stool. "Sit." She looked at Leedles. "You may stand in that corner, but please don't touch, those are my silks, and they are worth more than Sella's father's inn.

Leedles leaned on her staff and watched as Mistress Fall opened a closet and pulled out a dress. Leedles had never seen anything like it. Not only was the fabric fine and dyed a glorious shade of blue, it had tiny gems sewn on it, and designs traveled around the hem of the skirt and sleeves. It looked like silk, Leedles itched to run her fingers over it. She clutched her staff tighter.

"Some old men from the Queen's City came and tested everyone," Sella bounced on her seat in excitement. "They told me I was special and needed to go to the City for school. When I get back I'm going to marry Dirk. They paid for the dress and said when it was finished, they'd send for me. Isn't that grand?"

"Yes, dear." Mistress Fall nodded and sighed, "Grand indeed. Why don't you go and run some errands, your friend and I have business to discuss. You can come back and have tea with us."

Sella bolted out the door, and Mistress Fall closed it gently behind her.

"I remember my mistress sewing such a dress," The woman sank onto the stool Sella had vacated. "Don't remember the girl ever returning. But you aren't here to indulge an old woman's misgivings. Your shirt is the finest cotton, I don't know if I could match it, but what you've done to it." She shook her head. "What do you need?"

"I don't have any money to pay for anything new, Sella brought me here because I wanted some advice on how to fix my shirt better."

"Ah, advice." Mistress Fall shrugged her shoulders. "Advice has its own price. Sella won't listen, her head's in the clouds, I sew as slowly as I dare, but one day the dress will be complete, and we will lose our Sella. Will you listen?"

"It depends on what you say."

Mistress Fall laughed and pushed herself to her feet.

"An honest one, I like that, so refreshing. Here's my advice. If an old man offers to buy you a dress fit for a Queen, refuse." She shook herself. "Now, hand me your shirt, I'm an old woman, you're safe with me."

Leedles unwrapped the bandage and removed her shirt. The Mistress ran her fingers over the cloth and hummed to herself. She dug into a pile of fabric and pulled out a piece too small to do much with. Pulling out scissors and thread she started sewing the small section to the shirt.

The motions of Mistress Fall's hands were too fast to follow. Several times she held up the shirt and nodded to herself before returning to work. She suddenly tossed the shirt to Leedles.

"Try it on." the extra cloth formed a flap which could be pulled to the front and fastened with toggles, a smaller flap closed the sleeve. Leedles ran her hand over the seam. No air blew in through gaps in the side.

"It's marvelous." Leedles tugged at the shirt, straightening it. "But I can't possibly pay you for it."

"It's a scrap and a bit of time, nothing between friends." Mistress Fall waved her hands. "But if you do get to the Queen's City, you might keep an eye out for my Sella."

"I will do that."

The door flew open and Sella burst into the room carrying parcels.

"Oh, that looks better. I'll pour the tea."

***

Back at the inn, Leedles dug through the pack to find needle and thread. She didn't have the fast hands or tiny stitches Mistress Fall used, but she went through all the clothes sewing up tears and cutting off loose threads. The entire time she thought about the beautiful dress, and what it could cost Sella to wear it.

CHAPTER NINE

Karl was off woodcutting again before Leedles woke. She stretched and groaned. Weeks of sleeping on the ground gave her no problem, two nights in this bed was turning her into a cripple.

Downstairs she snatched a quick breakfast, then asked where she might find a bit of work.

"Not much work for a barbarian." The cook, Sella's mother winked at her. "Furd, our barman, sometimes has cleaning done for him. He might be due. He's...strange, but perfectly safe. All I know about him is he escaped slavery somewhere in the far south, and all the children in town adore him."

She gave directions to find Furd's house, then went back to chopping.

Leedles wandered outside. Chilly enough for her to briefly consider going back for her blanket. Maybe it would warm up as the sun got higher. The townspeople continued to stare at her, but today it didn't bother her. Attention for being different wasn't as bad as for being ugly.

Furd's place sat on the far edge of town surrounded by fantastical creatures made of wood or stone. Leedles peered at a frog climbing out of a rock, and a bird carved from a stump with creature in its claws that didn't look like a mouse. A grin grew on her face, and tension faded from her neck and shoulders.

"May I help you?" Furd's deep voice vibrated inside her. She felt as much as heard his words.

"I love your garden; I've never seen anything like it."

Furd clumped down the stairs. His skin shone like polished ebony, and he towered over Leedles.

"Let me show you around." He pointed to a tiny horse with a horn coming out of its forehead, then told her where he found the wood he carved it from, though he talked about 'freeing' the creatures.

Leedles followed in rapt attention until the sun was high in the sky.

"Oh, I was going to ask if you needed cleaning? I'm hoping to earn some money to buy more clothes."

"You'll be Sella's barbarian. Come, I'll show you what to do."

The inside of the house looked like a tent. Carpets piled on the floor and hung from the walls; fabric draped from beams in the ceiling.

"The carpets need to be taken outside and beaten with a paddle you'll find there. I could do it myself, but each one is like friend to me. Don't worry about putting them back in the same place."

Leedles dragged a carpet through the door Furd indicated, she tried using the paddle on the rugs, but her staff made it too awkward. She used the staff instead making sure she struck flat and not with the iron shoe. Huge clouds of dust flew up from the rug making her sneeze and her eyes water. After ten whacks the dust cloud faded to almost nothing.

She left it there and fetched another to hang it a little further down the railing. Dust had settled on the wood of the porch, so she used the broom leaning against the wall to sweep it away. After some practice, she could hold broom and staff together.

Drag, beat, sweep, Leedle worked through the day humming. She'd never hummed before, but the house had such a happy feeling to it she couldn't stop. Some of the carpets were too large for her to move, so she swept them vigorously with the broom. Last she swept the hanging cloths, making them rain dust.

Outside she breathed in fresh air and dreamed about the bath she'd buy for a penny.

Back inside she swept the dust out the door, she spotted a mop and bucket. In the garden, she'd seen a rain barrel on one corner of the house. Mopping the floor brought out marvelous grain in the wood. She finished by mopping the porch.

The sun had lowered almost to the horizon before she put the last rug back in place.

"My house is happy. She says you sing very nicely. Now you may clean yourself. If you are brave."

"What does bravery have to do with bathing?" Leedles pushed her hair back, stiff with dust.

"Come, see."

Furd led her around a corner to where a wall stood out an arm span from the house. Above it was an odd circular thing connected to the house with a pipe.

"You pull the string, water flows from there," Furd pointed to the circle. "Never know what temperature the water is, maybe warm, maybe cold. There's soap." He opened a cabinet. "and towels. If you give me your clothes, I will wash for you."

Leedles took two breaths to decide she wanted to be clean more than modest. After camping with Karl, then Cordin's intrusion, she hardly cared about undressing in front of Furd. She turned her back and quickly stripped all her clothes off, stepped under the bucket and pulled the string.

The water gushed out, hardly warmer than the mountain streams she bathed in. Leedles held back a scream and reached for the soap.

Wrapped in an immense towel she walked back around to Furd's door and into the house. Her clothes lay on a rack, already clean and dry. He must have other tricks about his place. She dressed and sighed with pleasure at being clean again.

"Will you eat with me?" Furd poked his head into the room.

"I'd love to," Leedles gave a last comb at her wet hair with her fingers. She followed him into another smaller room, also overflowing with carpets. Furd sat on one side of a low table, so Leedles knelt on the other side.

"You are very brave, when the water is cold, I roar like a dragon."

"It's ingenious, if you could make the water hot all the time, it would replace baths."

The food covered a huge circle of bread. They ate by tearing a piece of the bread and using it to pick up whatever they wanted. Furd only used his right hand to eat, and with her staff attached to her wrist, Leedles found it easiest to do the same. The tastes danced on Leedles tongue, nothing burned, but heat and bitter, sour and sweet mixed in ways she didn't expect. Soon nothing was left of the meal but crumbs.

"Sweet?" Furd asked, he had a glint in his eye which made Leedles wonder what he was up to. He lifted a covered dish from a side table and placed it in front of Leedles.

She lifted the cover to reveal a collection of insects in perfect condition. They looked like larger versions of the hoppers she saw in Peace during the summer.

"What are they?" She picked one up and peered at it closely.

"Honey roasted locusts, very rare. They come a long way to be eaten by golden barbarian."

"We'd better not disappoint them." Leedles steeled herself and bit off half of the locust. Sweet and crunchy, with a bit of a nut flavour. She'd have thought them baked if Furd hadn't told her different. She finished the locust and brushed off her fingers.

"I'd better get back to the inn," Leedles said and sighed. "Thank you so much."

***

"You are forgetting you worked for me, a worker is due their wages." Furd dug in a pocket and pulled out a silver coin.

"Oh no, that's far too much."

"We did not settle on wages, so I pay what I wish. You are brave, and underneath your troubles you are content. You try new things and bring joy to my home." He placed the coin on the table in front of her. Leedles picked it up, still warm from being in Furd's pocket. It looked like no coin she'd ever seen, so beautiful she'd be reluctant to spend it. She clutched in her hand.

"I'll hold it safe." She held up her hand. "I don't have any pockets."

"Put it in here," Furd handed her a tiny bag. The scent of spice drifted out of it. "My spices come in these, I have many, many of them." He found a cord and tied it so the bag could hang around her neck and be tucked inside her shirt.

"I will walk you back to the inn, it is dark and not all people are good." Furd stood up effortlessly and Leedles pushed herself to her feet.

They walked through the darkness. Leedles fighting to keep her eyes open, just before they reached the inn. Furd stopped her with a gentle hand on her shoulder.

"Advice is dangerous," he said, barely visible in the night, "but I give you this. Beware of what you desire." He pushed her toward the door, then followed her into the inn.

Karl sat in a corner with a beer in front of him and a couple of empty ones to the side.

She went over and slid in beside him.

"How was your day?" She picked up his beer and drank from it. Sharp and bitter, she almost made a face, but instead put the mug in front of her.

"Long, harder than I remember." Karl reached for the mug and Leedles slid it away.

"I don't remember you ever getting drunk in Peace, but last night you forgot who I was and tried to throw me out. Tonight, you're a fair way to drunk again. Whatever demons are eating you; I will help fight them if you let me."

"I threw away my sword." Karl put his head in his hands and ran his fingers through his hair. "What good am I?"

"You lived without it for fifteen years in Peace."

"I knew it was buried under my floorboards. Half of why I guided you away was to carry it again." He clapped his hand over his mouth and looked wide eyed at Leedles.

"I don't love you less because you wanted to carry your sword again, nor do I love you less because you threw it away. My father, it was your wisdom and caring that won my heart." She put her hand on his. "I still need your wisdom."

"It's bedtime, daughter." Karl stood up and wobbled.

Leedles took his arm. "Tonight, *I* sleep on the floor."

CHAPTER TEN

The sun woke Leedles. Karl had got up much earlier and tiptoed past her. She'd mumbled something and gone back to sleep.

Now she got up and put on her shift and dress, then bundled her pants, shirt and a pants and shirt from Karl's kit into her pack. The pack bounced on her shoulder as she walked down the stairs. The cook served up a bowl of hot cereal.

"That's a different look. Sella will be disappointed to lose her barbarian."

"She's just taking a day off. I have a job I'd like Mistress Fall to consider."

"You must have worked hard yesterday." The cook eyed her carefully.

"He said I made his house happy, I also made it very dusty before I finished cleaning." Leedles poured honey on her cereal and ate it quickly.

"He's always talking like things are people with thoughts and feelings." The cook went back to wiping down the bar.

The fastest way to Mistress Fall's led through the town square. While she walked through, Cordin stepped up beside her.

"See, there's the Queen's Guard building. Impressive isn't it? It'd be more impressive if there were Queen's Guard in it, but there is a clerk, and he's usually bored. Tad could liven up his day by reporting an unlicensed wizard on the loose."

"What proof, aside from the word of a couple of thieves, is there that I'm a wizard?"

"I'm wounded, we're not common thieves, we're artists, but I digress. The Guard has a device, given them by the wizards. One look through the device and they will know whether you have the ability to wield magic. If you do, they whisk you off, never to be seen again."

Sella's dress popped into Leedles' mind. Did she look through a device? She never said what the test was.

"You aren't listening to me," Cordin put his hand on her arm. The strength of his grip surprised her, but she only turned and smiled at him.

"The baker is watching us."

Cordin stepped away. "Meet me in the cemetery late in the afternoon." He disappeared into the crowd. Leedles refused to rub her arm in case Cordin was watching. The rest of the walk to Mistress Fall's shop, Leedles looked over her shoulder and peered into shadows, her heart pounding painfully. She sighed with relief when she arrived.

Mistress Fall answered her door on the first knock and welcomed Leedles in.

"That's a different look on you." She circled Leedles again. "I like you as the barbarian better."

"So do I," Leedles unpacked her bag, "Which is why I need a few more clothes. A shirt for sure, pants, and if there's enough, a shirt and pants for my father."

"What do you have to spend, my dear?" Mistress Fall picked up the clothing and looked at it carefully.

"I have this coin Furd gave me for cleaning his house." Leedles pulled it out of the bag and held it out to Mistress Fall.

"I know what Furd usually pays the children to beat his rugs, and it isn't silver."

"He said I made his house happy."

Mistress Fall nodded as if that made sense and took the coin from her hand and peered at it closely, then tossed it a couple of times.

"Ok, but I will choose the cloth."

"It needs to wear well, I'm a bit rough on my clothes these days."

Mistress Fall laughed and slipped the coin into her pocket.

"Let's get to work." She took a string with knots at regular intervals and swiftly measured Leedles, muttering under her breath the whole time.

When Leedles arrived back at the inn, a message waited for her.

Remember the graveyard before the sun goes down.

"Cordin." Leedles crumpled the paper and stuffed it in a pocket. She walked out of the inn and looked for a place to think. Messing this up was not an option. When the sun moved toward the western horizon, her head hurt, but she had the beginnings of a plan.

Rubbing her temples, Leedles headed for the cemetery.

Leedles wandered around looking at headstones. while Cordin sat on one reading a book. He looked up when she stopped in front of him, then went back to reading.

"You don't act like a normal person." Cordin had closed the book.

"What's normal? Yesterday I was a barbarian because I wore pants and a shirt and have a blanket for jacket."

"Really?" Cordin's eyes lit up.

"Here are the rules," Leedles held up a hand with three fingers up. "You don't steal from me or my friends, so far that is Mistress Fall, Furd and the inn where I'm staying." She put one finger down.

"Cloth is hard to fence, you couldn't pay me enough to go near Furd's, and the inn has nothing I want." Cordin shrugged and brushed dust off his sleeve.

"Second." She dropped another finger. "I will make you three things. No more, if you come back and try to force more out of me, I will take my chances with the wizards, and you will be a toad."

Cordin didn't look nearly as nonchalant about the second rule, but he nodded again.

"We'd like something to make us, not invisible, but not noticeable, so people, like guards, don't pay us much attention. Then something which will tell us if there's magic about. Last is a bag only we can open. Don't want anyone lifting our hard earned swag."

"I think I can work with that." Leedles stifled her inner panic, telling her stomach this was not the time to lose her lunch.

"Third." Leedles put the last finger down. "You don't sell, trade or give away the things I make. They are your responsibility. I've told you I'm not sure about what I'm doing, so you, and only you will live with the consequences if I mess up."

"Now listen here," Cordin stood up and reached to grab her. Leedles held up her hand as if to throw something.

"How many headstones do you think you'd knock over if I tossed you through the cemetery?"

Cordin went pale. "Tad is waiting..."

"At the Guards building, I've got that, but I'd rather take my chances with them than with a couple of thieves." She muttered something and held her hand out, letting only the thinnest thread of magic add glow to it. Pain spiked into her temples, but she forced a pleasant smile on her face. "Let's shake on our agreement, shall we? If you break a rule, I'll know, and there will be consequences."

Cordin tentatively reached out and poked the light on her hand, when it didn't burn him, he gave a dramatic shrug and clasped her hand. A spark made both of them jump.

"Give me a day for each object, then meet me back here, same time." She stood up and brushed her dress off. "Give my regards to Tad, remember the rules bind him as well as you, whether he was here or not."

Leedles shook like a leaf as she left the cemetery. She had no idea what that spark did, the magic always had a mind of its own. With any luck, she'd never need to find out.

CHAPTER ELEVEN

Mistress Fall worked quickly and had basted a shirt and pants together for Leedles the next day she went back, once more wearing what she now thought of as 'her barbarian outfit'. The shirt was made of dark green cloth, which, while not as soft as her shirt, would be very comfortable. The pants were of some tough material, a bit stiffer than what she wore, but Mistress Fall assured her they would soften with wear.

The first day in the field, Leedles considered how to make the thieves unworthy of notice. She sat, eating nuts and trying not to cry in frustration, when a squirrel ran up and stole a nut.

"You rat..." A broad grin crossed her face. Anywhere there were things to steal, there'd be rats. If she made something to make them look like rats. She have to figure a way to turn it on and off, they wouldn't appreciate looking like rats all the time. If she made it so it only worked while it touched their skin? She picked up an uncracked nut and began to concentrate.

The magic fought her every step of the way as she carefully explained what she needed and how it would work.

"When one of them holds this, or it's touching their skin, the people around them will only see a rat, not a person. When it's in their pocket, they will be visible as people. Got that? Pocket, they're a person. Skin, they're a rat."

A sharp pain ran up her arm and the nut flashed bright white before turning coal black. The magic laughed at her as she shook off the pain. Tomorrow, she'd set the thing on the ground.

:Sloppy.:

She ignored the feeling of ants crawling inside her.

Next day she tried on the clothes and Mistress Fall wanted to make some final adjustments. Karl's clothes were ready, just copies of what he already had. Leedles' shirt had a more sophisticated wrap around system on the left side. Mistress Fall didn't like how it hung. Leedles couldn't take her eyes off the cupboard with Sella's dress in it. What would they do to her? Train her, or lock her away? She had to get this bargain done and get away from the thieves.

Out in the field, Leedles decided to make a stone glow when it was near magic. Only it glowed all the time. She put it in her pouch around her neck, it might be useful. What she needed was to show when magic was being used. When she used it, she formed it into a different shape, so revealing when magic was being manipulated would work.

She laid the rock on the ground and forced the magic to do her bidding. No flash of pain this time. The rock glowed if she held it near her staff or her glowing rock. Two down. No judging voice inside her head, but the ants got worse. She only had one more thing to go. They would leave town and it would be only her and Karl again. Maybe they could stay away from other people.

Leedles gave Karl his new clothes that evening in their room. He looked bewildered, then delighted and had to try them on immediately. They fit perfectly, as she'd expected.

"We'll leave tomorrow." Karl ran his hand down the front of his new shirt, a dark blue cloth the same weight as her green shirt.

"I need one more day to let Mistress Fall finish my clothes, they aren't quite ready yet."

"Fine, I could use a day to rest."

Leedles showed up at Mistress Fall's shop the next morning with her pack.

"They are ready, try them on." Mistress Fall looked as eager as Leedles felt.

When Leedles pulled off her shirt, Mistress Fall frowned. She touched the bag around Leedles' neck.

"You have magic in here."

Leedles pulled out the stone and it lit up the workroom.

"Oh my," Mistress Fall touched it in wonder, then dug into her pile of scraps. "Here, Leedles, wrap the stone in this." She handed Leedles a tiny square of cloth.

The cloth ran like water across Leedles' fingers. It was so dark a blue as to look black even in the stone's light.

"Silk will hide the magic from any but the most discerning eye. Don't show it around or word will spread. There are those of us who don't like what the wizards do with magic, but we only have power to resist in small ways. Stay away from them."

"Thank you."

Leedles wrapped the stone in the silk. She tried on her new clothes, then packed her old ones in the bag. If Mistress Fall could see magic, how many others could? She'd have to be more careful around people. She didn't need more like Cordin and Tad, or to be reported to the wizards before she was ready.

Out in the field she put down a nondescript bag she'd bought with the bit of change Mistress Fall had insisted on giving her. Just canvas with a draw string. How to make it so only Cordin or Tad could open it? She needed something from them to tell the magic it was them.

Leedles closed her eyes and tried to think where she'd find them. Immediately the magic tugged at her, so she followed it. It led her in a winding path through town until she rounded a corner to find Cordin and Tad sitting on upturned boxes playing a game with cards.

"How did you find us?" Cordin dropped his cards and Tad rolled his eyes.

"She's a wizard, you nit. I told you not to mess with her."

"I need a hair from each of you, so I can make the bag open only to you. We're leaving tomorrow, so meet me at the cemetery in two hours, both of you." Leedles took the hairs the men reluctantly plucked from their heads, then left them arguing over what they would have done if they were bald.

Back in the field, she put the hairs in the bag, then told the magic only the people who owned those hairs could open the bag. The magic sullenly did what it was told. The ants were bad enough Leedles' hands shook and her head ached.

:You don't learn do you?:

The bag wouldn't let her open it, so it must have worked. She headed toward the cemetery.

Cordin paced about the gravestones while Tad sat on the ground whittling a stick with a small knife.

"Here's your magic," Leedles handed them the bag. Cordin opened it up and looked at her.

"How do I know it will only open for me?"

Leedles took the bag and tried to open it and failed. Cordin nodded.

"I don't know how it would react to someone trying to cut it open." Leedles said. She handed the stone to them. "When this is near magic being used, it will glow. It shone dimly in her hand, brightened near the magic bag, and Cordin grinned broadly.

"Last." Leedles held the cloth wrapped nut in her hand, suddenly reluctant to give it to them.

"Yes?" Cordin held out his hand.

"I have to warn you, I think this one is dangerous." Leedles handed it to Cordin. "When it is touching your skin, people around you will see a rat. Wrapped in cloth it will have no effect."

Cordin immediately unwrapped the nut and held it in his hand. A rat sat in his place and Tad scurried backward.

"I don't like rats," he said.

Then Cordin stood there again. He put the wrapped nut in his pocket.

"Last thing, if you can, wrap these things in silk, it will make it harder for others to see them. Won't work against wizards, so stay away from them."

"No argument here." Tad shuddered. "They give me the creeps."

Leedles turned to walk away and stumbled. She tried to catch herself but hit the ground hard. She lay trying to catch her breath. The ants were scurrying madly and the world with them.

"Hey, are you all right?" Tad came over but didn't touch her.

"No, I'm not all right. Did you think magic had no cost?" She pushed to her feet and used her staff to steady herself. "Go steal whatever you're going to steal, and leave me alone." Leedles hobbled back to the inn and crawled into bed.

CHAPTER TWELVE

Karl had them up early. He frowned at Leedles' pale face, and hands which still shook slightly.

"I'll be fine." Leedles dressed in her new clothes and packed her bag. "Once we get walking."

She said farewell to Sella and her mother, then followed Karl out the door. They walked through town and gradually the tingling subsided until it was only an unpleasant buzz and her hands didn't shake. Furd waved at them from his garden and Leedles hoisted her staff in salute.

"The next town is two days walk, then they are about a day apart until we get to the river. Last I traveled through there, you could pay a penny to cross the bridge or a half penny to be ferried over the river. I preferred to walk, the river is treacherous."

Karl talked about places he'd traveled, but never about the wars he'd been in or even much about himself. By the end of the first day Leedles felt fine, full of energy and ready to keep going. They camped at a spot used by other travelers, then set out again in the morning.

Then a gray fog settled on Leedles, which even Karl's stories couldn't lift. She struggled to get up in the morning, and didn't say much during the day. People stared at the staff chained to her wrist, but she or Karl explained it was a religious thing. No one pointed at her and shouted she was a wizard.

A week after they'd left Dunstown they reached the river.

Leedles stopped on the road and stared. The entire village of Peace could be dropped in the river and not touch both shores. The bridge arched to a pillar set in the river, then to another until it reached the far shore. The entire structure glowed with magic.

"Riverport, on the other side is not near the size of the Queen's City, but big enough. We'll need to be careful. They say it took the wizards a year to build the bridge. No matter how much water or ice comes down the river, it won't move."

"They built that with magic?" Leedles struggled to imagine how she'd do it, and how she'd survive the ants after. The pain that went through her after the avalanche had been fearsome. But the staff had taken it away, how? She'd have to think about it, later.

Karl nodded and walked forward again.

"Never had much to do with wizards, they didn't associate with the common soldiers, but can't argue with the things they can do."

They reached the shore and Karl led them down to the docks.

"I thought you liked the bridge better."

"Might be wizards up there, or spells to spot magic, let's get you to the Queen's City before we face them."

The air got thicker as they walked down to the docks. Leedles' head spun so she made sure to plant her staff solidly in the mud. Her ears popped and the spinning subsided enough for the smell of the river to overwhelm her. Fish, alive and dead, were offloaded on wharves. Birds fought over guts and dead fish floating in the water.

If she could shake off her lethargy, maybe she could use the magic to block the odours. She followed Karl to a dock with no fishing boats, instead a flat boat waited at the end of the dock, already loaded with people, a horse and cart, and a pile of packages.

"J'st the two of ye?" A man approached Karl and held out his hand. "A penny to cross. W'leave soon's yer aboard."

Karl dropped the coin in the man's palm and led Leedles onto the ferry.

Leedles found a space on the side where she could see the bridge and settled in.

A mother who constantly told her children to behave and stay away from the water, stopped to stare at Leedles.

"It's a religious thing." Leedles dreaded the day when someone would ask about the religion, but the mother rolled her eyes and yelled at toddler who ran too close to the water.

The ferry started with a lurch as two men at least the size of Furd walked around in a circle holding bars connected to a massive wheel.

"The wheel has a wrap of the cable which runs under the water to the other side." The speaker looked at Leedles through lenses balanced on his nose. He carried a bag at his side.

Leedles nodded but turned to the water. Last thing she wanted was conversation.

"I'm not aware of any religion which requires a staff to be chained to one's wrist."

Leedles dragged her gaze back to the man, he didn't look dangerous.

"It's long and complicated," Leedles said, "easier to tell people it's religious."

"May I?" The man leaned close to the staff and peered at the wood and steel. He ignored the acorn on its twig proving Leedles' theory that only she could see it. "Interesting workmanship, and I can't say I've ever seen this wood before. You might get a good price from a collector."

"If I take it off, I die." Leedles tucked the staff between her and the side of the boat.

"Oh my," the man said, but didn't continue the conversation.

The air freshened as they pulled away from the shore and a breeze played with her hair. The children had fallen asleep around their mother, so the only sounds were the lapping of waves against the side of the ferry and the creaking of the wheel.

As the ride grew more pleasant, Leedles' mood sank. Great sadness filled her, and tears splashed into the river. Worse, she couldn't think of any reason for her grief. Karl's hand rested on her shoulder, but even connection with her adopted father didn't lift the gloom.

A shadow moved in the water beneath the boat. It curled and swam around them gradually growing brighter and larger. Other people pointed at it and murmured. Then a huge head lifted out of the water in front of Leedles.

:Greetings, magic one.: The gentle voice filled Leedles' head, leaving no room for sadness.

"I'm not magic." Leedles said and the murmuring around her grew.

:You are and must be. Go east across the sea to the testing lands.:

"How?"

:You will find the way, or the way will find you. Refrain from working wonders, little one. The magic will consume you otherwise.:

Leedles' tears returned, so much she didn't know.

:You carry a wise one with you.: The great head glared at her. :Let it guide you.:

"I'll try," Leedles reached out to the creature as it put its head beneath her hand. She expected cold slimy scales, but she touched warm skin. The heat traveled up her arm, at the same time a gentle light lit the gloom in her heart.

"Thank you," Leedles whispered. The great head bowed to her, then disappeared beneath the surface.

"I've heard rumours of the dragon fish living beneath the bridge, but to see it with my own eyes..." The man with the lenses looked to be at the point of tears. He bowed to her and retreated to another part of the ferry.

The crowd left a bubble of space around her. Leedles let her hand trail in the river, imagining her sadness floating away, replaced by the light given her by the river dragon. She'd caught a glimpse of his life, ancient beyond her imagining, but he encountered each moment as if it were his first.

CHAPTER THIRTEEN

Leedles and Karl were the first off the ferry. Karl led them at a brisk pace up the hill.

"We need to get ahead of the rumours," Karl said. "We'll find a place you can change your clothes, be less recognizable."

"Changing my clothes won't remove the staff from sight." Leedles let the calm from the river drown her anxiety. "But I have an idea."

Karl found a tavern and paid for a room with the last of his coin. Leedles sat on the bed with the staff in her lap.

"You're the wise one, the river dragon talked about." She shook it slightly

:I never could keep my mouth shut.:

"How do I hide the staff?"

:You can't, it's part of the spell.:

"Spell?"

:Yes, the spell forcing you to carry me until you die, which at the rate you're going won't be long.:

"Can't you do anything about it?"

:The fish is right; you have to go east to the desert.:

"How?"

:For a start, no more magic. If you must cast a spell use a focus, not yourself. It will keep the magic burn down.:

"But the wizards-"

:*Stay away from them.*: The voice dripped with contempt.

"Why?" The voice didn't respond and Leedles sighed. What was the use of a wise one if it didn't talk to her?

She went downstairs and sat with Karl.

"I'll have to try something else."

Karl looked at her and Leedles squirmed. Her father shouldn't have that half-scared, half-in-awe look on his face.

"I will always be your daughter, no matter what happens." She put a hand on his shoulder. After a moment, his hand covered hers.

"There's something else we can try," he said.

They left the tavern and wound through the streets to a market. Leedles glimpsed a familiar face in the crowd and groaned.

"I hate stealing," Karl said.

"Wait a moment." Leedles reached for the connection she had with Cordin and tugged. He appeared out of the crowd with a scowl on his face. He looked different, not so sure of himself.

"What a surprise." Cordin waved his arm. "I thought we were through."

"Not quite." Leedles steeled herself to speak calmly, as if she were completely in control. "There are some rumours about a river dragon talking to a woman with a staff chained to her wrist."

"Really? Not my problem." Cordin turned to go.

"It is if the wizards capture me and find out about those little things I made for you."

"You wouldn't."

Leedles looked at him.

"Ok, what do you need?"

"A robe with long sleeves, something to make Leedles' hair grey, and make up for her face." Karl rattled off the list.

"Sure thing, gramps. Looks like you lost your sword, probably's for the best."

Leedles swung her staff and caught Cordin on the ribs.

"Respect, he's my father."

Cordin rubbed his side and nodded, then vanished into the crowd.

"What kind of deal did you make with him?" Karl grabbed her hand.

"Let's get to somewhere more private and I'll explain." Leedles said. "It's a long story."

A short time later Karl glared at Leedles as she finished her story.

"You should have talked to me. I would have straightened them out quick enough."

"You had no sword, and you'd thrown away your confidence with it. How was I to ask you to face them again? You aren't that fighter anymore. You left that path long before you threw your sword into the rocks. Be who you are now, not who you were then." Leedles wanted to throw her arms around him and find comfort in his strength. But since they'd come down from the mountain, he'd been fragile and uncertain.

Cordin swaggered into the alley, interrupting whatever Karl might have said. He carried a bundle he presented to Leedles.

"Now, can we please be done? I have work to do." He tossed Leedles a purse. "A bit of coin to ease your passage out of my life."

"A word," Karl stayed seated on the barrel. His hands on his knees, but a portion of his ability to wait in the present might have returned.

"Make it quick, gramps."

"Magic is chancy, and it will betray you at the worst time. Why me and my mates never trusted ought but ourselves and our swords."

"Lovely, my eyes are tearing up at your words, but what does this have to do with me?"

"Remember who you are, remember your skills, don't depend on the magic. You're linked to Leedles now. Mess up, we're dragged in with you."

Cordin gave a salute while rolling his eyes, then left the alley and vanished into the crowd.

"We will want to be far away from here when he fails at whatever he's going to fail at." Karl stood up and took the bundle from Leedles.

"How do you know he'll fail?" She lifted her arm so Karl could feed the long wide sleeve over her staff.

"When you're that cocky, failure is always waiting in the wings." He dusted grey powder into Leedles' hair and massaged it in.

"Great, my head is going to itch something fierce." She lifted her head so he could put make up on her face.

"Now you'll be my mother instead of my daughter." He pulled the hood over her head and had her grip her sleeve as well as the staff.

"What was your mother like?" Leedles tried to walk like the old women in Peace.

"Never stopped giving me orders, worse than a Sergeant. Was why I ran away to fight."

"I think I can do that." Leedles rasped. "Now help me along, this is no place for an old lady."

Karl switched shirts then offered his arm to Leedles. He walked with small steps as if he was uncertain of the ground. Leedles bent over as much as she could with the staff and shuffled along.

They used the money Cordin gave them to stay in a small but respectable inn. Leedles kept up a litany of complaints while Karl apologized profusely for his mother. The only looks they got were pity for Karl.

They went up to their room early and Leedles sighed and let her old woman persona drop.

"I don't like being your mother very much." She stretched and her back clunked as it fell back into place.

"Good, then you won't grow up to be like her." Karl lay down on the bed and put his hands behind his head.

Leedles removed the robe but left her hair and makeup as it was. She lay down and closed her eyes.

CHAPTER FOURTEEN

Karl tried to sleep, but Leedles' words kept running through his mind. Who was he now if he wasn't a fighter? It had never been an issue in Peace. He'd done odd labour jobs and acted as a constable the few times it was needed. As soon as he left, the fighter tried to come back, but it didn't fit right.

He dropped off to sleep no closer to an answer. Leedles woke him when she sat up with a shout.

"They're in trouble." She stumbled to her feet. "Hiding from the guards in an old building." Leedles pointed through one of the windows.

Karl's fists clenched, he'd warned them, but he let his anger go. At their age, he wouldn't have listened either.

"Stay here, if you can create some fog to make it harder for them to follow us." He pushed her to sit on the bed. "Put the robe on so you're ready to go. Now give me the best directions you can, and I'll find them."

Leedles pointed again. "That way, almost at the river. It's an old building, no one uses it anymore. It used to store cloth. I don't know."

"You did fine. I have a good idea where they are. The guards will tell me the rest." Karl looked out the window. It let onto the roof which gave access to a shed. In the old days, he'd never have accepted such a room. He'd never even checked. Though he didn't carry his sword anymore, he couldn't get sloppy.

The window opened easily. Karl climbed out then crept along to drop to the shed then the street. He took off at a run, keeping to the shadows. The old habits of spying and covert action came back. The last mission before he went home to find Cassie dead had been a deadly game of cat and mouse. Never knew which he was. Glad he'd kept Cassie out of it, poor girl. Didn't have time to think about her now.

Fog poured up from the river thickening from tendrils of mist to soup which left beads of moisture on his eyelashes. A vision of the mountain coming down on them made him worry Leedles may have over done the fog.

Mission first, worry second.

In the warehouse district his feet knew the streets better than he did. He slowed, puffing hard. Forced himself to breathe through his nose to quiet it. Shouts and the clatter of armour sounded ahead. Just what had those fools done?

Get them out, then deal with it.

Shadows kept him hidden from the men running through the street. Once he'd have worn charcoal coloured clothes just for this. His dark blue shirt would have to do. They were searching the warehouses one by one. Moving as a line through the district using a huge number of men. The good news was once Karl got the idiots away, there'd be fewer guards to chase them.

Out in the fog, a roar came which made every guard turn to face the river. Echoes bounced around the buildings hiding Karl's footsteps as he ran to the old weaver's guild building and climbed up onto the loading dock. He rolled under the door which had jammed most of the way closed.

He heard scurrying off to his right. The rats would have run for their holes with all the noise going on. He followed them.

A young man Karl didn't know looked around with a pale face.

"What do we do now? We're trapped, Cordin."

"Hush, Tad and let me think." Cordin's voice came from where a rat scurried, but never went anywhere.

"Gentlemen," Karl whispered. "We have maybe a minute before the guards get here. I suggest we move."

"Who are you?" Tad stared at him wide eyed.

"Leedles' old man," Cordin said.

"You'll have to leave one of your magic things here to let them think you're still about. It won't give us much time, maybe an extra minute.

"No thanks, we risked our lives for this thing, we're not giving it up."

"We have to." Tad whispered and shook something Karl couldn't see. "That or get taken, you know what that will mean."

"Very well." A canvas bag appeared on the floor. "The dragon take them. Good luck opening the bag. Let's go old man."

"It might be better if you gave up the rat thing." Karl waved them toward the door he'd come in.

"Can't, it's stuck."

"Right, escape then. The cordon is moving through each building with guards running sweeps ahead looking for runners. Weren't looking for someone coming in. Harder to get out. Don't have time to loop around them, we'll have to chance it."

"Stay in the shadows, keep it quiet. Move when I move." Karl dropped to roll out through the door.

"Right, teach us the basics, old-" Cordin's voice came from the floor.

The roar of the river dragon sounded louder, closer. The guards looked around fearfully, some started to run, then stopped. Just as Tad rolled through the door, the fog turned to a heavy rain.

"Perfect," Karl said, "We run, now." He sprinted through the shadows, letting the noise of the rain cover his footsteps and breathing. Confusion reigned behind him as orders were shouted then retracted.

One last roar from the river dragon sounded more grieved than angry. Karl caught a shout saying half the river had disappeared.

He arrived at the inn and jumped up on the shed only to almost slide off again. Tad leapt up beside him and a rat ran beside him, strangely dry in the downpour. Karl led the way to the room.

Leedles lay in a heap on the bed, for a second his heart stopped thinking she was dead. Then he spotted the tiny movement of her robe.

"Meet me around front." Karl didn't wait for an answer but swept his pack on, then picked up Leedles. He opened the door and ran out into the hall.

"My mother is dying!" He shouted as loud as he could. "She needs a healer."

At the bottom of the stairs the innkeeper met him.

"What can I do?"

"Do you have cart, a wagon, anything?"

"We have a small cart, I can get the boy to hitch it for you, but I need some surety it will be returned."

Karl dropped Cordin's purse on the counter. It thudded heavily enough the innkeeper didn't hesitate to run to the kitchen door and shout to the stable boy. Karl follow him, then ran through the rain to the stable.

The boy staggered through the motions of harnessing an old horse to a tiny cart. Karl had probably overpaid for it. He placed Leedles gently in the cart, then covered her with a horse blanket he snatched off a rail.

Though sleepy, the boy worked quickly, then fell back into his straw bed. Karl drove the cart out into the rain, not too fast at first. Two thumps behind him were followed by Tad's quiet voice.

"We're on."

"Stay down." Karl snapped the reins and set the horse and cart traveling as fast as he dared out of Riverport. The road they were on went straight for a short way before making the wide loop around the lakur nest. If the lakur didn't catch trespassers, the Queen's Guard did, then hung them on the border.

Either way meant a certain if not quick death.

Once, a long time ago. Karl had fought the lakur. He never wanted to see them again. He'd been lucky to get out alive. Most of the army hadn't.

He let the horse slow to a walk. No need to wear her out. They had a long way to go. With any luck the guards wouldn't connect a man and his old mother with the fleeing fugitives, but if they had wizards with them, it could be in deep trouble.

At least they'd be past the lakur in a couple of days and his dreams wouldn't be troubled by old memories. The rain slowed then stopped, the water returning, Karl guessed, to the river.

They came to the section of the road which ran through an outcropping of the forest the lakur claimed. It spooked Karl every time he passed through it, knowing the monsters were only a few miles away. Signs warned travelers not to wander into the woods on the east side of the road. Fortunately, it only lasted for an hour's travel by horse. Maybe a bit longer for this old nag and cart.

Leedles sat up and screamed. She jumped from the cart as the old horse panicked and ran away at full speed. Karl hauled on the reins to no avail as he looked behind him.

Leedles disappeared at a run into the forest on the east side of the road. Karl's heart cracked a second time. He dropped the reins and wept into his hands.

CHAPTER FIFTEEN

The river dragon was coming for her. Leedles jumped out of bed and ran as fast as she could away from the river. Suddenly she ran through trees, her staff catching at branches and tripping her up. The robe caught on a branch, so she wiggled out of it and ran on.

She hadn't meant to anger the dragon, but like the wind which blew the mountain down, her magic ran wild lifting most of the river into the air. No wonder he raged at her. As soon as she could think past the knives of pain, she turned the fog into rain, but the effort had thrown her into darkness.

:No, turn back. Fool, you'll kill us both.:

If she could have thrown the staff away, she would have. *Some wise one, full of riddles and empty advice.* If she died, she'd be rid of it and the pain. Leedles ran faster.

Exhaustion made her slow and finally stop. She leaned against a tree and gasped for air.

:Listen, to me. Remember, you need a focus to cast magic. The magicburn will kill you otherwise.:

Something rustled in the dark. Leedles' heart leapt into her mouth and she staggered into a run again. Every time she stopped the rustle would come. It gave her no rest. She pulled on the magic to bolster her strength. The voice of the wise one in her head screamed at her, but she couldn't take in the words.

The river dragon was near, he said he'd punish her for her actions. She kept running. Daylight made the forest easier to see. It didn't look much different than the one she and Karl traveled through. She wished they'd stayed there and never entered this nightmare world of thieves, dragons, and magic.

Even in daylight she couldn't see what followed her. Leedles stumbled on, leaning on the staff for support. Soon, she'd fall over and whatever chased her would destroy her. She tripped on a root and fell. This time she didn't have the strength to get up.

***

Karl carried her out of the darkness. But his arms didn't feel right. Leedles looked around at his face and saw the river dragon looking down at her. It opened its mouth to swallow her. She screamed and struggled, but the arms held her tight.

Leedles opened her eyes. She was being carried by giant ants. They'd finally escaped her and now were going to eat her alive. Her staff had no effect on their hard backs. There were dozens of them, hundreds As a child, she'd watched ants carry larger insects away, and wondered what had become of them.

Leedles opened herself to the magic. The voice said to use a focus, she pulled the magic in through the staff.

:No!:

Fire bloomed from her staff incinerating the ants and the trees and everything else as far as she could see. Soot and ash blackened her clothes and filled her hair. She coughed in the acrid air, managed three steps and collapsed.

***

Karl brought his tears under control, then the horse.

"We need to go back for her." Cordin sounded panicked.

"That's the lakur nest." Karl snarled each word. *If it weren't for these thieves and their plans...*

"So, she needs to fix -"

"She's dead, or as good as. No one comes out of there alive. The lakur eat trespassers, including wizards. I've seen them." Karl turned away and concentrated on driving.

Tad and Cordin argued in the back, but neither jumped out. Karl didn't care. Maybe he should have stopped, gone back, died with her. Visions of Cassie taunted him. He'd let two daughters die; did he deserve to live?

The sky brightened. They were a day's hard ride from the Queen's City. So close.

He should dump the thieves and let them make their own way, but they were the last connection he had to Leedles.

Just after dawn the ground shook and a fireball bloomed over the lakur's forest.

Maybe she wasn't dead yet. Karl's heart lifted and he snapped the reins.

Before mid-day a man in uniform galloped past them. Karl paid only enough attention to get out of the way.

If she made it out, she'd go to the Queen's City.
Karl would be waiting for her.

CHAPTER SIXTEEN

A firm hand shook Leedles awake. She opened her eyes and gasped. Everything she could see had burnt. She'd burned it. The giant ants-

"Easy," The man wore a grey uniform with darker grey markings on it. He looked friendly, with concerned blue eyes and almost bald head. "You're safe for the moment. The queen wants me to see how dangerous you are." He looked around and smiled crookedly. "I'd say pretty dangerous. Was a half-hour ride through the burn to reach you."

He helped her sit up and gave her water to drink.

"You have one chance to live, and that is to convince the queen you are too dangerous to eat. Wondered if you hadn't gone out in a last gasp. Surprised to see you sleeping peaceful as a baby in the ashes."

"Hardly peaceful," Leedles croaked. The man gave her another drink. "I remember these giant ants carrying me..."

"The lakur, this is their nest. Sacrosanct according to the truce for the last two hundred years. What got into you? Everyone knows about this place, at least that it's death to trespass."

"I'm not from around here." Leedles pulled her knees up to her chest. "Can't we leave before they get back?"

"No, they're already watching us, and they'd nab us before we got out of the burn, not to mention starting a war which might take another hundred years to end.

Don't care what the wizards say, the lakur aren't to be trifled with."

"Come out then." Leedles jumped to her feet and turned in a circle. "I can't talk to shadows."

They lifted out of the ash, only a few feet away from her. Leedles stepped on her fear and looked more closely at them. They didn't really look much like ants. They had feelers coming from their heads, but those heads were more doglike than insect. They only had four legs like a dog but had a hard shell on their back. Their feet were a mix of paw and claw.

"This piece of your Queen has trespassed. Much destruction, many lakur dead."

"She isn't one of us." The man bowed to the speaker. "Not one of my Queen's nest."

"Who is her Queen, shall she not be punished? She came through your Queen's land. Does that not make her your Queen's piece?"

"I don't belong to any Queen, I'm my own person and I'm responsible for my own mistakes."

Both the man and the lakur looked at Leedles before turning back to speak.

"She claims to be a rogue." The lakur shivered. "Dangerous not to have a Queen. Best if she perishes here."

"My queen can't be responsible for the damage if you fail to eat her." The man waved at the devastation around them.

"Your thoughts are confused as always. I am unsure of your intentions, but the surface words are true. You don't know this piece. You may go and we will deal with it in our own way."

Leedles poked the lakur with her staff. She didn't have any tingling from the magic, but she didn't trust it. The magic moved oddly in this place; the whispers dissonant. She gathered some in her hand and it ran out like water.

The lakur turned and walked up close to sniff at her.

"Your magic will not work in this place. It is forbidden."

"I've never been good at following the rules." Leedles twisted the strange magic and made red flames leap from her hand. The magicburn started instantly, but she held the flame until the lakur stepped back. "I want to talk to the Queen, not some flunky. This guy doesn't speak for me either."

"You speak to the Queen, I am the Queen as the lakur your magic destroyed were the Queen. We are one."

"Then how do I get you to understand? I don't want to make trouble, but I'm not going to die here."

"There is a way."

"No don't." The man stepped forward, but a lakur stepped in front of him.

"Fine, tell me." Leedles stepped up to the lakur. The magicburn ached and made it hard to think.

The lakur reared up to snatch her right hand with its claw, then it leaned forward and stabbed its feeler through her hand.

Agony exploded in her mind and she lost her grip on the magic. She could think of nothing but the pain. Then she felt a different ache, not her own. Huge, beyond even the River Dragon in age; the damage from her fire a blister on her hand. The grief drove Leedles to her knees. So many gone, so much talent become ash. Leedles' awareness encompassed the nest, she felt each piece as individual, yet bound inextricably in one mind.

"I'm sorry," Leedles sobbed. "I didn't know."

She became one with the lakur, their grief the same. Then the Speaker for the Queen pulled its antenna from Leedle's hand and she became just a girl sobbing in the ashes.

"The lakur will not eat this one. It trespassed unknowing and attacked in fear. It is an egg trying to hatch. The lakur desire to see what emerges. Your Queen must not eat it."

"You know, Queen to Queen, I will request, but she will decide."

"The ways of your nest are sloppy, but the truce is kept. There will be no punishment."

"My Queen is pleased." The man bowed to the lakur, then hoisted Leedles onto the horse and jumped up behind her. "Put that stick between your leg and the horse. Don't want it catching a branch." He snapped the reins and the horse set off at a walk.

"I'm Captain Theodore, closest thing I have to a job is Speaker for the Queen. The lakur have a long history of living with humans in one way or another, but the concept of individuals unruled by a Queen sets them into a panic. Happened way south I heard, and no one came out of that well."

They reached the unburned part of the forest and the Captain set the horse to a canter.

"Let's get out of here, then we'll talk more. Hold on tight."

They rode through no path Leedles could discern, yet they never slowed or hesitated.

"You joined with the lakur too." Leedles turned her head to talk to the Captain.

"Part of my job, most of the time, my thoughts are my own, especially outside the nest, but when the lakur call, I come at full gallop. Means none of the people around quite trust me. Never know when the lakur might be listening in on secret councils. So I spend my days trying to keep order in the City and doing nothing of import. I suggest you don't talk too much about joining with the lakur."

"What did it mean about the egg?"

"The lakur hatch from eggs, the only reason for waiting to see what hatches is if the egg is another Queen."

"What happens if it is?"

"Have no idea, even the lakur can't remember the last time it happened."

They rode out of the trees and the Captain let his horse rest.

"We'll change at the nearest station, but there's no need to ride the poor beast to death." He walked around and stretched while the horse cropped grass nearby.

Leedles' hand ached, but nothing close to the pain when it had been pierced by the lakur. The hole had already closed, leaving a puckered scar.

The staff remained stubbornly silent. Good, it wasn't much of a wise one in Leedles' opinion.

They climbed back on the horse and rode to a stable beside the road where they changed horses. The Captain kept a pace just slow enough not to hurt the horses, but when Leedles wanted to sleep, he told her to sleep in the saddle.

Finally, she leaned back and let her exhaustion carry her away.

CHAPTER SEVENTEEN

The Captain shook her awake with one arm wrapped tight around her.

She woke hoping to see Karl, but sighed. Likely she'd never see him again. Grief tore at her, but she pushed it away. The only hope she had was to stay alive.

According to the Captain, she didn't have much chance of that.

Leedles looked around, they rode through land covered with crops or animals grazing in the fields. Up ahead the City wall dominated the landscape. The fields continued up to the wall with no building in sight. Guards in black uniforms waved the Captain through the gate then returned to searching a wagon while a man protested beside the road.

Inside, the City was paved with cobblestones and the horse's shoes struck sparks from them. They rode straight to another wall, so Leedles only saw people starting their day, some waved at them, some flung cruder signs. At the next gate, they entered an area of large estates and huge houses. No one stirred here, though smoke wafted from chimneys. They reached a third wall.

For the first time, the guards spoke to them, these were in blue uniforms.

"The Queen awaits."

"Very well," the Captain replied.

He stopped the horse in a courtyard and tossed the reins to a man who ran out to meet them, then jumped down and lifted Leedles down.

"Behave yourself in there." Captain Theodore pointed toward the doors as he walked. "Very powerful people will fight over you. They are more dangerous than the lakur."

"How can they be more dangerous?" Leedles had to run to keep up.

"Because they think they understand you and can use you. Don't disappoint them."

Leedles saved her breath to keep up with the Captain, who wasn't even breathing hard at the end of the hall.

"If you'll announce Captain Theodore and his prisoner." He nodded at one of the guards who slipped through the door while the other one glowered at Leedles.

"Prisoner?" Leedles voice squeaked.

"Did you think we would put you up in a fine hotel? You almost caused a war. Stay silent unless you're asked a direct question, speak respectfully and whatever you do don't try any magic."

The door swung open and the guard waved them in.

"They're waiting for you. Can I have your job if they take your head?"

The Captain lifted his scarred hand in front of the guard's face.

"We're rooting for you, Sir." The guard stepped back into place while the other smirked at him.

Captain Theodore pulled Leedles through the door, as if he hadn't seen the byplay between the guards. He held her by the right hand, covering the scar from the lakur.

He walked slowly up the aisle giving the guards standing around the Queen plenty of time to assess them. They wore the same uniform as Captain Theodore, not the blue of the rest of the guards they'd seen. None of them looked happy. Two had crossbows aimed at Leedles as they walked.

Leedles calculated if she could stop the bolt before it hit her.

"Don't even think about it." Captain Theodore spoke without moving his lips. "Some of the wizards claim to read minds."

When he mentioned wizards, she looked for old men in grey robes and long beards. She didn't see them, so focused her attention on the queen.

Grey streaked the woman's hair, her face had lines on it suggesting she didn't laugh often. Instead of fancy robes, she wore a plain version of the grey uniform, with no insignia at all. A sword lay on a pillow beside her. Leedles didn't think it was just decoration.

The Captain stopped at a line set in the floor and went to one knee, pulling Leedles down too. Her staff scraped across the floor.

"Why haven't you removed the weapon?" The Queen sounded more bored than angry.

"The prisoner is chained to the staff," the Captain said, his face still lowered. "It didn't set off any of the alarms."

"Apoxthenis?" The Queen looked to the foppishly dressed young man standing beside her.

"She has a rather quaint bauble around her neck, the staff is inert, but there is a spell binding it to her. It might be wise to leave it be, for now."

"If she makes a move with that thing, I want her skewered."

Leedles opened her hand and let the staff fall to the floor. The Queen nodded as the echoes subsided.

"Captain, report."

"The lakur queen called in the night and I rode to the nest arriving in the late morning. I found the prisoner sleeping in the centre of a burned out circle an hour's ride across."

A murmur went through the hall, though Leedles didn't see anyone move.

"The lakur let the attack go unpunished?" The wizard asked. His eyes held a gleam which made Leedles queasy.

"They were unsure of the wisdom eating such a powerful wizard. They released her into your custody."

"Letting us deal with how to dispose of her. Lovely."

"If I may point out." Apoxthenis leaned toward Leedles as if he were examining a joint of meat. "She is uncontrolled, yet immensely powerful. If she could be trained into your service, she would be a valuable asset."

"Prisoner, what do you have to say for yourself?"

The Captain squeezed her hand painfully, Leedles swallowed the words she wanted to say.

"However I may serve." The words tasted bitter, but they were her only chance to find Karl.

"Very well. Apoxthenis, you have a month to either train her or dispose of her. I will hold the Guild accountable for damage caused by your failure." She stood up and walked away. Everyone watched Leedles so she was the only witness to the fury the wizard directed at the Queen's back.

The wizard sauntered down the stairs and looked down his nose at Leedles.

"Thank you, Captain. I will take her from here."

"As you will." The Captain stood up and walked away without turning back. The guards never took their eyes from Leedles.

"Come," The wizard reached down his hand. Leedles reluctantly took it and he hauled her to her feet with surprising strength. "Since you appear to like chains..." He waved his hand and the magic around Leedles screeched. Chains formed to attach Leedles right hand to her waist, shackles joined her feet. She shuffled after the wizard until the exited through a side door.

The chains vanished.

"Always good to impress the guards." Apoxthenis spoke with a constant edge of contempt that grated on

Leedles' nerves. She kept her mouth shut and followed him.

"Good," he said, "you've already learned your first lesson."

They walked along a long hallway to a door leading to a small courtyard. The guards at the door saluted Apoxthenis as he ignored them. Another man ran out leading a horse and closed carriage.

"After you," Apoxthenis waved Leedles in. "The Guild," he said to the driver before he stepped in and closed the door. The interior of the coach let no light in from outside. The magic whimpered dolefully from where it was tied in intricate forms.

"Let me see that bauble you carry with you."

Leedles dug it out of her bag. It glowed brightly revealing leather seats and plush walls.

"How quaint." Apoxthenis clenched his hand and the light vanished. "You will need to do better than that if you expect to live."

The carriage stopped and Apoxthenis climbed out. Guards in red uniforms saluted as he dragged Leedles past them. They walked along a long corridor to a door where another wizard met them.

"I thought we agreed the council would assign students."

"Circumstances made it prudent to take her under my wing."

"The council will hear of this."

"She burned a section of forest an hour's ride across, then convinced the lakur to free her. Most likely she's the one who emptied the river and set the River Dragon raging. Think of the power she will bring properly controlled."

The second wizard paled and stepped aside.

"Do give the council my regards," Apoxthenis pushed Leedles through the door.

They walked onto a high narrow bridge. The wind buffeted Leedles, though not a hair on Apoxthenis moved. She listened and whispered to the magic until the wind left her alone. The tingle of magic burning her flesh was the least of her problems. Apoxthenis grunted, but didn't slow his walk.

The bridge took them to a tower on a rock set in the midst of roaring waves. Leedles stopped and stared. The bridge led to a solid stone wall. The tower had no windows she could see. The top faded into the clouds.

"Take a good look," Apoxthenis grinned at her. "That is the training tower, and where you will live or die." He led the way forward laughing as if what he'd said was a joke.

Part Two

CHAPTER EIGHTEEN

Karl drove the cart through the gate after the suspicious guard searched all through it, including under. Cordin had dropped off while they waited in line saying they'd meet inside.

Though the City was full of rats, the guards wouldn't be impressed at them bringing another.

"What's your business in the Queen's City?" The guard looked disappointed at not finding anything.

"Just visiting an old friend." Karl crossed his fingers.

"And who might that be?" The guard raised his eyebrow.

"Theodore Brenson, we served in the south together years back."

"Yes, Sir." The guard went from bored to carefully respectful in an instant. Theo must have moved up in the world. "Would you like me to send a message to him?"

"Is the Unkissed Toad still in business?" Karl kept his voice casual.

"Aye it is, hasn't changed much neither, you know your way?"

"Unless you've completely rebuilt the City in the last fifteen years, yes I know how to get there. Let Theo know I'm there."

The guard saluted and waved the cart on. Tad looked at him suspiciously.

"What was that all about?"

"Last thing we need is guards keeping a watch for us. They don't like things they can't explain, and an empty cart pulled by an old nag is not the usual thing asking entry into the City. You'll find they're a suspicious lot."

"Tell me something I don't know." Cordin's voice came from the back of the cart.

"The Unkissed Toad is an informal meeting ground between the Guard and the less savoury guilds of the City."

"You do realize we're thieves, and thieving without permission in this City is a death sentence?" Cordin's voice dripped with sarcasm while Tad had his head in his hands.

"You'll have to find some honest work, then."

Both the young men laughed.

"Do we look like we have skills an honest employer would want?"

"Your knowledge cuts both ways," Karl took a breath. Would do no good to get angry at them. "There are those who don't want to be stolen from, your – unique – set of skills might be handy."

Blessed silence greeted his words, and the rest of the drive to the Toad, Karl spent spotting old landmarks and how the City had changed over the years. The smell hadn't, neither had the edge of desperation tingeing the faces on the street. More windows were bricked in. The places with open windows had men standing nearby with hands on swords. The private guards were new, and not a welcome sight. They suggested the City Guard no longer controlled the streets.

Karl pulled the cart up behind the Toad and a boy sauntered out to greet them.

"You want her stabled or sent to the knackers?"

"Be respectful, she's pulled us from Riverton."

The boy shrugged but led her off to the side. Henrik hired good people, so Karl put the nag out of his mind.

"Tad, you're my son-in-law, looking to get into the security business. There's a surplus of hired guards, so there will be a market for your more esoteric skills. What you do with that is up to you."

"Sure thing, gramps and what am I supposed to be?" Cordin said beside him.

"Silent." Karl pushed through the door into the bar that had the reputation of being the toughest place in town. He tried to relax his shoulders, but one of the traditions was to challenge the new guy to a fight. Until they remembered who he used to be, he'd be the fresh meat.

He walked through into the dingy bar. There was a seat open at a table, mostly because its back faced the door. He grabbed the seat and twisted the chair so he could lean an elbow on the table and keep an eye on the door. Tad stood beside him, looking about nervously.

"Go get me a beer, kid," Karl said.

"What am I supposed to pay with?" Tad whined.

"You think I'm going to pay you and pay for your beer? Next you'll want me to pay for your women too." The others at the table laughed.

"While you're there fetch a pitcher for these gentlemen."

As Tad wove his way to the bar, a man stomped up to Karl. He looked to weigh twice as much as Karl and stood at least a head taller.

"Y'er in the wrong bar, gramps."

"You're in my light." Karl leaned back.

"I'll break ya in half and toss you in the street, then you'll have plenty of light."

"No, you won't. You're standing too close. I'll break both your knees, then snap your arm for fun. Tossing you out's too much work; your friends, if you have any, will have to carry you out."

The man puffed up, but a grizzled hand stopped him.

"He'll do that and more if I recognize the voice. Karl cleaned out the entire bar when someone insulted his unit."

"Karl Barduson? The Black Dragons?" The big man switched from menacing to puppy-eyed in an instant. "I've heard about you."

"We all know the stories, Bart, let some old friends get caught up." Henrik walked away through the crowd. Karl followed him.

"What am I supposed to do with this?" Tad waved a beer at him. Pitcher in the other hand,

"Drink it, s'what beer's for." Karl raised his voice a bit. "Don't cause the kid any grief, I promised my daughter to bring him back alive." He was collecting children at a great rate, maybe he'd have better luck with this one.

Henrik kicked the door closed behind them and the noise from the bar cut off. He stood shorter than Karl, a bit heavier, and covered with more scars than even Henrik could count. The deadliest fighter Karl had ever met, but he had a soft spot for his old companions.

"The Karl I knew would have had that oaf's balls on a platter before he said anything." Henrik eyed him up and down.

"I'm not exactly the Karl you knew, aside from my ability to gather trouble wherever I go."

"Like old times, huh?" Henrik poured a couple of glasses and handed Karl one. They drank the liquor in one shot, and it hit him like a kick from a horse.

"Still serve the good stuff," Karl turned the glass around in his hand. "Went home after that last bit of work fifteen years ago, found my daughter dead and house burnt. Lost my mind for a bit and ended up across the mountains in this village they call Peace. Big golden tree in the centre of it. No fights, no war, no more blood on my hands."

"So you've gone soft." Henrik looked at Karl like he'd stepped in horse droppings.

"No, not soft." Karl looked Henrik in the eye. "But I learned there are better ways to solve problems than leaving a trail of bodies. It's a lot harder than killing people, Henrik. Days I wish I could go back."

"Hmmph," Henrik sat on the edge of the table. "What good are you to me?"

"Saw the guard is losing control of the streets."

"Losing? Never had it. They're as like to start a fight as stop it. No training to speak of. No discipline, the thieves' guild is more honest."

"Remember I used to talk of taking over the guard, making it work?"

"Yeah, but you had to run back to your family." Henrik paused, then hooked the bottle to him and poured another drink for each of them. "To Cassie, may she rest in peace."

Karl slugged back the drink and wiped the corner of his eye.

CHAPTER NINETEEN

"Theo's the one running the City Guard," Henrik spat into a bucket in the corner. "He's the Queen's man, so no one trusts him as far as they can throw him. He isn't soft, but he's a bureaucrat and has to kiss ass along with the rest of them."

"I sent a message asking him to meet me here."

"Well, that ought to be interesting. There's a fellow or twelve who'd like a piece of our Theodore."

"You might want to put away the fine china then."

Henrik laughed and moved to pour another drink, then stopped.

"You aren't the only one getting old. I'm starting to look for someone mean enough to run the Toad so I can go off and raise goats."

Karl shook his head.

"What is it with you and your schemes?" He stood up. "I'll need a room if you've got one. I'll share with the kid."

"He really your son-in-law? Cassie would have died before marrying age."

"No, he's just trouble I picked up. He's looking for a rather special security job. You know anyone who looking not to get robbed?"

"Isn't that all of us? Let me listen around."

"Last thing," Karl took a deep breath. "Is Widdershins still around?"

"Thought you didn't like him, he being the one who got half your unit killed." Henrik shook his head. "You're up to more than your usual trouble if you're thinking of talking with him."

"He owes me. Time I collected."

"I'll send him word, tell him to bring some of his love poetry."

Henrik pointed upstairs. "Don't know if my heart will take any more tonight. Your usual room happens to be empty. Get the kid out of there before someone loses their mind."

Karl dragged a mostly drunk Tad away from the table of his new best friends and headed upstairs. He set the kid on the bed, eyed him doubtfully and kicked the biffy pot over beside him.

"Cordin, time to shut it down for the night."

"How'd you know I was here?" Cordin's voice came from the bed beside Tad.

"Cause the same mangy rat is sitting under the bed. I told you not to depend on magic."

"It was your daughter who screwed it up."

Karl found himself standing beside Tad with Cordin's throat in his hand.

"You forced her, even after she warned you. Don't put this on her. Or I toss you out on the street and we'll find out how long a rat will live in this city."

"I thought you'd given up violence." Cordin's hands were trying to pull Karl's arm away from his throat.

"Don't make me forget it." Karl let go and shook himself. Did he want to go back there? Be that person?

Maybe coming to the Toad was a bad idea, but it was the only idea he had.

***

Widdershins walked into the Toad, and seasoned fighters turned pale and turned away. He didn't look like much. An overly thin kid wearing clothes that might have been stolen from his father's wardrobe. One look in his eyes revealed the most callous killer Karl had ever met.

"I hear you have a sudden desire for my company after all these years. I'm touched." Widdershins sat down in the chair that became vacant seconds before he claimed it.

"You owe me," Karl sat across from the wizard.

"Unfortunately, I do, to my eternal regret. I hate unpaid debts. What picayune problem do you want me to solve?" A bottle and glass floated from the bar and set on the table. Widdershins poured a glass and swirled it under his nose.

"Bring it upstairs, where we can talk in private." Karl's fists clenched, he wanted nothing more than to wipe the fatuous grin off that face. Wasn't going to happen, not today, not ever.

In the room, Widdershins sneered at the furnishings, then leaned against the wall.

"Cordin." Karl pointed to the middle of the floor.

"How darling, you've picked up a pet. It suits you too. Do you call it Cassie?"

"Look closer wizard," Karl's knuckles popped, but he kept his voice level.

"A hiding spell! How clever, not very elegantly done, but very thorough, how long have you been a rat?"

"Three, four days." Cordin said.

"How were you supposed to control the spell?"

"I have a nut, when I hold it, I look like a rat to other people. When I put it in my pocket, I should be myself again."

"Nut," Widdershins shook his head, "I suppose one must work with what is available." He put out his hand, suddenly covered with a glove. "Give it to me." He pulled his hand back and examined a black ball in the palm of his hand. "The problem with using rough objects for such spells is they collect things, like bits of skin, which is enough for the magic to keep you a rat." He blew on the nut, and Cordin appeared where the rat had been.

"I'm back!" He looked at his hands in horror. "Why are my hands covered in fur?"

"You can't expect to be under such an open-ended spell for so long without some consequences. Now, that the nut is not next to your skin, the transformation will slow, but in a year or two, you will be more rat than human. The wizard who made this delightful object might be able to put you right, but then maybe not."

He tossed the nut in his hand then put it in his pocket.

"I'll be keeping this as a souvenir of this most delightful day. Don't let me ever see you again." Widdershins sauntered out the door.

"What am I supposed to do? I'm half rat."

"The first thing is to settle down." Karl sighed and pushed the door closed. "A least it's just fur, so you can shave it off. You're lucky, I've seen much worse come from playing with magic."

"Great," Cordin slumped on the bed, "I'll be a laughingstock."

"There are worse things." Karl closed the door as he left. He needed a drink.

CHAPTER TWENTY

Leedles followed Apoxthenis into the tower. The wall opened for him and closed behind her. A spiral stair ran along the outside wall of the tower. They climbed until her legs ached. She listened for magic, but it told her nothing. They passed floor after floor until they arrived at the open roof of the tower. A hut stood to one side.

"Server."

"Yes, great one?" A man in a grey robe stepped out of the stairs they had just climbed.

"Take this one and have it bathed, dressed in suitable clothes. Burn everything it's wearing."

"And the staff?"

"Leave it for now."

"As you will." The server turned and walked back to the stairs.

Apoxthenis looked at Leedles with a raised brow. She ducked her head and followed the server. He led her to the floor below and directed her to remove her clothing. Leedles reluctantly removed her clothes and dropped her pack on the floor. Everything she valued was in the pile another server swept up and carried away. Her heart ached and she had to breathe past a lump in her throat. Yet better to lose things than lose herself.

The first server led her to a door and pointed to the pool. Leedles walked into it. It wasn't hot, but not cold either. She felt something touching her and looked down, hundreds of tiny fish swarmed about her.

"Remain still," the server said his voice never changing tone.

After a while the fish left her alone and the server ordered her out of the pool. She went through a series of pools, each strange and humiliating. She came out of the last one completely bald, her golden hair floating away in the current.

The server handed her a white robe to put on, then led her up the stairs again to Apoxthenis, who looked like he hadn't moved.

"Now, we begin. You will learn to focus the magic properly."

Leedles gathered in the magic around her.

"No." A shock struck her. "You have too much magicburn already. You must work the magic outside your body."

He worked her for hours, shocking her anytime she reached for the magic around her. If she tried to send the magic through an outside object, he shocked her.

"You mustn't depend on a thing for your focus. If you lose it, you lose power. Create a lens in front of you. Use that to focus the magic."

Leedles lost track of the days. The Queen had given her a month, but Apoxthenis woke her in the middle of the night to practice, or had her sit in darkness for hours at a time. Meals appeared at his whim, and always the servers stood by to do his will. Not one would answer a word Leedles spoke.

During one session in the dark, the staff stirred beneath her hands.

:Never do that again.: The staff's voice in her head sounded weak.

"What happened?" Leedles whispered.

:Speak in your mind.:

"What happened?"

:You channeled your power through me, using my power as well as yours. You're lucky I didn't burn to ash in your hand.:

"Sorry, I woke up and panicked."

:Now you're worse trouble.:

"What do you mean?"

:You'll find out.:

The staff refused to talk to her again. Apoxthenis worked her to distraction. She took to using the magic to spy on him, to see how he worked.

"It is the simplest of things." Apoxthenis spouted his usual incomprehensible words about lenses and focuses, but what he did was pull the magic from a specific source. Almost as if he couldn't see the magic around him – when she gathered the magic surrounding them, he'd see an empty gesture. He could feel magic being worked, he'd known when she'd worked magic to stop the wind from pushing her off the bridge, but he didn't know where she got the power from.

More of what he said made sense. If he was working blind, all the mental exercises were necessary to build the construct, then force the magic into that shape. No wonder the magic screeched and moaned around the tower.

She went to the edge of the tower and peered out over the ocean. A bird flew far away across the water. According to Apoxthenis, she needed to create the line to fling across the gap to compel the subject to come. At the last second, she didn't compel, but begged, pleaded for the bird to come to her hand.

It turned in the sky and flew toward her. It grew larger and larger until it darkened the sky above her. It landed gently on the edge of the tower.

:Why do you call me, child?:

"I am trying to learn this wizard's magic." Leedles sighed, "For all my effort, I am failing."

:Does a hawk seek to become a sparrow? You have no need of these wizards, though they have need of you. Take care, child. If you escape, call on me.:

It dropped from the tower as Apoxthenis appeared, face white.

"What are you doing?" He yelled at her, and for a second Leedles expected him to push her over the low wall.

"Practicing the summons as you command, great one." She bowed her head.

He stared at her for a long time, probes of magic struck her, but fizzled away on her skin.

"Bah, continue." He stood away to the side.

Leedles chose a closer bird and called it to her. It circled crying forlornly until she released it.

When she looked to Apoxthenis for approval, or more likely reproof, he'd vanished.

She sat on the stone deck of the tower and tried to make sense of what she knew. The huge bird must be another wise one, like the River Dragon and her staff. None of them liked the wizards, but all of them stayed clear.

As if the wizards posed a real threat to them. But how could even the wizards harm such powerful beings? She had a ghost of an idea, but it skittered away before she could grab hold.

Never mind. Her first concern had to be surviving the month.

CHAPTER TWENTY-ONE

The sounds of breaking furniture told Karl Theo had arrived. He ordered Tad and Cordin to stay in the room, then went down to watch the fun.

Theo stood in the centre of the room in his immaculate greys tossing men twice his size about. Henrik sat on the bar taking bets. Karl sidled over and leaned on the bar.

"What are the odds?"

"Not worth betting." Henrik shook his head in mock sorrow. "The young these days, they have no instinct for self-preservation."

The last attacker backed away and Theo sat himself at a table. Henrik handed Karl a pitcher of beer and two mugs.

"Good luck."

Karl stepped over moaning patrons as Theo stood up again.

"Karl!" He grinned widely and landed a solid punch to Karl's gut.

Waving the mugs and the pitcher, Karl sat down.

"A little early in the morning for beer, isn't it?" Theo sat down across the table and dusted off his sleeve.

"I should have brought wine?"

"Where have you been the last fifteen years?" Theo poured a mug full of beer and took a slug.

"Cassie died." Karl looked across at Theo. "I needed to think."

"For fifteen years?"

"I think slowly." Karl poured himself some beer and drank deeply. "I'd like to accept your job offer."

"What makes you think the job's still open?"

"I drove through town, Theo, I've heard the gossip."

"Great, you start today. You're late for work, better get to it."

Karl finished his beer. "You haven't gone and moved the garrison?"

"Same place." Theo poured himself another beer. "Good luck."

***

Outside the City Guard's garrison, Karl took a deep breath, then strolled in.

"Sergeant, get your feet off the desk. I want anyone who's not walking the city assembled in the yard in five."

"Who are you?" The Sergeant in a black uniform leaned over the desk, big man, but probably slow reflexes. The best always went for the Palace Guard.

"New trainer." Karl kept moving toward the yard.

"Who says? I didn't get any memo."

"You want to wait and ask Theo?" Karl turned to look at the Sergeant. "You have four minutes to assemble the Guard." He continued his stroll toward the training yard as the Sergeant's footsteps faded behind him.

He picked the side which would put the sun in the guard's eyes and took an easy stance. Guards started pouring into the yard, mostly men, a few women. He'd warned Theo he needed to recruit more women.

They looked around, spotted Karl and lined up facing him. The last two straggled in and joined the lines. Maybe sixty guards, figure another thirty out walking the city, Theo was short at least fifty, if he let Karl run things his way.

"Sergeant, send someone to work the desk." When the Sergeant pulled a woman out of the ranks, Karl shook his head. "Not her. You," he pointed at the last man to enter the yard. "Desk."

"Who says?"

"Didn't you hear me? Sergeant, please explain just why these good people are standing here?"

"This is our new training instructor. He is in command of the garrison, second in command of the Guard."

"Then why ain't he in uniform?"

"I haven't been to see my tailor yet." Karl strolled around the assembled guard, feeling their eyes on him. He stopped ten feet from the man. "You look like an intelligent individual. What do you think is going to happen when the commander finishes his beer and decides to check on how his new trainer is doing? And finds him needing to explain himself to someone who is consistently last to the yard?" He raised his voice. "How many of you want to be City Guards?"

Everyone in the yard raised their hands.

"Liars," Karl let his voice drop to conversational tones. "City Guards shouldn't be afraid of the truth. How many of you want to be City Guards? I know what the other units call you, I know what you call yourselves when you think no one's listening. I know what the people on the street call you." Hands dropped as he talked. "Most of you are here because you can't get into one of the other units. You aren't good enough, you aren't a man, you don't talk with the right accent." He stared the man in front of him in the eye. "Most of you are here for the paycheck, and if you want to continue collecting that paycheck, you will obey me." He raised his eyebrow at the man, who'd turned green.

"Yes, Sir!" The man saluted and broke and ran for the door. Karl returned to the front of the formation.

"We will start training by putting away your swords. If sword is what you train on, it will be the first thing you reach for when trouble starts. You will train with batons, and you will train with them until they become your tool of choice for doing your work on the street."

"We're going to get slaughtered." A woman shouted from the ranks. "Sir."

"In the average shift, how many times do you encounter trouble?"

"At least once, maybe twice. Depends on the zone." The woman answered.

"And that once or twice, how many times do you face trained soldiers?"

"Sir?"

"You are a City Guard, a trained soldier in the service of the Queen. There should be no one aside from another trained soldier you cannot handle with a baton and the proper training."

"And you are going to be training us?" A man in the front row spoke up.

"That's what trainers are for."

"Then why are we still talking?" The man had been one of the few who'd refused to put his hand down.

"Good question. Swords on the racks. Batons at the ready. We'll begin with fifty repetitions of each move..."

***

"How'd it go?" Theo sipped at his wine and made a face. "I'm supposed to be cultured and drink this stuff, but I don't like it."

"Don't drink it then."

"Politics." Theo grimaced and put the glass down. "The Queen's Guard is jealous of their position and resent any encroachment by the Palace Guard, so they refuse to exchange information or even a 'hello'. None of them want to have anything to do with the City Guard in case they'll have to wipe something off their shiny boots."

"May I make a suggestion?" Karl picked up Theo's glass and sipped. "First, if you're going to drink wine, buy stuff that isn't half vinegar. Second, show up at the Palace in your blacks."

"They'd throw me out."

"Really? What happens to the Palace Guard if the City riots? They close the gates and hold the Palace. What good is that if they lose the City? How long will they last without their daily deliveries? If the commanders have forgotten, you can be sure the Queen hasn't. When she was Princess, the City Guard was her particular concern.

"Wouldn't know it from the funding we get." Theo looked at the ceiling.

"You're an old campaigner, you know you have to twist the client's arm to get a decent contract. No different here. Wear your blacks, remind them the City Guard is what stands between them and a return of the riots from twenty years ago. Ask for more money to put the unit into shape." Karl took a deep breath and leaned back in his chair. "If they throw you out, you can always come work for me, we're short guards."

***

Tad answered the knock to see Henrik standing in the hall.

"Someone wants to talk to you."

"About what?" Tad's heart sank. Could they have connected them to that fiasco in Riverport already?

"A job." Henrik leaned toward Tad. "If you're going to play a role, play it all the way. Don't stop to relax, or let yourself get sloppy, that's when trouble will find you."

Heat traveled up Tad's face and he nodded.

"I'll be right down."

"What's this about a job?" Cordin stood by the basin, shaving the fur from his hand.

"Security." Tad closed his eyes and focused his thoughts. "I'll tell you about it after the meeting."

Downstairs the newcomer sat at a table alone. Behind him stood a huge man with hair so blond it looked white. His hard, blue eyes swept the room. They paused on Tad, dismissed him and kept moving.

Tad forced himself to walk slowly. He was a young man, new in business, he needed this contract to get a start. A bit nervous, but no puppy dog submissiveness.

"Mind if I sit?" He pointed to the chair across from a man in elegantly cut clothes. Rich enough he didn't care what the chair in the bar might do to his outfit. Smart enough to know the effect those clothes would have on this crowd.

The man nodded and looked over Tad.

"I hear you're looking for some special security."

The man raised an eyebrow.

"Straight to the point. A little eager are we? What does this place have to drink?"

"The beer is passable, I wouldn't recommend the wine. Henrik is rumoured to have some fine old distilled liquors hidden away."

"Interesting, I haven't had a beer in a long time."

Tad waved at the barman, who wiped out two mugs, then filled them from the keg. He placed one in front of Tad and the other in front of the man.

Tad gambled and took a sip first, the man in rich clothes smiled slightly and emptied his mug in one smooth drink.

"Refreshing, I should try it more often." He leaned forward. "What do you have to offer me?"

"I spent some time in the business." Inspiration hit Tad and he almost grinned, instead he put a mournful look on his face. "My partner's unfortunate accident convinced us it was time to look for other work."

"And how do I know you will stay convinced?"

"The accident made my partner somewhat, noticeable. He's sensitive about it. We had accreditation, but not for the City. I'd prefer not to go through the expense."

"Very well, you will take it as understood I will not allow a double cross to go unpunished."

"Of course."

"I have a rather unusual object. What it is doesn't matter. The guildmaster of the overly expensive City guild desires it. To save time and bloodshed we have made a bet. He will have three nights to steal the object. It will be located on my property where I have my warehouse and offices."

"Is the object magical?"

"What does it matter?" The man picked up Tad's beer and drank it down.

"Magic has to be hidden differently than other things. It also depends on who's looking for it. We don't need to know what it is, but we do need as much information about how it might be detected as possible."

"Very well, my man here will show you to my offices. Bring whatever you need with you. Once you're there, you won't be leaving until we're done." He nodded once, dropped a coin on the table and walked out of the bar.

"Five minutes," the big man said.

CHAPTER TWENTY-TWO

Leedles concentrated on threads of magic. She'd discovered them connecting everything in the tower, but couldn't figure out what they did. None of them pulled any magic from what Leedles named 'wild magic' as opposed to the 'tame magic' of the wizards. The tame magic didn't fight back or try to twist the spell to its own ends. Colourless, soundless, like the servers unless Apoxthenis called them. They too were connected by the threads.

She could see the value of the tamed magic, results were predictable, thus one could try much more powerful spells without fear of them falling apart. And there was no magicburn when she used them.

Creating magic without paying the cost had its attractions, but Leedles worried about the price. Like Sella's dress, it was just too good to be true. There had to be a catch somewhere; she needed to find it before it jumped up and bit her.

Apoxthenis was approaching. Leedles had set strings of magic to warn her. They tingled as they broke, tiny amounts of magic burn.

She raised her head to watch him come out onto the terrace. He was smiling and the hairs on the back of her neck rose.

"You are ready for the next step in your training." He dangled a crystal on a thin chain. "We all wear one of these, they are keys to unlock doors you haven't found yet." Before she could respond he crouched down and fastened it around her neck. A shock ran from the base of her spine into her head making her dizzy. He was saying something, she should listen, but couldn't focus.

Leedles woke with the cry of the sea birds in the morning.

:Beware of wizards bearing gifts.:

"What are you talking about?"

:That bauble around your neck, it's doing something to your mind.:

"Don't be ridiculous, I've had this forever, my mother gave it to me."

:The wizard gave it to you two nights ago. You laid here senseless until now. Remember your grief at the bath?:

A pang struck Leedles heart, the servers had taken everything she owned away to burn. How did they miss her necklace? Confusion wrinkled her forehead, then a breeze blew across her scalp and wiped it away.

She had much to learn. Breathe in magic like air, change it, make it her own, store it for use. The voice in her head shouted at her, but she ignored it. The great one would be pleased with her progress.

Leedles worked on her lesson for the next three days until she imagined she'd burst if she took in any more magic. Holding all the magic made her tired, so she lay down to rest.

***

Sharp pain woke Leedles. Her heart raced. Where was she? This wasn't home. Memory flooded her, making her shake. Karl, the lakur, the wizards. The pain came from a magic thread leading from her throat to a wizard she didn't recognize. His face contorted in pain or ecstasy as he absorbed power from Leedles.

The lines made sense, the wizards used other people as batteries to store power, remove magicburn, then they could draw on it without consequence.

Fire exploded in Leedle's gut. *How dare they. All their ritual and smugness, and they are nothing more than parasites.* Fury drove her to sit up and scream at the wizard. His face paled and he waved his fingers trying to knit the thread into something to contain her.

Leedles threw all the power she had in her at him. It exploded in a ball of magic sending the wizard through the stone wall behind him, and the next, until he flew out over the ocean. The magic raged uncontrolled, burning and twisting her out of her shape. Leedles clutched a tiny handful and worked a shield between her and the raging magic.

:Get out. You can't possibly hold against this.:

She crawled out of bed, magicburn already stabbing in her gut. At the door, the spiral staircase greeted her. At least she was going down. The tower changed around her as she crawled, wearing thin the shield she put up. At the main level the bridge had twisted into sculpted shapes belonging in a different world. The stairs continued, so she crawled. At the bottom of the stairs she found a boat. Leedles fell into it and snapped the ropes tying it up with a brief spell. Magicburn consumed her, but she twisted one last piece of magic to send the boat away from the tower - east, toward the beginning glow of the rising sun. With that, Leedles gave into the pain and screamed until darkness took her.

CHAPTER TWENTY-THREE

Tad followed Cordin into the warehouse compound. A high wall ran around the entire property, leaving only one gate big enough for a heavy wagon. Guards stood on either side looking as professional as any Queen's Guards. They peered at the pair but didn't challenge them. The bodyguard must have given a good description. Odd, they didn't know the name of their client or any of his men. The less Tad knew the better.

Past the gate they walked on a cobbled courtyard in better shape than the road. Large enough for heavy wagons to turn easily, Cordin's nose twitched. Tad expected he smelled the stables on their right. The warehouse formed the left wall, the office took the space in between.

Tad led Cordin up the stairs to the double doors with more guards.

"Boss is expecting you." One said and pulled the door open.

"Thanks." Tad smiled at the guard and stepped over the threshold. The door closed behind Cordin with a thud. *Well-built door.*

More stairs, why did rich people love stairs so much?

The bodyguard met them at the top and gave them a once over before opening the door to let them into the office.

Tad raised his eyebrow. He'd bet himself he'd see ostentatious grandeur, but the room was disappointing.

Basic chairs, table, file cubbies along one wall. A massive safe box took up half one wall. The Boss sat at the table with a bottle of wine and glasses.

"Hello, Boss." Tad took a seat across the table, Cordin one on the side.

"Boss?" the man said.

"You failed deliberately to mention your name. Since you are our employer for the next three days, Boss allows us to communicate clearly."

"Fair enough." The man poured wine into the glasses and pushed two toward Tad and Cordin. He picked his up and sipped. "Since you were kind enough to treat me to your beverage of choice, allow me to give you mine."

Tad picked up the glass and swirled it a bit, sniffing. He'd had wine before and thought vinegar would be easier to drink. He wasn't going to be rude before he'd even started.

The wine exploded with flavour in his mouth, and he couldn't hold back the look of delight on his face.

"I've never tasted anything like it." Tad took another sip. Cordin still sniffed at his glass, but sipped it gingerly. The magic had done odd things to him. Neither of them knew the extent of the change.

"Down to business then." The Boss set his glass to one side.

Tad reluctantly followed suit.

"The wall is good enough, it will stop street ruffians, but not determined burglars. There are weak points where the warehouse joins the wall, and again where the stable does. Both spots allow access to higher level entries in the office and the warehouse. It helps they are in line of sight of the gate, but you'll want three guards instead of two – one to walk perimeter while the others stand. If they are professionals, they will know how to vary their stride to change the timing around the building.

"Line of sight is good in the daytime, but night will give solid shadows for stealth. Unless you have more lights than you appear to, that's going to be an issue. The other option is to have no lights and let the men use their night vision.

"I'm sure I haven't told you anything you don't already know, but we'll need to look around to get a better feel for the setup."

The Boss nodded once.

"I'm guessing from the safe your strategy at this point is to block any entry into the building, and if they do gain entry to make the object impossible to remove by placing it in the brand new safe you have against the wall"

Tad took a breath and told his heart to slow down. It didn't listen.

"I will tell you now, there is no way to prevent entry into either the compound or the buildings. You could have men on every floor and the burglars would still get in. I'm hoping you've agreed to no deliberate killing, but incapacitating people temporarily is not easy."

The Boss frowned and sipped at his wine. Good, Tad was now telling him things he didn't know. Now it came down to whether the man trusted them or not.

"For successful completion of the job, we need your complete trust. The rules, as you explained, state the object must remain in the compound. You can't know where it is at any given time. Your subconscious reactions will give it away. We can't, of course, guarantee success, but if we fail, we won't collect our fee."

"Give us some menial job to do." Cordin said. "If we are just hired labour, no one will pay attention to us."

"If making the compound impregnable is impossible, how do you plan to keep the object safe?"

"Misdirection." Tad pulled out a deck of cards. He fanned them quickly to show all the cards were there, then shuffled the deck and held it out to the Boss.

"I'm not in the mood for parlour tricks." The Boss's frown deepened.

"Indulge me." Tad held eye contact.

The Boss picked a card looked at it and put it back in the deck. Tad picked up the cards and shuffled them.

"Call your bodyguard in for a moment."

The Boss sighed and called the big man into the room.

"Please look in your pouch," Tad said, still shuffling the deck. "and let us see what card is in there. The bodyguard's frown would have been frightening in any other circumstance, but Tad lived for these moments.

The bodyguard checked his pouch and his eyes riveted on Tad when he felt the card. He tossed it on the table. The Boss clapped slowly.

"Well done, and what is the purpose of this exercise?" He tapped his fingers on the table. "I'm familiar with switching decks and pickpockets."

"You may want to take a look at your safe." Tad couldn't keep the grin off from his face.

The Boss's eyes widened, and his mouth dropped open when he saw the door hanging open.

"There are layers of deception we need to invoke. The safe is a good beginning place. Put the object in the safe tonight for the first night. This model has a feature which prevents it from opening except during daytime hours."

"But your partner opened it easily, why..." The Boss stopped himself. "You do what you do. In three days if the object is still in the compound, I will pay your fee."

"Now we have the matter of determining that fee." Tad grinned again. "What did you have in mind?"

They settled on a figure lower than what Tad asked, but considerably higher than what he'd expected to get.

The Boss pulled a package the size of a small book from his coat and placed it in the safe. He spun the dials and muttered the words to activate the daylight only spell.

"Now, I have work to do. My man here will escort you to the warehouse and give you each a broom."

"Perfect," Tad said.

CHAPTER TWENTY-FOUR

A load came in late in the afternoon. A ruckus ensued when the warehouse manager didn't show at the dock. After a few minutes of arguing with teamsters who wanted to get to their serious drinking the man arrived still pulling up his pants and red in the face. The cargo got off loaded quickly and the men sent off. Guards took their positions with grim faces as the sun dropped below the horizon.

Tad and Cordin were still sweeping the warehouse as night fell. They finished up their aisles then found a comfortable corner to rest in.

Nothing disturbed their rest, at least not until the Boss arrived in his office to discover the safe missing. Tad grinned at the volume of the man's voice. Impressive.

He left Cordin sleeping and wandered out to see the Boss.

"They stole the safe!" the Boss still shouted. He waved his hands as well, so Tad kept a respectful distance.

"They did. I was counting on it."

The Boss stopped in mid-tirade and stared at the book-sized package in Tad's hand. He snatched it up and immediately smiled.

"Boss, you might as well ask for the safe back, you did spend a fair bit of money on it."

That afternoon two carters brought the safe through the gate and pushed in out onto the cobbles. It landed crooked with the door swinging open. They turned their wagon and left.

Tad handed a note to the bodyguard. He looked at it and shrugged.

"No, you can't have a raise." He waved a fist in Tad's face. "You've only worked one day."

Tad hung his head and returned to sweeping. One of the loads that afternoon had an extra box. The teamsters wouldn't take it, as that would mean driving back to their warehouse before they could start drinking. The warehouse manager pushed it aside and decided he'd deal with it when he felt better.

Once again Tad and Cordin swept until dark, then found a corner to rest. This time they didn't sleep. About midnight six men in black climbed down from a window in the warehouse wall. One of them held a device she proceeded to wave about.

She pointed at a crate, and the other forced it open without making a noise. The woman with the device picked up something and threw it across the floor. Back to the device, she spotted another crate with the same result. She cursed and pointed to half a dozen crates also failing to find what they wanted. The group spent considerable time opening crates before they got sloppy and made too much noise. Guards rushed in from outside and the six burglars retreated.

Tad stayed on high alert until the sun lit up the windows. Again, he made a show of handing the Boss the package to the Boss's delight.

Nothing untoward happened that afternoon, though the warehouse manager worked Tad and Cordin hard getting all the goods back in the crates and sealed up again. They decided the collection of charms and baubles belonged in the mysterious extra crate. Probably meant for some cheap magic shop.

Once more Tad and Cordin swept the warehouse, but as soon as the manager left, they went to work on the warehouse. Using the things they'd found in the crates and some ingenuity they created a maze of traps and snares. In the centre as if to mock the thieves, Tad placed a book sized package. This time they took perches high up in the rafters of the warehouse and waited for the show to begin.

The thieves came in a different window, but their rope cut on the blade set in the sill. They cursed and rubbed bruises. One of the group brushed up against a crate and stuck fast. The others had to cut his shirt off to free him. Nets fell, drugged darts fired, charms went off creating confusion. The burglars worked their way through the maze to the goal.

Tad figured they had five minutes or so before the sun rose when they reached the package. Only for one of them to scream silently into the dark. He looked around and pointed up into the rafters.

"You're on," Tad whispered and watched Cordin scamper across a beam. The burglars swarmed up the walls and crates to chase him around the warehouse finally cornering him. The one who'd done the silent scream stepped up and searched Cordin. He finished the search just as light came in the windows.

"Ok, brother," the man said in a mellow voice, "you win." The burglars dropped to the floor. Cordin ran back to Tad and they climbed down. The Boss and his bodyguard came into the warehouse, the boss grinning broadly.

"You've had my people chasing circles around themselves for the last three nights. I think I deserve to know how you did it."

"These gentlemen here." The Boss pointed to Tad and Cordin. "Are my special security team."

"So where is it?" The burglar asked.

"Follow me," Tad had to force himself to keep a straight face. They walked out into the sunshine and over to the safe. He lifted the door and Cordin reached under to pull the package out and hand it to the Boss.

Tad couldn't hold his laughter in any longer; he had to lean against the safe to keep from falling over. The Boss and the burglar joined them.

***

Tad and Cordin sat in the room at the Unkissed Toad and counted their money. The Boss had thrown in a bottle of wine as a bonus.

"We did good, mate." Tad thumped Cordin on the back. His mate grinned, but didn't say anything. "And no one's chasing us."

"Hey, you two," Henrik yelled up the stairs. "Guy here has a security job for you."

"Well, maybe not no one." Tad hid the money away. "We are going to make a mint."

***

Karl looked at his guards. They stood straighter and more confident. They carried swords sealed in the scabbard with lead wire. Easy enough to draw; hard to explain to the shift Sergeant. They worked with batons and other ways of subduing people without risking themselves or causing injury.

The most important change was Karl instructed them to be deliberately helpful at odd times. Holding a horse or helping to unload a wagon. It would be slow, but the inhabitants of the City would start to trust their Guard again.

Theo wore his blacks to the Palace. The results there were mixed, but the Queen didn't so much as bat an eye when he showed up the first time. Karl had heard the talk. The others would follow the Queen, at least in public, and then habit would carry it over into other areas.

Karl wished he'd done this years ago, but then he didn't have the skills to make it work. Leedles had been right, what he learned in Peace was who he was now.

As it always did, the thought of Leedles sent a pang through his heart. Theo told him of finding her in the lakur forest and the wizards snatching her up. No one had seen her since.

Tad and Cordin had made a name for themselves. The gossips were full of their antics.

"Brooding again?" Theo knocked on Karl's door and stepped into the room. He joined Karl in watching the Guards go through their exercises.

"Recruiting is up," Karl said. "We'll need more money for pay, some for equipment too. We are almost ready to start the specialized training."

"Let's hope we don't need it." Theo sighed and cracked his fingers. "That's what working with the sword for a lifetime will do to you."

"We'll need the training; I just hope we're ready." He pointed out into the city. "There's always someone planning trouble."

"Ever the optimist." Theo thumped Karl's shoulder, "Look at what you've accomplished in just a few weeks. Another month-"

The sky over the harbor bloomed into a white ball. Karl's eyes hurt trying to focus on it.

"Don't look at it," Theo pushed him away from the window. "The magic can mess with your head."

"Leedles." Karl didn't know whether to laugh or cry.

"Either she's dead, or lost control, which would amount to the same thing." Theo put his hand on Karl's shoulder. "I'm sorry."

"She brought a mountain down, emptied a river, burnt up a huge swath of forest. If she died, most of the city would have gone with her. She's alive, but someone made her angry."

"I'll ask around, but the wizards will never tell us what happened."

"Not the truth any way." Karl smiled grimly.

***

Apoxthenis stood relaxed in front of the council. He was supposed to look up at them and tremble. Everything in the room had been designed to intimidate.

"You blame me for this, but I had her primed and ready to be a source such as we have not seen in centuries. That one of our own decided to tap her prematurely is not my responsibility."

"He is not here to defend himself." One of the tribunal leaned over his tall desk to peer down at Apoxthenis. "Someone must be punished for this travesty. We have not only lost this source you brag about, but a score of other sources. It will take great efforts to replace and prepare them."

"True," Apoxthenis said, "but you are missing one important piece. She still wears the conduit, and if she survives will go to the desert in the east. When she transforms, we will have a wise one as a source. Is that not worth the gamble?"

When no one spoke, Apoxthenis bowed and backed out of the Council Chambers. He had work to do.

CHAPTER TWENTY-FIVE

Leedles woke to a thud and a vibration which ran beneath her. She pried her eyes open only for them to water in the bright sun. Shading her eyes helped. Water stretched as far as she could see. As she turned in circle water surrounded her on all sides.

Without knowing what time of day she'd awakened, any direction might be east. At least the water was calm.

The thud came again and the bottom of the boat shook. Leedles leaned over the side. A fish shaped creature at least the length of the boat popped its head up and spat water at her, then laughed.

"Ok, you're funny," Leedles wiped water out of her eyes. The salt stung her face. Blisters covered her body, the robe hung in tatters. Thirst hit her, but the boat had no supplies on it. She floated alone in an ocean.

The boat shook again. Not quite alone.

"You don't happen to know which way is east?" Leedles hoped the laughing creature might be another wise one. It squirted more water at her, but didn't speak or do anything else useful.

She had to do something, but the magicburn hurt as much on the inside as her blisters did on her skin. Whatever she'd done had made a good job of cooking her.

Cross-legged on the bottom of the boat, Leedles reached for magic. It ran through her fingers like water. Maybe if she stirred instead of gripped? The creature spat more water at her, creating a puddle in the bottom of the boat. Water first, then.

The magic fought her, but there were no convenient obedient lines out here. Leedles wrestled until the magic drew white salt out of the puddle and dropped it overboard. She knelt down and slurped up the fresh water before more saltwater arrived. The creature didn't spit anymore. It swam a short distance then did a flip and came back to the boat.

"So that's east, but I don't have enough energy to push the boat with magic." She tried paddling with her staff, but even without it moving any water she tired in minutes.

The ropes on each end were cut short. Leedles wrestled the one in the back off and tied it to the one in the front. She tossed in the water. The creature took it and the knot gave way. The creature tossed the rope back into the boat.

"I really should have a name for you," Leedles said to the creature as she tied the rope again. "Maybe Squirt?" The thing laughed and splashed water at her.

"Ok, Squirt it is, let's try the rope thing again." She threw the end in the water and this time it held. The boat followed Squirt and the moving air let Leedles know how hot she was getting.

The fragments of her robe wouldn't protect her from the sun. She laid them out and stirred the currents of magic again, this time making weaving motions. The resulting blanket looked fragile, but pulled over her head, gave her shade.

They traveled at a steady pace until the sun sank low in the sky behind them. Leedles freshened more water and drank her fill. The temperature stayed warm, so she lay under the blanket and slept.

Flapping woke her. A fish struggled in the bottom of the boat. Leedles snatched it and hammered its head against the edge of the boat until it stopped moving. Its skin split open so she dug her fingers in and tore most of the skin from one side. It might take more energy to cook the fish than the fish gave her. Leedles had a harder time moving this morning.

The pain had dulled, but not enough to let her work bigger magics. Each spell made the magicburn worse, but not using the magic would mean she'd die sooner. She bit into the fish and chewed it raw. Squirt paused in its work to laugh at her, then resumed pulling her east.

They could reach land today, or it could be a month. Leedles didn't have a month, she wasn't sure she had a day. Time for a gamble.

"Look Squirt, if I don't make it, know I'm thankful for the help, and the company."

Squirt left the rope and circled round so she could run fingers down its leathery back. It sped off and did a series of leaps and twists. Leedles hoped it meant encouragement.

She lay on the bottom of the boat under her blanket, already coming unraveled, and focused on the summoning spell. The watery magic didn't cooperate, but Squirt chittered at her and suddenly the spell came together. Leedles cast the call out into the world asking the great bird for help.

Squirt made a last leap over the boat before exhaustion claimed Leedles.

***

Cool air woke her. She lay in the shade of a large rock, the overturned boat beside on the ground. Just being cool and in the shade was achievement enough for the moment.

:Are you planning to lie there all day?:

"It depends on what getting up will accomplish."

:More than lying like a stick.:

"True." Leedles sat up, pain from her burns, inside and out, made her gasp. "What happened?"

:You released enough magic at one time to twist the wizards' tower into nothingness, and incidentally, to almost kill you. You're tougher than you look.:

"I don't feel tough." Leedles used the rock to help her stand. "Any water around here?"

:Dig into the ground.:

"I just stood up." Leedles dropped to her knees and scrabbled at the ground, a mixture of sand and rock. A flat piece of rock made a shovel. She'd dug down a foot before she saw darker sand, another foot before water collected in the bottom. Cupping her hands, she got a good drink before the water vanished.

A little strength returned to her legs and she stood up again and peered up at the bird perched on the rock above her.

"What do I do for food?"

:Wait:

Since she was on her feet anyway, Leedles walked around the extent of the shadow. The ground beneath her feet felt cool, in the sun, it burned.

When she'd finished her tour, the shadow had shrunk.

"Sun is rising, got it, so this pleasant spot will disappear with the noon sun." Leedles turned around, looking for other rocks. Heat made the air about the ground waver, but even so, none looked close enough for her to reach if she had to walk through the sun.

"The boat." She walked along the rock back to where she'd started. The boat lay half in shade. Leedles crawled under it. Stuffier than by the rock, but cooler than in the sun. With nothing else to do, she fell asleep.

Her shivering woke her, and for a second she was back in the cell thinking no one cared about her. Karl did, but he probably thought she was dead. From what the wise one said, she had been very lucky to get out of the tower alive.

She rolled out from under the boat and hopped about until she stopped shivering. Movement in the sand caught her attention. A mouse hopped away from the rock and found something in the sand to eat. While

Leedles watched, and owl swooped down and snatched up the mouse.

"So that's how it is."

A snake moved in the sand near her feet, she pounced on it and beat it against the rock. A sharp sliver of stone made a crude knife.

"Dinner is served."

It didn't taste any worse than the fish. She carried the sliver and the remains of the snake and went exploring. The rocks to the east were strangely formed and glasslike. Little moved around them. To the west, they were shaped by wind and sand. She found a rock with a hole running completely through it. Good for avoiding the noon sun.

The wise one landed on the sand outside her new home.

"So, what happens now?" Leedles pulled more meat off the snake and chewed on it.

:You live, or you die.:

"People keep giving me that choice."

:Life is that way.:

"What should I call you? I don't want to keep saying 'bird'."

:If you must call me something, call me Roc.:

"You sound like you don't have a name."

:Wise ones become different, and our names no longer fit. Ask the stick.:

Roc leaped into the sky and quickly vanished.
Leedles put her staff on her lap.
"It's just you and me."

CHAPTER TWENTY-SIX

Tad looked at his friend's hunched over form. The transformation hadn't slowed much. Fur covered Cordin's body and his fingernails were now claws. Tad's gut twisted with the knowledge he was losing his friend, more than a friend if he was honest.

Cordin put a hand on Tad's knee. Cordin had stopped talking completely, but had gained an eerie ability to sense feelings. Tad stroked the fur on Cordin's back. When they were kids in the slums, Cordin had bragged how one day he'd have a fur coat to keep him warm in the winter.

The twist became a yawning gulf and Tad hugged his friend tightly.

"We're going to go find that wizard and make her fix you."

Cordin nodded then shrugged. He stood up and awkwardly put on clothes which no longer fit. Tad didn't trust any tailor to make custom clothes without gossiping about the rat-man.

Tad threw his clothes on without worrying how he looked. They were done with impressing clients. It had been fun, but Cordin's life was more important. He packed everything he cared about in a bag, then put their money in pouches hidden around his body. He gave some to Cordin too.

When he was done, he still had a pile of smaller coins. Too heavy to carry for their worth, he needed to get rid of them. He pushed the pile onto a shirt he wasn't taking, then made a crude bag to carry it downstairs.

"Morning, Henrik." Tad leaned against the bar. He'd never bothered moving from the room above the Toad. He liked the place.

"Leaving us?" Henrik stopped wiping the bar to face Tad.

"You heard about the magic burst over the wizard's guild?"

"Who hasn't."

"The wizard who did this to Cordin is still alive, I'm going to find her and make her fix him."

"The talk is she died, and that was a deathburst."

"Nah, she's alive, I'll find her and hold a knife to her throat until she makes it right."

"You'll need a good knife then," Henrik reached under the bar and pulled out a knife and sheath. They showed their age, worn and scarred, but when Henrik drew the blade, the steel was unmarked by nicks or rust. He put the knife back in the sheath and pushed it over to Tad.

"Thanks," Tad closed his hand around the knife.

"Carried that when I still fought in the wars. It's tasted wizard blood before. Bring it back to me when you're done.'

Tad shoved it into his bag. He dropped the shirt full of coins on the counter.

"Settling up my bill," he said. "There may be a bit extra, put it to good use. Anything left in the room is yours too."

"I'll have to charge you extra for the cleaning." Henrik's smile looked a little crooked.

"Put it on my tab." Tad started for the door.

"You'll always have a room here, kid." Henrik said.

Cordin followed Tad out into the street. The sun shone warm, making a mockery of Tad's dark mood. He headed down to the docks where ships from the eastern countries landed with exotic goods.

He found a ship, just loading cargo for the voyage east.

"Like to talk to the Captain."

"Captain's busy, talk to me." The sailor stood no taller than Tad but had scars from old battles and steely grey eyes.

"Need passage to the east." Tad put his pack down and stretched. "Have some business over there."

"What country you headed to?" The sailor didn't look excited at the prospect of letting Tad aboard the ship.

"Don't matter, business is with a person."

"How you going to find her?"

"Does it matter?" Tad's gut churned, he opened his hands and deliberately kept his voice level.

"Guess not, passage is twenty weights of gold." The sailor turned away to continue his work.

"This should pay for us both." Tad dropped a few of his pouches on the ground beside the sailor.

The man picked up the pouches and looked in them. He yelled at someone to take his place.

"I'll just go check this, shall I?"

"We'll wait."

The men worked closely as a team, shouting at each other in a language Tad didn't understand. He'd have time to learn on the voyage.

"Planning a trip?"

Tad didn't bother looking around.

"Going to find your wizard, Karl, and make her fix Cordin."

"Could be hard to find."

"Figure I'll listen for stories of disaster and look there." Tad's hands shook, the wizard had destroyed Cordin. She'd pay.

"Might be a plan." Karl sighed and patted Tad's back. "Good luck." He put something in Tad's hand. "If you see her, give her this letter."

"I owe you for helping us get set up. I'll see she gets it." Tad stuffed in his bag beside the knife.

The sailor returned and showed them to a tiny room near the bow of the ship.

"You stay here, and out of the way." Tad held the door for Cordin, then followed him into the room. Not much smaller than their room over the Unkissed Toad. Darker, with only one small round window to let in light, hammocks swung by the wall opposite the window.

"This'll be home for a bit, Cordin. Make yourself comfortable." Tad climbed into the upper hammock and closed his eyes. Visions of how he'd make the wizard pay for her mistake ran through his mind.

***

Karl sat in his office. His fake son was off on a mission to kill his adopted daughter. Cassie might have been smart. He wasn't much of a father.

"The ship sailed, Karl. Nothing you can do about it now." Theo swirled his glass. "You're right about the wine, the right bottle is very drinkable."

Karl swept his arm across his desk, sending papers flying. Theo jumped back with both glasses in his hands. Heat burned in Karl's gut. He kept failing people who cared about him.

"I don't want to listen to you natter about wine." Karl slumped and dropped his head into his arms. He couldn't focus on anything. He raged one second, despaired the next.

"I'm your commander and I'll natter about whatever takes my fancy." Theo set Karl's untouched glass beside the bottle on the sideboard. "You have work to do. That burst in the wizard's tower is going to upset them something fierce. They've been working some deep game since we were snot-nosed recruits. This has got to set them back." He walked around the desk and kicked Karl's chair.

Karl looked up at him and snarled.

"Would this Leedles of yours be impressed with your sulk?" Theo stepped away to a safe distance. "In the lakur forest, she stood up to the queen. She might have almost started a war, but she certainly was the one to stop it. The queen thought she was special." Theo shook his head and headed for the door.

"If you aren't up and doing your job before sundown, you can clean out your desk and get out of here." Theo slammed the door behind him.

Karl looked around at the mess in his office, then at the closed door. Was he going to fail Theo too? He wanted to rage and tear the place apart, smash everything. And then what?

He sighed and started to pick up the papers and organize them again. Henrik had given Tad the knife; he'd given him a letter. It would have to do. Leedles was out of his reach he couldn't do anything more to help her.

Time he focused on helping his City.

Once his office looked like it should, Karl went looking for Theo. He had a confession to make.

CHAPTER TWENTY-SEVEN

Leedles had sat in the hole through the rock and watched three days pass with no response from the staff. Time to get creative. The only time she'd truly affected the staff was when she channeled magic through it.

She pulled in threads of magic and whispered to them, and sent them through the staff. It glowed and gave off a gentle heat to offset the chill of the night. Should have done this early.

:What do you think you're doing?:

"Getting your attention."

:Stop it.:

"You're supposed to be training me, or something. Roc said as much, the River Dragon said the same thing."

:Oh, all right. Why are you talking out loud again?:

"It reminds me I'm human."

:That's going to be a problem.:

"Why is that?" If Leedles could have backed farther away from the staff, she would have. She'd traveled with it all this way, but didn't trust it.

:You are an artesian; magic naturally flows through you. When you want to cast a spell, you don't need fancy rituals or preparation to call up magic. The wizards use magic as a tool; magic is part of you.:

"That's why they wanted to tap my power, to make it easier for them to use. But they'd need dozens of sources to do all the things they do."

:Hundreds, most aren't as powerful as you. They can sense magic around them, but can't bend it to their will. Still, they can be taught to store it.:

"How long have the wizards been doing this?"

:How long have there been wizards?:

"So why haven't you done anything about it?"

:There are few of us, and while powerful, we have our weaknesses.:

"You're afraid."

:We need to talk about the next step in your evolution.:

"What does that mean?" Leedles would let the staff off for now, but the conversation wasn't over.

:You need to become a wise one.:

Leedles leaned against the rock, her mind blank as it tried to process what the staff had said. A wise one, like Roc, and the River Dragon? She glared at the staff, or the Golden Tree.

"Why did you become the Tree?"

:I lived in a time of great unrest. I was tired and wanted nothing more than to be left in peace. When I transformed, I planted myself in the valley you called home. People found their way there and settled around me.:

"How did you get from here to that valley?"

:I walked, in the form of a human, but gold, like you.:

"What happened to my parents?" A yawning pit opened in Leedles. She knew the story, her mother had given birth to a baby with hair and skin dusted with gold.

Her father killed his wife in a rage for betraying him then, when he was exiled, had hung himself. No one ever speculated about who had really fathered Leedles.

"It's not an accident I'm an artesian is it?"

:The ability can be passed from parent to child.:

"What did you do? Leedles ran out of the tunnel, but the staff followed attached to her wrist. She tugged at the shackle sending pain up her arm.

:Stop it! When you transform, none of this will matter. I was lonely, so I stepped out of the Tree. I had done it before, but this time a woman caught my eye. We wise ones are supposed to be above concerns of the humans, but I made my form to look like her husband. What would the harm be?:

"What harm? Murder, suicide, my life as a pariah!" Leedles gave up fighting the shackle holding her to this staff, this betrayer of everything she'd grown up believing. She fell to her knees.

:His rage wasn't because she'd slept with another man, but because she insisted she hadn't. The impossible nature of the dilemma drove them mad. You weren't expected.:

"You could have come out and explained, but you hid. You killed my family."

:People would have wanted things from me...:

Leedles screamed with inarticulate rage. All the pain of her life gathered into a ball spinning her chest. She gathered magic from as far as she could reach. The staff whimpered and threatened, predicting she'd kill them both.

Full beyond even what she'd held in the wizard's tower, she glowed like a flame in the desert night. Standing now, she reached for more, then slammed the staff into the ground releasing rage and magic together.

Light burst from the impact and spread like a wave across the landscape. Creatures paused in their endless fight for survival as the magic passed them, then resumed their lives. Rocks twisted into strange forms, then faded back to what they had been.

Roc screamed as he flew over the jungle, then turned to speed north. The River Dragon roared and the people in Riverport trembled in their beds. In Peace the Tree shook as if it was buffeted by mighty winds; leaves tore from the branches and swirled through the town.

In the centre of the explosion, Leedles lay motionless on the ground, the staff lying beneath her body.

CHAPTER TWENTY-EIGHT

Karl woke screaming, then looked around his room. His heart raced painfully, but he couldn't say what woke him. He walked through the quiet barracks, more than half his guards lived here, with no other home or family.

They'd worked hard, and he'd work them harder, but he wouldn't abandon them, not again. Tonight, he didn't need to choose between duty and family. Up in his office he opened the drawer of his desk and reached to the back. He could just reach the switch. He closed his eyes and flipped the switch. Pain shot through his hand, but he held on for a count of five. When the pain vanished a panel on the inside of the desk opened.

Widdershins never knew why Karl had asked for the locking spell fifteen years ago. If he'd known, Karl wouldn't be alive. Inside the small compartment lay two black bolts. He lifted them out, then wrapped them in cloth and put them in his shirt.

Theo didn't live in the City Guard barracks; they weren't convenient enough to the Palace. *They aren't convenient to anything.* An old joke, that the people who protected the City could hardly reach it. They were tucked up against the City Wall, part of construction so old, Karl figured it predated the City.

When the Guard was created, some bureaucrat decided they should use existing structures instead of building near the centre of the City where land was expensive. To get to the City, the Guards either had to navigate through a labyrinth of alleys, many of them blocked by new buildings. Or travel on the road running inside the wall to the West Gate, then take the road into the City from there.

Karl took the time to think, probably why he didn't see the men step out with knives in hand to block his way.

"Give us what you got, mate," the larger one waved his knife in Karl's face. The smaller one hung back, his knife held to throw.

"Ok." Karl slapped the knife away and drove a blow into the first assailant's stomach. The man dropped gasping for breath. Karl shifted enough to avoid the blade hitting his heart, but not far enough to avoid it completely. He left the knife in his arm and stepped toward the other man.

The second assailant squeaked and ran off. Karl returned to the first and hauled him to his feet.

"You have just tried to rob the Vice-Commander of the City Guard," Karl spoke in a conversational tone of voice. "You may want to warn your mates, the Guard will be walking the night. They mightn't be as gentle. I'm getting old and soft." He dropped the man back to the pavement and walked on.

The knife in his arm hurt like blazes and his shirt was probably ruined by the time he knocked on Theo's door. The night staff opened the door and her eyes widened when she saw Karl.

"I will fetch a surgeon right away, Sir," she said.

"Wake the Captain Theodore first, then the surgeon." Karl saw himself into the room where Theo entertained his rare guests. Theo walked in minutes later, still doing up his shirt.

"Good grief, man. You should be seeing the surgeon."

"Your aide has gone to fetch him." Karl sat in a chair. "Sorry for bleeding all over your room."

"I'll get the kit and do what I can while we wait." Theo ran out of the room and returned a few minutes later with a bag. He wrapped a bandage tight around the arm above the knife.

"The surgeon always says to drink lots to replace lost blood." Karl poked at the bandage. It would do.

"I don't think he meant fine wine." Theo frowned but headed toward the cabinet.

"I'd prefer beer, if you still keep any around the house." Karl waved his finger at his friend. "You're taking this wine thing much too far."

Theo rang for an aide and sent them to the kitchen to draw a pitcher of beer. The aide returned with the beer and a couple of mugs and the surgeon walked in behind him.

"That will be all," Theo waved his staff out.

"What were you doing?" The surgeon opened his bag and pulled out a handful of moss. He removed the knife in one swift move without warning Karl and pushed the moss into the wound.

The bleeding stopped immediately, and the pain receded. Karl grabbed a now full mug and drank half of it down.

"At least you haven't gone cheap on the beer." Karl saluted Theo with the mug, then finished it. He refilled it from the pitcher.

"What do you think you're doing?" The surgeon looked sternly at Karl.

"Replacing fluids."

"No more than half a pitcher, or the alcohol will interact badly with the moss."

"Define badly." Karl sipped his beer this time.

"Your arm will rot and fall off." The surgeon's face didn't change in the slightest.

Karl pushed the mug aside.

"Just in case."

Theo rolled his eyes, but his worried look relaxed. They thanked the surgeon, and Theo saw him out before sitting across from Karl.

"What happened?"

"Walking here to talk to you. Couple of bully-boys tried to relieve me of whatever I had. Dropped one, the other ran after his knife didn't slow me down."

"I hope the one is in the gaol."

"Nope, sent him with a message the Guard would be walking the night. Not a bad idea, actually. Keep 'em on their toes."

"The Guard or the bully-boys?" Theo took a swallow of the beer and smacked his lips.

"Both." Karl shook his head. "Not why I woke you." He pulled the bolts out of his shirt and dropped them on the table.

"Are those what I think they are?" Theo reached to touch them then pulled back his hand.

"Wizard-killers." Karl pushed them over to Theo. "I have a notion you'll be needing them."

"You have the knife too?"

"Henrik had it, gave it to Tad. The kid doesn't know what he has."

"Leedles?"

"She destroyed a fair section of the Wizards Guild buildings. Power like that can change a person. Besides, Henrik had one of his hunches the kid would need it."

"Henrik had a hunch, huh?" Theo leaned back. "Did he have a hunch about these too?" He pointed at the bolts.

"Had a feeling it was time." Karl rubbed at his arm, and Theo frowned at him. "They'll fit a standard arm rig. Wizards can't spot them and magic has no effect on them. They'll kill a wizard without the usual side effect. Wonder if that's how the lakur eat them."

"I'll get a rig out tomorrow. I'll need to get my sleeve adjusted to make for a clear shot."

"Do what you need to do."

"Should I be informing the Queen of what we know?" Theo tapped his fingers on the table.

"What do we know? The wizards meddled in the wars in the south. They were behind the disastrous attack on the lakur down there. We don't have anything linking them to politics up here. My gut tells me we need to be ready for any eventuality."

"You turning into another Hendrik?"

"Maybe it's growing old." Karl stood and waited for the room to stop spinning. "I need to get back to the barracks."

"I'll have someone drive you. Don't want you passing out on the road. It would spoil the tough guy image."

"Not much of that left." Karl ran his fingers through his hair.

"Enough."

***

Cordin woke with a start. Tad slept above him, poor blighter. He had given up the business and his new start for Cordin. A bit of light came in the window, more than enough for him to see his surroundings. Being on the ship suited him. A rat on a ship – as long as they didn't sink. Never thought he'd make the City, never mind travel across the ocean.

The sailor's voices floated down to him as they did whatever sailors do in the middle of the night. One voice came a bit sharper, then there was a commotion up on deck. Someone ran through the bunks where the off-shift crew slept, yelling about all hands on deck and prepare for battle.

Cordin thought about waking Tad, but he'd want to go up on the deck and get heroic, probably get killed. Cordin set himself to listen for a bit.

Things got quiet above with no voices shouting orders. The silence lasted so long Cordin wondered if the thing had been a false alarm. Then the Captain shouted for archers to fire and it got chaotic. Sailors groaned, bodies fell into the water. The others whoever they were must be firing back. A bump on against the ship woke Tad, who sat up with wide eyes.

Open battle raged on the ship's deck with the clash of steel and the scream of dying men. Couldn't tell by listening who was dying.

A bump on the other side spelled doom. The battle faded as the victors finished off the losers. Cordin had a very good idea which was which. He signed to Tad to pretend to be asleep again and climbed into his hammock and closed his eyes.

Bumps and crashes sounded as the intruders searched the ship. They got closer and Cordin could feel Tad tensing up. He reached up and bumped the hammock. Tad reached down, they clasped hands for a moment before the door crashed open and two men stepped into the room

They talked to each other in a language Cordin didn't understand. Then one of them shouted back along the ship. A larger man stooped to enter the cabin.

"Fight, and die, slaves, and live."

Tad rolled out of the hammock with his hands visible. He kicked his pack over to the man, then knelt on the floor. Cordin knelt as best he could beside him. The men chattered away in their guttural language after they saw Cordin. The big man shrugged and left the room. One of the others tied Tad and Cordin's hands, then tied them together.

The other went through the back. He grinned when he found the bags of coin. The knife he looked at, then stuck in his boot. When he found Karl's letter, he turned it over in his hands a few times, then shoved it into his shirt. The clothes went back in the bag, then he tossed it in the corner.

They led Tad and Cordin out of their room onto the deck. Bodies lay everywhere. The attackers were efficiently moving cargo from the ship to their own low-lying boats. Two more came out of the mist to help. Cordin's gut heaved at the smell, so when he and Tad were loaded like cargo onto one of the boats, he breathed easier.

The strange men hoisted a single sail and left the ship burning behind them.

It looked like it would take longer than they'd hoped to find Leedles.

***

Apoxthenis sat bolt upright in bed and restrained the urge to shout in triumph. He'd gambled everything on this moment. Time to collect the rewards before the council organized to take over his pet project.

He dressed quickly, then went down to the basement of his home, set against the wall of the Wizard's Guild for convenience. A source lay semi-comatose on the mat in the corner. It was new, barely trained but would be enough for the task. He sat on the floor and began to draw power to create something very few wizards had ever attempted.

When he succeeded, he'd have power enough to rule the world.

CHAPTER TWENTY-NINE

Leedles fought her way to consciousness. Agony ran through her veins and pounded in her head. She rolled over and sat up. The sky lightened in the east. Morning wasn't far away, and she needed to be in shelter.

The staff lay on the ground beside her, the chain shattered. The steel shackle fit around her arm, but the magic which bound her to the staff had been broken.

:What did you do?:

"I will not be bound to a murderer and coward." She climbed to her feet.

:Don't leave me here.:

"I should, I should leave you to rot and burn in the sun. Though I may be the fruit of your passion, I am not your daughter." She picked up the staff, the gold colour of the wood had faded almost to grey, the wood lighter in weight. Leedles plucked the acorn from the twig at the top of the staff and dropped it on the ground.

"I wish you'd go home." She ground the acorn under her foot and the staff disintegrated in her hand. Leaving the remnants on the desert floor, she staggered back to the tunnel through the rock. Walking was harder without the weight and support of the staff.

The tunnel's gloom welcomed her as the first rays of light beamed across the desert to set another day on fire. Leedles collapsed against the stone wall, and wept for her parents.

A painful tug on her throat yanked her out of her misery. In the rock across from her a window opened into a room lit with candles. Apoxthenis sat near enough she might have touched him had they been in the same room. The pull got worse and she staggered.

"Now that you are a wise one, my power will be limitless." The wizard smiled and licked his lips. "I would have expected you to choose a shape of greater power."

"I'm no wise one," Leedles gasped out the words. "I will die before I become such a monster."

Apoxthenis frowned, then shrugged.

"So be it. You will still give me more power than any other source. No matter how far away you are."

Leedles picked up a rock and threw it at him. It bounced across the room behind him and Apoxthenis winced.

Leedles wasn't looking at the wizard. Sella lay on the bed behind him pale and barely breathing, dressed in rags.

Fire burned up from Leedles' heart. She gathered magic to her, but Apoxthenis siphoned it off as fast as she could take it in. *The rock had traveled through the portal.*

Leedles lunged toward the portal and reached through to grab Apoxthenis by the throat. With the last of her strength she hauled him toward her. His head and one shoulder made it through the portal before he screamed, and it collapsed. A burst of power slammed Leedles against the wall, by reflex she absorbed the magic.

The stone returned to stone, and Leedles dropped the head of the wizard on the ground. Something at her neck burned. She yanked at it and tore off a necklace with a darkened and cracked crystal hanging from it. A fog that had lain on her mind since Apoxthenis gave it to her lifted.

She'd been used, by the Tree, by the wizards. No more. Leedles gathered the magic, but through a focus she created outside of her. Weaving the strands together she created clothes for herself. Her favourite shirt and pants Karl gave her, the blanket which changed her life. She breathed in more magic and stored it within herself, made it hers.

Ironic the wizards taught me how to live with the magic after all.

"Thanks for nothing," she said to Apoxthenis' head, face frozen in a rictus of pain and fear. "I was going to give you a message that I'm coming after you, but I guess your friends will find out for themselves."

Leedles tucked the stone chip she'd been using as a knife between shackle and wrist, then left the rock with its gruesome occupant behind and walked north. Magic shielded her from the full heat of the sun; her boots insulated her from the burning sand.

She lost count of the days she hiked, catching food where she could in the evening before resting through the night. One day a faint green line appeared on the horizon. As she walked it become more solid until she moved through waist high grass. Trees dotted the plain and as they became more plentiful, she found running water and a pool at the bottom of a waterfall.

Swimming in the pool made her laugh with delight. The echo coming back strange to her. Leedles treaded water and tried to remember the last time she'd laughed. So much time spent in rage or in tears, but she couldn't remember laughter. She ducked her head and went back to swimming. She wouldn't forget this day.

Roc fell out of the sky and landed on the rocks above her.

:Greetings, wise one.:

"I'm no wise one, Roc. I won't be, not if it means forgetting what it means to be human."

:Not all of us are like the stick.:

"No, I know you're not." Leedles climbed out of the pool and let her clothes form around her again. "Yet, even so, I will wear this shape and let it remind me."

:You will die.:

"We all die." Leedles climbed up the rocks to sit beside the great bird. "The wizards fear death. In their last moments they release all their power in an attempt to thwart it. I am not a wizard either."

:Whether you take a shape of power or not, I count you among the wise.: Roc bowed to her, then flew away over the plains to the desert.

Leedles stood up and headed north.

CHAPTER THIRTY

Karl stood beside Theo at the edge of the hole where a wizard's house once stood. The remaining stones were twisted by magic and the street overturned. Neighbouring buildings had taken damage from the burst, but nothing that couldn't be fixed.

Most of those neighbours were wizards, or those who served them, but the burst damage wasn't why Theo had been called in. He'd sent a message for Karl and they'd met at this hole.

"There's a body of a wizard down there?" Karl peered into the shadows.

"Most of one." Theo pointed to a corner where a shape lay. Even with limbs distorted by the magic, it was clear the body's head had gone missing.

"Is it safe to go down there?" Karl walked around looking for a route down.

"Seems stable enough." Theo waved over one of his aides. "Fetch a rope, a ladder would be better."

"Yes, Sir." The aide trotted off to consult with a bystander before heading toward one of the neighbouring houses.

"I guess even wizards must trim trees." Karl pointed to a spot halfway around. "That's our best bet. Not much overhang, so nothing to fall on us."

The aide returned along with a man in grey coveralls, carrying a ladder on their shoulders. Under Karl's direction they lowered it into the hole. They steadied the ladder as Karl and Theo climbed down into the pit.

The effect of the magic was clearer here. Stone and brick took on a glassy, brittle look. Wood twisted into odd shapes.

"This wasn't just a burst." Karl rubbed his arm. The climb hadn't done it any good. "There had to be an explosion of some sort as well."

"Maybe the explosion is what killed him." Theo bent down to pick up a piece of paper. The words were written in a different language. He put it in his pocket. He'd find someone to read it.

"Explosion wouldn't make such a clean cut." Karl crouched down by the body. "Even a sword couldn't cut like this." He pointed to the line. "Right through bone, and not small ones either, yet there are no fragments in the wound."

"Some kind of magic attack?" Theo clambered over some furniture to stand beside Karl. "His name was Apoxthenis, advisor to the Queen, but not popular with other wizards."

"Do even other wizards like wizards?" Karl stood up and looked around. "If this was an attack, it was a risky one. Wizards aren't immune to the effect of the burst. They're still flesh and bone, like the rest of us. No matter what they'd like us to believe."

"Hold up." Theo raised a hand. "You hear that?"

"Sounded like someone moaning." Karl pointed. "Over there."

A slab had fallen at an angle creating a space behind it. Another moan came from behind it.

"We're going to need some equipment and more hands down here." Theo waved to his aide. "Make it quick."

The work of moving the slab without collapsing everything around it went on into the night. By lantern light, Karl could see the form of a young girl curled into a ball. He reached in and picked her up.

"They're eating me!" the girl screamed, and he almost dropped her. Then he got a look at her face and his blood ran cold.

"Look like you've seen a ghost." Theo came and helped Karl lift the girl onto a stretcher.

"I know her," Karl sat on a misshapen chair. "The cook's kid in Dunstown. We stayed there a few days."

"What's she doing here?"

"Don't know, but I plan to find out."

***

Their captors didn't mistreat them. Tad might have felt better if they had. Instead he and Cordin were fed and watered. Blankets covered them when the air grew cold. The kindness made their fascination with Cordin harder to understand.

Fear and loathing, Tad could have understood. Cordin didn't look very human anymore. Only Cordin's eyes hadn't changed. Somehow, they had to get away and find the wizard. Not even seafaring barbarians were going to stop them.

They sailed into a mist which defied wind and wave to hang like a wall in front of them. The ships sailed through as if it weren't there. The air became freezing and more blankets were tossed on Tad and Cordin, but the seafarers laughed and bared their chests.

A day of moving through the mist made Tad so disoriented he couldn't be sure he was still in the same world. At times the fog became so thick that even the men nearest him on the boat were only faint outlines.

He slept fitfully, cuddled against Cordin to share his heat. His friend lay so still, Tad feared he'd given up completely. Once in a while a hand would pat Tad's shoulder.

The mist cleared and land loomed over them. Mountains leapt straight up out of the ocean. Waves broke against them and exploded into spray. Far above a hint of green promised at least some life inhabited the place.

The boats sailed toward the cliffs. Tad saw an opening, like an ax had sliced into the rock. They traveled along the inlet to a sandy beach. Past the beach, houses packed a green hill leading up to a winding path to the top of the cliffs. The inhabitants swarmed the beach as the boats pulled in, seafarers roaring in victory.

There were no docks, instead the men hauled the boats onto the sand, then began tossing out cargo to the eager people below. The big man, Tad guessed the equivalent of their Captain came and cut the ropes binding them.

"You run, you die." He pointed over the side of the boat.

Tad helped Cordin over the side, then jumped to the beach. He fell to the sand as his legs gave out. People around him laughed but left him alone. They pointed to Cordin and muttered to each other.

An old woman came up to them and motioned for them to follow. Tad looked at Cordin and shrugged.

She led them to a longhouse, one of many. Tad couldn't see any houses like he was used to. Inside the longhouse a fire burned, and unshuttered windows let light in. The reek of men, dog and sour mead made Tad gag. The old woman took them to a corner with sleeping mats then brought them bowls of stew and chunks of coarse bread. The mats smelled as bad as the rest of the place, but Tad made sure Cordin was comfortable before lying beside him to sleep.

The big man came to check on them while the village celebrated outside with singing and dancing.

"Want to learn to talk." Tad said to the man.

"We talk."

"Speak like you. Your language."

The man roared, and Tad's heart skipped. Had he insulted the man? But a little girl, no more than eight or ten years ran up and hugged the man. He spoke to the girl, pointing at Tad and Cordin. Then pushed her toward them.

"Teach."

***

The Wizards met in their hall; one wall made glassy from the burst when Apoxthenis' source escaped. One of them died in that escape. Now Apoxthenis was dead.

"They have a source." An older wizard thumped the floor with his cane.

"It wears a conduit. It cannot be removed. It can tell them nothing," another said.

"The new Vice-Commander recognized her." The old wizard looked around. "I remember him. He has no fondness for us."

"We will not let fear stand in the way of our goal. We are close." A council member leaned over his desk.

"We have been close before," the old wizard said. "We must not be careless."

"Not careless, but not fearful either." The council member looked out at the gathered wizard. "We need the power. We continue as planned."

CHAPTER THIRTY-ONE

The sounds of fighting ahead made Leedles pause. She wasn't sure what she wanted to do next, though a vague tug pulled her north. Getting involved in a conflict wouldn't help her.

Voices yelled at each other; screams sounded. Leedles understood none of it. She needed to know what was going on before making any decisions. Plucking some threads from around her, she created her focus and sent the magic out. It came back to whisper in her ear and the shouting voices became clear.

"Watch out, the lakur is going to break out. Hold the line, hold."

A beast burst out of the trees and spotted her. It looked a bit like the lakur she'd met in the forest, only at least four times larger and with tusks sticking out of its mouth. It roared and charged her. Leedles froze the lakur in place and went to talk to it.

"I need to speak to the queen."

The lakur foamed at the mouth and, incredibly, moved closer to her. Leedles stepped back and tripped. The spell holding the lakur failed and it lunged toward her. She sent a bolt of fire through its skull.

"Please don't move, lady," one of the voices from the battle spoke quietly behind her.

"I would rather talk face to face." Leedles stood up and turned around. The bolts from the crossbows bounced off her shield. "I'm no threat to you."

"You are no friend either." Two other men joined him and fanned out around her.

"I have some experience with the lakur, I may be able to help."

"Help us now, then rule us and suck the life out of our children." One of the other men said.

"I am no friend of the wizards." Leedles held her hands out. "If you don't wish my aid, then I will continue my way north and leave you to your battles."

"North is where their nest is." The first man lowered his crossbow.

"As I said, I have experience with the lakur, I don't fear them."

"You have to be crazy," the third said.

"I have been accused of that before."

"This is beyond me," the first man slung his crossbow on his back. "The lakur is dead, our mission complete. We'll bring her back to the King and let him decide." He turned to Leedles. "Since we'll be traveling together a ways, you can call me Chen. That's Ying, and the one trembling in his boots yonder is Kan."

"I am Leedles."

"An odd name for a wizard," Ying said.

"I'm not a wizard." Leedles took a slow breath. Life would be frustrating if this was the greeting she received everywhere.

"Then what are you?" Chen led the way into the woods to where several horses were tied.

"I'm not sure." Leedles shrugged and went to greet the horses.

"Can you ride?" Chen looked up from tightening the cinch on his saddle.

"The horse says she will carry me." Leedles tightened the saddle as the horse instructed, then jump up onto its back.

"I think that's a 'yes' boys." Chen slapped his reins against his horse's neck and rode west along a barely discernible trail.

"How long have you been fighting the lakur?" Leedles asked her horse to move up closer to Chen's.

"It started in my great-grandfather's day; we been fighting ever since. They're getting worse, crazier, like they don't care if they live or die."

They reached a fortified town before the sun set. Chen tossed his reins to a boy as he jumped off his horse.

"Thanks for carrying me." Leedles patted her horse and it snorted and shook its head.

Ying stared at her. "I think the horse understood her."

"You're as crazy as she is, Ying." Kan slapped the other man's back. "We better report in while Chen talks to the King."

"Follow me," Chen led the way into town. "Normally, the King is not so near the front, but he took a notion to see the situation for himself. We've got roving squads out keeping the lakur far enough away they can't get to the King. The problem is, because he can't see them, he doesn't think they're that big a problem. He wants to put more units to the east where he's afraid the Lovaris might invade. They're not going to bother. No one wants to live in a lakur infested country."

He opened a door and waved her in. Two guards stood in a short hallway.

"How's his majesty today?" Chen asked.

"Grouchy," one guard said. "His hunt got cut short."

"Lovely." Chen looked at the ceiling. "I keep telling myself if I can survive the lakur, I can survive talking to the King."

"Keep telling yourself that." The guard opened the door.

The inside of the room bulged with pieces of animals. Heads hung off every available space, rugs covered the floor, birds dangled from the ceiling. Leedles tried to avoid stepping on the sprawled rugs, but Chen marched across them as if they weren't there. Sella loved fur, she'd adore this place, or maybe just the coats that could be made from the skins here.

"My hunt was interrupted again." The King leaned back on a huge wooden armchair with one leg over an arm.

"Security must come first, your Majesty. Losing you would be a terrible blow to the country."

"Security, bah," The King pouted, not a regal look on a man only slightly younger than Karl. "I've yet to see one of these ferocious lakur."

"We've been working hard to keep it that way."

"I don't want to sit safely here and have my hunts ruined. It's time I met the lakur.

"A good idea, your Majesty," Leedles said. Chen frowned at her, but the King grinned and pointed at her.

"Who is she? I like her."

"She's...Leedles," Chen said. "We met to the east of here while fighting a lakur."

"Why did you bring her here?" The King looked at him suspiciously. "Are you trying to distract me again?"

"She killed the lakur, with magic."

The King sat bolt upright and just about fell out of the chair.

"A wizard? You bring a wizard here?"

"Not a wizard, your Majesty, something else."

"How do you know?"

"The wizards from Lovaris are all men and arrogant. She's a woman and appears reasonable."

"I can see she's a woman, Chen." The King got up and walked over to Leedles, then around her. "She isn't dressed like a wizard, more like a peasant." He plunked down on the chair again. "Show me some magic."

"What would you like to see?" Leedles kept her voice pleasant.

"How about you show me what a lakur looks like?"

"Very well." She whispered briefly, and the lakur she'd killed filled the room. It roared, bringing the guard stumbling through the door, swords in hand. The King stared enraptured at the lakur.

"I must hunt one. Chen see to it."

Chen glared at Leedles and talked to the guards.

"You will be informed when the scouts spot an incursion."

"How do you kill them?" The king walked around the frozen illusion of the lakur.

"With great difficulty," Chen said. "We're fortunate they've been coming in ones or twos. If these came in an organized charge like my father's day, we wouldn't stand a chance."

"But this is so much bigger than the records say."

"They've been breeding for war." Leedles dismissed the illusion. "The longer they fight, the bigger and nastier they are going to get.

"Bigger than that?" The King looked uncertain for the first time.

"To the south of our land, there was a war between the lakur and the men of the region. The men lost and the lakur rule, and that was with wizards fighting in the battle."

"We've been holding them for three generations." The King jumped up to pace about the room. "We'll hold them as long as we need to."

"They're changing, your Majesty. Getting bigger, meaner. The only thing going for us is they seem to be getting less organized."

One of the guards ran into the room.

"The lakur, an incursion from the north!"

"How many?" Chen looked ready to launch himself from the room.

"Hundreds of them, Sir." The guard looked sick. "They'll be here within the hour."

"Prepare the ballista!" Chen ran from the room shouting instructions. "Every available man on the wall."

"I would ask a favour, your Majesty."

"Eh, what? Sure."

"I'd like to meet them before they reach the walls."

The King looked at her like she'd grown an extra head.

"Meet with them? Why?"

"The lakur are not beasts, or not the ones I knew. They are intelligent and mostly peaceful. There is something not right about this. If I can speak to the queen, I may be able to sort it out."

"Go then." The King waved her out of the room. "Guards, I need my armour."

Leedles walked back through the town. She climbed up on the wall and looked north. The lakur were there. They were coming for her because she'd asked to speak to the queen. It didn't look like such a great idea anymore.

"I hear you're going to meet them." Chen stood at her side, carrying his crossbow and a quiver stuffed with bolts.

"Yes."

"Then I'm going with you. The King will expect a report."

"I'll try to keep you safe," Leedles said. "Don't kill anything unless you have to."

CHAPTER THIRTY-TWO

Karl sat beside Sella in the infirmary. They'd taken her to the City Guard one behind the barracks. The smaller and more remote site made keeping her safe easier.

"The wizards will know we have her." Theo sat on an empty bed. "We need to find out how she survived the burst."

"She was such a bright young thing," Karl brushed her hair back. "Called Leedles a barbarian, never went anywhere but at full speed." Her hair tangled in something he couldn't see.

"Sir," an aide stepped into the room. "You're wanted in the report room."

"You go," Theo stood up. "I need to get to the Palace to listen for rumours about the burst." He looked at the aide. "Someone sits beside her day and night. She is never to be alone. No one sees her except the surgeon or one of us without my express permission."

"Yes, Sir." The aide followed them to the door and whistled sharply, another trotted over. Karl left them conferring and climbed the stairs to the report room.

The Guards in the room stood when he entered, and he waved them to sit. One of the guards, he took a moment to remember her name, Sopha, had red eyes and a suspiciously damp face. Her partner, a newer recruit Karl couldn't put a name to, didn't look much better.

"Reports." Karl sat on the desk and waited.

"Guards, Wadd and Birn," The two stood up, not at attention, but alert. They were the senior guards in the room. "We patrolled the docks, nothing much to report. Did hear some rumours about the Vice-Commander being a fearsome monster."

"Not rumours, Guards, the truth." Karl kept his hand from his arm.

The Guards laughed briefly.

The others reported, the usual until Sopha and her partner stood.

"Guards, Sopha and Crom." She took a deep breath and her partner put his hand on her shoulder. Not according to the rules, but Karl wasn't about to interrupt them. "We patrolled the Weaver district, mostly small merchants and their homes. Reports of missing children from five families. One family lost three. All of them taken from their beds. None of them slept alone in their rooms."

"How did the parents know they were missing?"

"Nightmares, Sir. Each mother related the same nightmare a monster come to snatch their child. When they checked, they found a child missing." She stopped to collect herself again. "You can imagine their panic. After the third report, I sent a runner asking for extra help and we started going from house to house asking folks to check on their children." She started crying. "Sorry, Sir."

"Sopha's sister's boy was one of them was snatched. I told her she could stay with her sister, but she wouldn't have nothing but she continue to work." Crom looked belligerently at Karl.

"Thank you, Crom, when we finish report, you have permission to escort Sopha to her sister's and provide what support you can." Karl stood up and looked at the others.

"Almost twenty years ago, someone or something snatched children from their homes. None were recovered alive. You will know the stories; you may even know someone who lost a child then. More than a hundred children were taken. Guards, we are not going to let that happen again. We are going to triple patrols where there is the highest risk. You will report the slightest thing unusual immediately." Karl restrained his desire to break something. He remembered being thankful Cassie lived far from the City while companions mourned their loss. "Get some rest, it's the last you're going to have until we stop this."

***

Terteky corrected Tad. Repeating the word of the day again for him. For a ten-year old, she was an extraordinarily patient teacher. She picked a word and drummed it into Tad's head for the rest of the day. The words themselves were an odd collection. *Skola* meant a cup to hold wine. *Fanrus* a dog. Her father was *Beow*, but Tad hadn't figured out whether that was his name or his title. Cordin she called *wulfkin*. Tad told her over and over his friend's name was Cordin, but Terteky wouldn't be moved. She picked up Tad's name quickly enough, but turned red and giggled whenever she used it.

Just my luck to have name which is a dirty word.

She called him *Kinsul,* which Tad guessed meant slave. There were other slaves in the *lanse* at the end of the fjord. He wasn't allowed to talk to them, though he listened to them talk in his language like a thirsty man looks at a mug of water.

They weren't mistreated. No chains or ropes, Beow made sure they had good warm clothes. They could wander around the longhouse as much as they wanted but were not allowed to leave.

Terteky pointed at Cordin, "wulfkin" she said, made a scared face then pointed outside and shook her head.

Aside from the language lessons, Tad spent his days bored to tears. The other seafarers who ate and slept in the longhouse treated him much the same as the fanrus who slept under the tables.

Eventually he had enough words to try brief conversations with the seafarers. They'd laugh and say something back too quickly for him to follow. He took to watching the other kinsul as they followed their captor's orders. Between that and Terteky, Tad pieced together enough of the language to make him decide he'd pretend ignorance.

The wulfkin was to be a gift to the *Spellska.* He thought it meant king or ruler until one of the kinsul disappeared. Two other kinsul talked about it, one angry, the other trying to keep her friend quiet. Tad only overheard one phrase before they returned to heated whispers, but it made his gut hands shake.

'Gone to the wizard' the woman said.

Time to get Cordin out of here. Never mind that they were on an island surrounded by warrior seafarers and a wall of mist. Tad began to work on a plan.

CHAPTER THIRTY-THREE

Leedles rode out the gate with Chen beside her. The guards looked at them like they were crazy, but weren't willing to disobey Chen.

"I've been trying to corral the king into a strategy of containment," Chen talked as if they were on a pleasant excursion instead of riding to meet a horde of murderous creatures. "His father built a line of fortified villages to stake a claim to the northwest of the country. The rest of our land would be remarkably peaceful if it weren't for the constant demand for men and resources to fight the lakur. We could gradually build a wall to keep them in. At least I thought so until you pointed out how they were changing. A wall won't hold them back."

"So you follow a complete stranger on a mad mission to certain death."

"It seemed like a better option than facing the King with the news we can't win this war."

"Can't win it, but there is a slight chance we can stop it."

"Good enough to risk death."

They reached the top of a slight hill in an open area.

"Let's stop here." Leedles jumped down from her horse and whispered in its ear. It neighed at Chen's and they carried on for a bit before Chen's horse nodded its head and stomped a foot.

"What was that about?" Chen stood beside her bemused at the interchange.

"Telling the horses not to panic when the lakur come. It will be dangerous enough without them running wild through the lakur. We may need them later anyway."

Leedles tried to show the same calm as the horse who grazed on the grass. Her palms sweated and her heart raced. She absorbed as much magic as she could without glowing, but didn't believe magic would solve this war.

The lakur were running at them from a distance, then suddenly they surrounded Leedles and Chen. The huge lakur panted, showing their array of teeth, but they didn't attack.

"What now?" Chen's voice didn't have the slightest wobble in it.

"We wait." Leedles failed to match his nonchalant tone.

He looked at her and grinned. "I'm relieved to see you're human. A wizard would never show fear."

"I've seen a few who did more than tremble under their fancy clothes." Leedles laughed, "But they were facing me, not lakur."

"I'm guessing you're dangerous when you're angry." Chen raised an eyebrow at her.

"You could say that." Leedles pointed to where the lakur were moving. "Something is coming."

Leedles watched the lakur shift as an unseen thing approached. It had to be smaller than the battle lakur. When it finally came through the last of the lakur.

Leedles gasped. The lakur looked like the ones she'd met in the forest, only weak and deformed.

"The queen must speak to you," it said without preamble.

Leedles gritted her teeth and put her hand out.

"Too weak for that, she barely holds this hatching from slaughter. You must come."

"If you'd warned me, I could have packed a lunch." Chen jumped on his horse.

Leedles climbed on hers and nodded to the lakur. It turned and hobbled back into the circle of battle lakurs. She followed with Chen beside her. The circle formed around them and moved with them north and west.

"What's in that direction?" Leedles needed to talk to still the fluttering in her stomach.

"Not sure, no one's been there in almost a hundred years. Low hills, more forest. Further east it gets rocky when you go north."

"How far north before you're clear of the lakur?"

"I've no idea. Our northern border is a big river, grassland and horse tribes on the other side. We trade a bit, raid a bit."

"How far away is the river?" Leedles tried to picture the landscape.

"A hard day's ride, two if you don't want to kill the horse. There are two or three outposts along the way."

"A larger territory than the lakur at home."

"How do you fight the lakur where you come from?" Chen looked at her sharply, reminding her he'd spent a lifetime killing lakur. They were the enemy to be feared. At home most didn't know they existed.

"We don't."

Chen didn't have a reply to that, and the conversation ended. Leedles went back to worrying about whether this had really been such a great idea. Though she found herself thinking about the man riding alongside her too.

The forest became thicker, more like the one Leedles had wandered into. Rocks poked out through the forest floor like massive sea creatures.

Most of the rock was shades of grey, but in places veins of colour ran through it. The trees began to change to pines and spruce.

They arrived at a hole in the ground leading into darkness.

"Your animals will be safe here." The deformed lakur looked at Chen. "The queen requests you leave your weapons here."

"And if I don't?"

"You may remain with the animals."

Chen dropped his crossbow, sword and surprising amount of weaponry on a bit of dry ground. He looked at Leedles and shrugged.

"Force of habit."

"What will happen if we succeed at stopping this war?" Leedles' fluttering butterflies took to gnawing. Convincing the lakur might be easier than changing the humans.

Chen looked over the pile. "I'd probably leave the crossbow at home."

Leedles rolled her eyes when he grinned at her.

"Let's go."

They followed the lakur into the tunnel.

Fungi glowed on the walls allowing them to see a little way ahead. Leedles concentrated on keeping her footing on the uneven ground. Chen beside her moved like he was walking across a town square.

They passed other tunnels and took turns apparently at random. Perhaps the queen wanted to be sure they couldn't leave without her permission.

At last the lakur limped into a cavernous space. It made it as far as a small delicate lakur standing in the centre of the open space before collapsing to twitch once and lie still.

"It made art with clay," the queen said, "and added much to our life."

"The lakur are individuals?" Leedles asked. The dim light hinted at a huge bulk behind the queen, then her understanding shifted. The bulk was the queen; trapping the delicate lakur here in the cave.

"Separate from the hive, they go mad. They may live, but not as lakur."

Leedles came close enough to see shades of gold on the queen.

"lakur live a long time, but this life is near its end. In digging tunnels generations of hatches ago, the miners struck a vein of poison." She pointed to the gold patches on her body. "It interferes with the mind, slows thinking, memory breaks."

"This war has cost both of our people." Chen stepped forward and bowed slightly.

"Yes, migration is difficult, impossible when hatching warriors."

"How do we end the conflict?" Leedles wanted to shake the queen, not a good idea. She wiped her hands on her pants.

"When this piece dies, the lakur will cease. The remaining pieces will attack with no reason."

Chen frowned and looked at Leedles.

"You didn't call us to tell us there is no hope." Leedles said.

"Correct." Another lakur came out of the darkness. It cradled something in one arm. "This one passes, but life is possible. This one felt your connection to a sister far away. The queen egg is untainted by poison. It is the last. Take it to sister; her drone may fertilize it to be planted in a new nest. Some memory may live."

"If we take on this task. Will you call back the lakur?" Chen had his fists clenched, as he balanced on his toes.

"As long as this one lives will hold lakur from battle. But this one needs surety."

Leedles stepped forward to kneel beside the queen and offered her hand. The queen stabbed her antennae through Leedles hand.

Awareness flooded Leedles. The lakur roamed through the forest, but many were sick or twisted. The poison left holes in the awareness. A piece wandered too far and vanished. The lakur's awareness briefly bridged the space between this land and Leedles. She felt the sharpness of the lakur's grief, and determination to help. The antennae pulled out of her hand and Leedles collapsed against Chen. He caught her and lowered her to the ground.

"I speak for my King." Chen gulped, the first sign of nerves Leedles saw in him, then knelt before the queen and offered his hand. He flinched when the antennae pierced him then twitched as awareness flowed through him. The queen pulled away and Chen slumped before standing to bow to the queen.

"I will speak to my King. Do everything in my power to grant what you ask."

Leedles took the egg from the lakur. The lakur led them out of the nest. Chen looked at Leedles and began picking up his weapons. Most of the battle lakur had left.

"Now we need to create a miracle between us." Chen said. "Life or death rides on our actions."

"That's life." Leedles created a sling for the egg then mounted her horse. "I must travel west."

"I will return to convince the King."

"The new nest will have to be far away from here." Leedles wanted to extend the conversation and stay with Chen a little longer.

"There is a large patch of scrub land between us and Lovaris, and the poison the queen spoke of is gold." He turned his mount south. "I've never met a King who could resist gold.

CHAPTER THIRTY-FOUR

Karl wanted to hurt someone badly. Seven children had been taken. No one saw a thing. No sign left behind. They'd vanished into thin air. Of course, the people were talking about magic, and any time magic came up, the wizards got mentioned.

Twenty years ago, the City rioted against the wizards. Citizens stormed the Guild. The Queen hired soldiers to suppress the riot because her own forces refused. At the end of it some of those who refused were hung, the streets ran red with the blood of angry mothers and fathers, and the wizards continued as if nothing had happened. Magic held too much importance to the Queen and the rulers of the land to risk losing it.

Twenty years ago, Karl had been sure the wizards got away with murder; but had nothing but his loathing of wizards to prove it. His commander had turned down the contract to quell the unrest, but Karl had saved a wizard from an angry mob. That wizard had owed him a favour until not quite a month ago.

He quashed the temptation to go speak to Widdershins. The wizard would spout the same line that came from the council. They had every sympathy for the bereaved families, but there was no information they could discern about the perpetrator. Those with a good memory knew it was exactly the same statement issued two decades before.

What was different was the City Guard, put in place under contract to Theo after the riots had finished, later made a regular part of the Guard. The men and women he'd trained combed the City, along with volunteers they searched every building they were allowed to enter.

"Still nothing?" Theo stepped into Karl's office and closed the door.

"Less than nothing." Karl glowered at the map he'd pinned to the wall. Pins marked the homes of the missing children. Chalked x's the buildings searched.

"The Queen is expressing concern. Her mother never recovered from the riots. She doesn't want a repeat of history."

"We need to pressure the wizards without triggering the riots."

"I have been speaking to the Queen on that very subject. If we can provide reasonable proof they have something to do with this, she will permit the Guard to search the Guild compound."

"A big step forward, all we need is the proof." Karl went to look at the map as if it would provide part of the answer.

"The Queen ordered me to keep it between you and me. The merest rumour the wizards are being investigated might set off the bonfire we're trying to avoid."

"Sirs," an aide put his head in the door. "A Guardswoman wishes to speak to you."

"Send her in." Karl sat behind his desk again. Theo moved back into a corner out of the way.

Guard Sopha entered the office as if she might find wild beasts instead of her commander.

"Sorry, Sir." She wrung her hands in front of her. "My partner, Crom, insisted I talk to you."

"I'm always open to hearing from my Guards. What do you need?"

"It's not so much that I need something, but it's odd. That's all."

"Odd?" Karl held still. The least wrong move could send her running.

"It's the children, the ones who are missing..."

"One of them is your sister's boy if I remember correctly."

"That's right, but another one is a cousin's daughter, a third the boy of my aunt's grandson..." She trailed off and wrung her hands even tighter.

"You're related to three of the missing children?" Karl leaned back and rubbed his arm. No one else had found a connection between the children.

"No, Sir." She looked at him with wide eyes and it hit Karl, it was him she feared. "I'm related to all of them."

"You're sure?" Karl leaned forward his heart pounded.

"We have a lot of relatives. I've been trying to create a family tree; something to do to take my mind off work. So I know about more relatives than most. I did more research, a lot of my cousins disappeared twenty years ago; the first time the Reaper came."

"I'd like to see your research, Guard Sopha. In fact, I would like you to carry it a step further and see if you can find family connections between the other missing children from twenty years ago."

"I don't know, Sir." She stood up and stilled her hands. "I will try." She pulled a crumpled paper out of her shirt. "This is what I have on the seven children missing now." She put it on the desk and pointed at a spider's web of relationships. "They all trace back to my grandmother."

"Anything special about her?" Karl followed the line with his finger.

"The stories are she could do things. Heal, fix stuff, find things."

"Thank you, Guard Sopha. Report when you have more information."

She left and Theo strode over to Karl's desk to look at the paper.

"Do stuff, like magic. The wizards act like they have the only access to magic, but we both know that's not true."

"Leedles," Karl felt the familiar pang when he said her name.

"Others too if old wives' tales are true."

"What if the wizards are collecting children with magic ability?"

"Why?" Theo paced around the office. "What good does it do them to steal children? If they were intent on keeping them from developing magic, they could kill them and not all at once."

"It's not about the children. It's about the power." Karl's hands shook. "You told me yourself this Apoxthenis practically drooled over Leedles."

"How do we prove it?"

"Sella." Karl jumped up. "She was one of them. We only found her because Apoxthenis blew up his house."

"Last I heard she's still comatose, except for nightmares."

"Nightmares of being eaten." Karl shuddered and led the way to the infirmary.

***

Tad watched the seafarers come for another celebration. The man who'd taken the knife and letter was among them. He pointed at Tad and laughed. He had the knife or something else stuck in his boot. Too much to ask for the letter to be there too.

Cordin didn't do much now but sleep curled in the corner, his tail wrapped around his waist. Tad would take any risk to help his friend, or get vengeance if help came too late.

His seafarer pointed Tad out to everyone who'd listen. Obviously bragging about capturing such interesting prisoners. From the actions, Tad was a better fighter in the stories.

The celebration involved a great deal of eating and drinking. The fanrus under the table gorged on the food cast off by the seafarers, even Tad was tossed a bone or two with meat still on them. He gnawed them clean. Pride gave way to necessity.

Night came and the torches were lit. The *sagaska* arrived dressed in furs with a skull stuck on his staff and a gold chain around his neck. When he told his tale, his voice filled the room and even Tad who understood less than one word in ten found his pulse racing with the cadence.

After the sagaska finished Beow presented a goblet of wine and a gold coin. The seafarers returned to the business of getting drunk. Perfect.

Tad caught the eye of the man who'd captured him and stuck out his tongue. The man frowned and looked away. But looked again at Tad after he'd downed more drink. Tad made another face. The man stood up, but his companion forced him to sit.

After a few more rounds, heads were hitting the tables. Even the sagaska waved his goblet, splashing Beow and anyone near him with wine.

One last time Tad made a face at the seafarer, he roared and climbed over the table. Tad forgot how big these men were. The seafarer shook Tad like a rag then threw him down and kicked him. He'd have kept kicking if Beow and the sagaska hadn't stopped him.

Tad lay groaning and holding his ribs, the sagaska's eyes passed over Tad and landed on Cordin.

"Wulfkin." The sagaska argued with Beow, pointing at Cordin. Finally, Beow gave in and stood over Tad.

"Wulfkin go." The man's face darkened with fury.

"I go with wulfkin." Tad crawled between Beow and Cordin.

"You go, you die."

"I die with wulfkin."

Beow waved his arms in disgust and stalked away.

"Young thief, your death will be neither easy nor honourable." The sagaska spoke with only a slight accent. At his command the seafarers searched Tad roughly, then the mats, finding nothing but fleas.

None of them searched the wulfkin sleeping peacefully a few feet away.

Part Three

CHAPTER THIRTY-FIVE

Leedles missed Chen, the only person aside from Karl who didn't fear her or try to use her. Even the lakur had their reasons for accepting her. Chen didn't have to come with her, but he did. He had little reason to trust her, but he did. His dry wit helped pass the time.

The pull north came stronger, and Leedles kept needing to correct her course to due west. It reminded her of something, but she couldn't recall what.

When she had been on her own coming out of the desert, loneliness hadn't been an issue. Walking away from people, she felt the emptiness of the land. One or two lakur peered at her from the trees on the first day, after squirrels and birds kept her company.

She ate off the land as Karl had shown her, killing a slow squirrel or bird when the chance came up. Not quite five days into her journey the forest cleared ahead.

Leedles came to a cliff towering over the ocean crashing endlessly into the rocks below. She sat on the edge of the cliff and looked out over the water. The lakur wouldn't last very long. Not long enough for Leedles to find a boat and cross the ocean. Even with her magic, it would take days maybe weeks, and she'd arrive exhausted. Then she'd need to take the return journey.

She hated what had to be done. The need of the lakur was greater than her pride.

Leedles closed her eyes and sent out a request, a plea for help. Roc had not been angry with her, but their parting had felt final as if by rejecting the transformation to wise one meant a rejection of Roc.

Night came. The stars lit the sky above the ocean while phosphorescent creatures lit the water.

What was she doing with her life? All very well to choose to stay human, but Leedles didn't know what that meant. Would she be doomed to wander the world seeking trouble to solve? It didn't sound much more inviting than living the moment to moment carelessness of a wise one.

She had Karl, but after the destruction of the tower by the City he must believe her dead. Leedles hung her head, thinking of the person she'd been, and who she'd become. Would Karl even recognize her as the daughter he'd adopted crossing the mountains?

Meeting again might be worse than letting him believe she had died. At least now he could grieve and move on, maybe find someone to share the remainder of his live.

:Gloomy thoughts for such a view.:

Leedles looked around to see where the wise one hid. A large wolf padded out of the trees and laid beside her.

:Itchy, just behind the ears.:

She scratched, expecting his fur to be coarse, but discovering it to be silky soft. The wolf sighed in pleasure.

:So hard to reach that just right.:

"Not that I don't mind the company, but why are you here?"

:Came to meet the wise one who shook the world.:

"I'm no wise one." Leedles paused in her scratching and the wolf nudged her hand.

:Wise one has little to do with shape, or power. Some flee the world, some watch it fall apart and despair, some,: he twisted his head and licked her hand. :Stay in the world and try to make it a better place.:

"So even though I stayed human, I'm a wise one? What about changing so the magic doesn't kill me?"

:The change makes you one with the magic, we don't wield it the same way you do. It would be like asking the rock to sculpt itself. Our power is held differently.:

Leedles ran the wolf's words through her head. Wise ones were as variable as humans, after all they began as human.

:One day, you may tire of the life you have, or have grieved too many passings. The desert will always be there.: The wolf's head lifted suddenly then he bounded into the woods.

"What are you doing here?" A man with a boy following him came out of the woods.

"Waiting." Leedles twisted to look at them. Rough clothing, but strong, healthy bodies. The man carried a bow, the boy a quiver of arrows.

"For what?" the boy asked.

Leedles moved away from the edge and sat against a tree.

"To see if a friend will come."

"Here?"

"Here."

"It's the boy's first hunt, he's a chatterbox." The man ruffled the boy's hair to take the sting from his words.

They sat, the boy looking like he wanted to burst with questions, but he kept silent and earned an approving nod from the man.

The world became slowly brighter as the sun rose behind the trees. Just as the first rays of light struck the water, Roc soared overhead, then dove below the cliff.

"I must go," Leedles said. "Good hunting to you." She ran to the edge of the cliff and dove off letting the magic slow her fall and take her away from the shore. Roc swept under her and she landed secure on the wise one's back.

"Thanks for coming," Leedles said into the rushing air.

:Always.:

CHAPTER THIRTY-SIX

Sella lay where Karl last saw her. Someone had put a clean shift on her, but her hair still tangled around her head.

"How is she?" Karl sat beside her.

"Much the same." The surgeon frowned. "If she doesn't wake soon, I don't expect she ever will. It is as if something is holding her back. Sometimes she twists in pain and clutches at her neck, and she screams during her nightmares, but fails to waken."

"Poor kid." Karl tried to straighten her hair. The Sella he knew wouldn't let her hair be such a mess. His fingers caught and he couldn't untangle her locks. "Wizards had her right?" He followed the tangles down to her neck. His eyes denied anything was there, but his fingers detected something on the edge of their perception.

"What do you see?" Theo leaned over to peer at the girl.

"Nothing," Karl put his hand out. "Hand me one of your bolts."

Theo shrugged and extracted one of the black bolts from his sleeve.

"Remind me not to accost you on a dark night," the surgeon said.

Karl ran the bolt gently up Sella's neck. She moaned and twisted as the bolt refused to move any further.

"Looks like something around her neck." Karl didn't have to ask for the second bolt. "See, where her hair moves, but nothing is there, trim it off."

The surgeon when to a cupboard and returned with a pair of shears. He carefully cut as Karl moved slightly. When no more hair shifted, he worked the bolts over her head. As his hands moved in front of her face, a chain with a crystal appeared hanging between the bolts.

Sella screamed and thrashed on the bed. Karl stepped back as the surgeon took over.

Theo looked at the necklace.

"Wizards' work." Theo reached toward it then drew back his fingers. Instead he pulled a handkerchief out of his pocket and held it under the necklace. Karl dropped it onto the silk and Theo wrapped it up quickly.

Sella stopped throwing herself about and curled up on the bed crying.

"I want to go home," she said.

Karl moved around to where she could see him.

"Can you tell me what happened?"

"The old man came; he was mad at Mistress Fall because the dress wasn't ready. He took me away and I never got to wear it. The carriage had no windows. I fell asleep. When I woke a man told me I needed to learn to hold magic. I didn't believe in magic, but he hurt me until I tried." She looked up at Karl with wide eyes. "It worked, I could feel it fill me up, like I drank too much water. He put something on me, and I don't remember anything 'till now."

"Power." Theo looked at the bundle of silk in his hand. He shoved it into his pocket, then took the bolts and reloaded the rigs on each arm. "We have her connected to magic, but I've never seen an old wizard. Maybe he works for them. Enough people do."

"Wizards?" Sella went pale and hid under the blankets.

"Surgeon," Theo said, "put the word out that the poor girl we rescued died without regaining consciousness. Then do whatever you need to do to change Sella's appearance. Karl will take her somewhere safe. You know nothing about necklaces or power."

"Certainly." The surgeon looked speculatively at Sella. "I think we can make you a very convincing boy."

Sella put her hands to her hair.

"Cut it off, cut it all off, whatever you need to do."

The surgeon could have made a living as a barber; soon Sella became Sam. Some clothes from a trunk in the corner completed the transformation. If he didn't look into her haunted eyes, Karl wouldn't have recognized her.

"Come on, Sam," Karl stood up. "We've a bit of a walk ahead of us."

He stomped out of the room, cursing at losing their only witness. He turned to look at 'Sam' and threw up his arms.

"Ok, you can give me your report on the way." Karl slammed out of the Guard compound yelling to the woman at the desk he was going for a drink and she was in charge until he got back. If the situation hadn't been so desperate the look of panic on her face would have been funny.

"Talk to me, kid," Karl said as they started walking. "Doesn't matter what you say as long as your mouth is moving."

All the way to the Unkissed Toad, Sella told him about the dress, her boyfriend and how she'd never leave home again.

Karl walked straight through the bar into Henrik's private room yelling for Henrik to fetch a bottle of the good stuff. Once the door closed, Karl slumped into a seat.

"I hope our act is good enough."

"I'm guessing you have a reason for all this fuss." Henrik poured a couple of glasses and handed one to Karl, who knocked it back in one shot. "Like that is it?" He poured another. "What's with the disguise?"

Sella's lips trembled and she looked ready to run.

"It's all right." Karl put a hand on her shoulder. "It would take a lot more work to fool Henrik here, but he's on our side."

"Safe keeping?"

"We rescued her from the wizards." Karl had never seen Henrik at a loss for words before.

"I'm not going back," Sella said.

"No, you aren't." Henrik smiled at her. The day was full of firsts. "I'll put her in the safe room. Give her some different clothes, those clothes will go on the back of a boy who runs errands for me regular."

Karl left Sella in Henrik's hands and went out to the bar. He sat at a table and yelled for a beer. Widdershins sat across from him.

"I heard you were storming through our city on a mission to get drunk." He took the pitcher from the barman and poured Karl a glass. "I had to come see for myself what upset you so much you'd abandon your post."

"The kid we rescued from the hole in Apoxthenis' house died." Karl picked up the beer and slugged it back.

"That's right, you have a soft spot for dead children." Widdershins leaned back and studied Karl.

Karl brought up the memory of Cassie the last time he saw her, begging him to let her come, screaming at him when he wouldn't. Leedles wide-eyed in a panic running into the woods to certain death. He didn't have to fake the loss on his face or the pain in his heart.

Widdershins put a coin on the table.

"Karl's drinks are on me today." Widdershins stood and looked into Karl's eyes. "Not all of us are monsters."

Karl was still trying to decide if he'd heard right as the door closed behind the wizard.

***

Theo took his carriage back to his home. He dismissed his staff then sat in his sitting room drinking a glass of wine. For twenty years he'd tried to bring fairness and order to the City. This year, he'd finally started to make progress. The citizens were asking the Guards for help instead of running away. The Guards shed the reputation of starting more fights than they stopped.

Then the children, again. He could recall with perfect clarity the ravaged faces of parents mourning their children. He refused the contract, thinking he'd never work in his home country again. No one was more surprised than he was to be asked by the old Queen to put the City back in order after the riots. He'd stayed out of it, his hands were clean, the people would trust him.

But then Karl left to visit his daughter and never returned. Theo didn't have the money or the time to train the guards properly. Palace politics swallowed up his time. He became Captain Theodore of the Queen's Guards instead of Commander Theo of the City Guards.

Theo looked up to see he wasn't alone.

"Took you long enough to get here." Theo said, "I was about to pour a second glass of wine."

The three wizards took position on either side of him and one in front.

"Give us the conduit, and you may die quickly."

"Conduit, that makes sense, and what makes you think I have it?"

"It is in your inner pocket on your right side of your jacket," the wizard on his right said.

"Thanks, I'd forgotten where I put it." He pulled it out and tossed it to the wizard in front of him. When the wizard moved his eyes from Theo to the conduit. Theo shot him with a wizard-killer bolt. He shot the wizard on his left before the first one hit the ground. Then was out of the chair with his hands around the third wizard's throat.

The man trembled in fear.

"They're called wizard-killers, undetectable by magic, unaffected by magic. Picked them up in the south a while back. I'm sure you remember that campaign? I remember you, standing in the rear, the first to run when your spells didn't work." He pushed the wizard into his chair and kept his left arm trained on the man. "You're going to tell me what is going on. Or you will die." He leaned over to check the pulse of first dead wizard. The wizard's mouth moved but no sound came out. Invisible hands clenched around Theo's throat.

"The wizards will rule as we should." The wizard stood up and reached for Theo.

He shot the wizard with the wizard-killer he'd pulled out of the corpse.

"Thanks for the information." He picked up the conduit and placed it in a safe hidden behind a frame. The seller assured him it would block magic from seeing what was inside. Theo hoped it stop magic from leaking out.

The wizards were a problem. If he went through channels, the Guild Council would know he could kill wizards without dying too. With only two bolts, that could be a problem. He couldn't leave them in his sitting room either. First things first, he removed the bolt from the bodies, wiped them clean and reloaded the spring-bows on each arm.

Theo washed his hands carefully. He pulled a sheet of paper from his desk and wrote a quick note, then looked out his door and whistled loudly. A boy ran up, the runners hung around wherever the Guard worked in hopes of being paid to carry a message.

"Take this to Karl at the Unkissed Toad, if he isn't there, give it to the owner." He handed the boy the note and a penny. The kid took off and Theo went back inside to pour himself another glass of wine.

***

The seafarers searched Tad again before he climbed into the wagon to be tied to a rail. He could sit, but not comfortably. Cordin already slept in a nest of blankets. Terteky stood stony faced beside Beow. She'd been angry at losing her student. Life couldn't be fun for a girl in this hard place. Tad hadn't seen any other children; maybe they lived elsewhere.

The sagaska's men formed up around the wagon, wearing armour and carrying weapons. A couple of them climbed into the wagon and started scanning the landscape. The sagaska rode a horse and carried his skull staff. The driver snapped the reins and the small shaggy horses moved forward.

The rest of the day, they spent slowing climbing the trail up to the top of the cliff, one switchback at a time. They rested at each one, the guards trading off who rode in the wagon. At sunset they reached the top and camped in a circle of stones. Tad and Cordin were allowed to go behind some bushes, but the men stayed close by.

Rough bread and cheese made up the meal. The men lay on the ground and wrapped themselves in their cloaks. Two walked around the camp peering suspiciously out into the night. Tad borrowed a blanket from Cordin's nest, but still shivered until Cordin shifted over to share his warmth.

The sunrise revealed a bleak landscape of short grass and stone. Tad and Cordin were given a slice of bread to gnaw on as the troop followed a faint trail through the rocks.

Tad didn't look around much as the wind whistled across the land, making cloaks and hair flap. The men ignored it other than tying their hair away out of their eyes.

Another stone circle, another cold camp. Tad huddled between Cordin and the side of the wagon.

They drove down off the bleak highland into a dark forest of spruce with moss hanging off the branches. The men went into high alert as the wagon creaked along the path. Even at noon, the gloom made it hard to see.

An arrow struck the driver in the throat. The horses kept walking forward as men in furs ran to the attack. They had the advantage of numbers, but only had sticks for spears and clubs. Two of them fell for every seafarer they killed. The sagaska flailed around him with the staff, crushing skulls and sending attackers staggering back with bloody faces.

The wagon left the battle behind. Tad tried to reach the reins to drive the horse, but he couldn't move. Cordin slept through the chaos in spite of Tad's shouts, barely visible under the blankets.

Men came out of the woods and cut Tad loose. They yanked him out of the wagon and dragged him away as the remaining seafarers charged them.

"We have to get Cordin," Tad begged the men dragging him through the forest. The answer was a blow sending him spinning into unconsciousness.

CHAPTER THIRTY-SEVEN

Leedles whooped as Roc flew away from the cliff. She hoped the boy didn't get too scared. The lakur queen didn't have long to live. There wasn't time to waste. Maybe pulling the battle lakur back would give the queen more resources and time.

Roc flew north and away from the sun until the cliff vanished over the horizon.

:Even I can't fly direct across the ocean. We will stop and rest on a series of islands spanning the water. In my day people rowed from one island to the next to cross the water.:

"How did you manage to find me and get me safely back?" Leedles hung on tight to Roc's feathers, her legs hooked in front of the wings. She felt so tiny in comparison to the great expanse of ocean, if she fell, Roc might never find her.

:You were closer to the shore than I imagined you could be. I had the boat to rest on before returning. It still wore me out. I rested for days after I left you with the stick.:

"The stick? Is that because he occupied the staff?"

:Having power is no guarantee of character.: Roc stiffened her wings and glided for a while. :Stick grew up in the midst of conflict, every side wanted to use him, he only wanted to get away. He might have stood his ground and refused, but he played them against each other until he could cross the ocean to the desert.: The bird's laugh vibrated in Leedles' stomach. :He became a tree, a stick in the mud, journeyed to that isolated valley of his and let it be known he wanted to be left alone.:

"I think he didn't know what he wanted. He came along with me, and he didn't have to. Then he wouldn't teach me much. At the end I sent him home." Leedles' anger had burned out; she no longer cared much about the Tree.

:There is only one way for an artesian to be born.:

"So he said. He was lonely, then he was afraid. He let my parents destroy each other rather than reveal the truth." Maybe the anger wasn't all ashes after all.

:The wise ones are a bit more than human, but we are a bit less too. Hard to care about people who will be gone too soon.:

"The River Dragon lives entirely in the moment, but he came and talked to me."

:Did he? He hasn't spoken to a human in centuries.:

"Then I emptied his river to make fog and he got very angry."

:Would love to have seen that.:

Leedles giggled. "I didn't see him, but his roar shook the town."

Roc flew on as the sun rose high in the sky, then fell into the ocean. Yet they might not have moved at all. Just before dark, Leedles spotted an island poking out of the water. Roc glided over and landed on a high cliff.

:Easier for me to take off in the morning.: Roc tucked her head under her wing and went still. Leedles jumped off and looked around. The ground reflected very little light making it hard for Leedles to see. Leaving the queen's egg with Roc; she created light on her hand and went looking for something to eat.

Trees grew farther down the mountain so Leedles walked toward them. Not much to eat. Nothing moved anywhere she looked. She'd go back up the mountain and wait until light, find some fish to eat.

She turned around to discover her way blocked by men in seal pelts. They pointed spears tipped with black rock that winked with the light from her hand.

"Magician." One stepped forward and bowed. "We need your help."

"What kind of help could I be?" Leedles' didn't want to get caught up in anything to delay her.

"A monster is driving away the fish and seals we need to live." The man pointed down to the ocean.

It couldn't hurt to look, maybe she'd be able to reason with the beast. Stranger things had happened. She followed them down to the village, her calves aching by the time they arrived. All her magic didn't make mountain hiking any easier.

The village tucked into a corner in the cliffs, with as many houses clinging to the rocks as set on the ground. An old woman waited for them by a fire in the centre of the half-circle village.

"Saw the great bird, and knew a powerful magician must be the one to tame it."

"She's a friend," Leedles' stomach twinged at the thought of Roc thinking Leedles had tamed her.

The old woman shrugged and sat down. Leedles sat across from her and the men brought bowls of fish stew. They dug in immediately as if this were the first meal of the day. Leedles followed suit. The stew tasted good, if the spicing was a bit odd. She opened her mouth to ask what it was when the world spun around her and she fell over.

The men looked askance at the old woman, but she gave them rapid orders to pick Leedles up and carry her toward the shore. A post had been set so it tilted over the water. The men tied her arms over her head, then one climbed up on the post and they hoisted her up and fastened the rope binding her wrists to the post.

"Sorry," one of them said before scuttling after the others.

Leedles tried to gather magic, but whatever they'd put in her bowl made it impossible to focus. The magic laughed discordantly just out of reach.

"Just more proof I'm no wise one." Leedles' arms already ached. She had no idea how long the drug would affect her and didn't want to wait until dawn.

The ropes chaffed at her wrist especially where she still wore the steel shackle. It had been too finely made to have a useful edge; she twisted her hand until it felt on the verge of breaking. Her fingers gripped the sharp stone she'd used to hack snakes and other carcasses open.

Cutting at the rope hurt worse than hanging from it. The stars moved overhead, glinting on the sea. Far out the water looked distorted. Leedles worked harder. The stone was no blade, but the strands parted one by one.

The waves formed a 'V' pointed straight in her direction. One of the ropes gave. It loosened enough she could free one hand, with that hand free, she could get enough lift to take her other hand out of the ropes.

Now she hung over the water from rapidly tiring hands. The shore might as well have been miles away instead of feet.

The wave vanished and a shadow in the dark water showed the monster diving but still coming toward her at tremendous speed. The thing planned to leap out of the water and snap her up.

Leedles had one chance, even though she didn't like it much.

The monster leaped out of the water coming straight up at her, mouth gaping wide, teeth glistening. Leedles let go of the rope and plummeted into the thing's throat.

CHAPTER THIRTY-EIGHT

Karl read the note the boy gave him, then read it again. Trust Theo to make things difficult. He gave the runner a penny then left the bar. If the wizards went after Theo, maybe they weren't following him too closely.

Widdershins showed up immediately after Karl left, much sooner and they would have passed through the door together. If Widdershins had been assigned to watch, Karl might have a chance.

He headed along the street to a less savoury part of the City which meant much smellier. The only place that stunk worse were the tanners outside the walls. Widdershins didn't strike him as the type to get too close to a place reeking of death and blood.

Down an alley and across a courtyard to another alley, the mournful cries of doomed animals filled the night. Karl slipped through a gate and knocked on a door.

"Wad ya wan?" The man who'd flung the door open filled it top to bottom, just enough light came through the door to highlight the blood still shining on the man's leather apron.

"Job for Wully the Knacker."

"Wait." The door slammed shut leaving Karl temporarily night blind. He looked into the shadows until the faint outlines of bricks and bones were visible.

"Let's go." A dolorous voice spoke behind him.

Karl followed Wully through a different door into a stable. The man hooked up a horse to a wagon then patted the seat beside him. Karl snagged a coat off a hook and climbed up.

The wagon rumbled out onto the street.

"Head for the gate for now, I'll tell where to turn as we get there."

Wully looked at Karl and sighed deeply.

Well into the early morning hours, Wully and Karl pulled into the back alley behind Theo's house.

"Took your time getting here." Theo stepped out of the shadows. "They're all wrapped for you."

Karl jumped off the wagon and helped load the three body sized shapes into the wagon.

"You okay?" He looked into his friend's eyes.

"Oh sure, I'll be fine." Theo went back into his house. Karl walked around to the front of the wagon.

"Usual price?" Karl fished coins out of his pocket. Wully snatched them up and twitched the reins. The wagon rolled out of the yard and away. No one would find the bodies.

The street began to lighten. Dawn was close. Karl headed along the alley. He followed back alleys and hidden doors until he'd penetrated deep into the maze of roads and building between the Guard Compound and the city. Few people lived here, but still clothes hung out a few windows and one doorway had a flowerpot beside it.

He came to a broken-down house with a bright red door. From there he took memorized turns left and right until he reached a door with wood so grey it blended with the wall around it. He took out a key and unlocked it and walked back into the City Guard building. The door locked when he closed it. Sidling around the stack of boxes in the quartermaster's storeroom, he headed for his office and bed.

As an afterthought he poked his head out into the front office.

"Anything happen?"

The woman shook her head.

"Good job," Karl leaned on the door. "I'm off to bed." He dragged himself up the steps to his room, then fell on the bed, asleep before he hit it.

The sun on his floor told him noon had come and gone when a knock woke him.

"Coming," Karl rolled out of bed and went to the door.

"Guard Sopha, reporting," She held a roll of paper under one arm.

"Very good," Karl smiled, he needed a distraction from last night's work. Guard Sopha and her genealogy would be just the thing. "Meet me in my office in five."

Karl sat at his desk, placing the plate of bread and cheese in front of him.

"Help yourself." He waved at the plate.

Guard Sopha looked shocked, then put her paper on one end of the desk and tentatively took a slice of bread and put cheese with it.

"Thank you, sir."

By the time Karl put the plate aside, Guard Sopha stood much less stiffly. She unrolled the paper and pointed to the mass of lines and names.

"I didn't have the same access to family information from twenty years ago, but I started with the records of the original crimes. They gave me the names of the victims and their parents."

"I didn't know we had any records going back that far." Karl looked at the paper, the lines converged on a few names.

"We didn't, Sir." Sopha turned red and gulped. "I went to the palace and told the chief archivist you wanted the information immediately. He appeared to be a little put out."

"Well done," Karl looked at Sopha more closely. She was blossoming under the pressure of her task. What other gems could he find among his guards? "Please, continue."

"Even with the names I only had conjecture, so I found the oldest people living connected with those families and sat down with them to ask questions. They were delighted to be able to tell stories about their families and how they related to each other." She began pointing to the chart. "You can see how the victims cluster around a few names, the Poole's, the Wells, the Springs, and then a scattering of other victims who didn't have a strong connection to each other." She looked up at him. "I wonder if many of those weren't crimes committed by other individuals and blamed on the Reaper."

"All too likely," Karl nodded. "Not much was done in the City other than making sure the inhabitants didn't disturb those who lived inside the Inner Wall."

"I think the people inside that wall may have forgotten the original purpose of their estates was to provide farmland to grow food in the case of a siege."

"Really?" Karl leaned back. "I didn't know that."

"Most people don't, Sir. Since the Kingdom stabilized not quite a hundred years ago, the likelihood of a siege fell, and the understanding of the Inner Wall shifted from being a refuge for the inhabitants of the City to a barrier between the City and the nobility." She shook her head sharply. "I'm getting distracted from why I'm here. The names of the victims lead back to a period before the wizard guild as we know it now. In those days people who wanted to work magic needed to work in pairs. One person who could access magic and even hold it for later use, and one who had the knowledge and ability to shape that magic into spells."

"So, when did this change?"

"Three wizards arrived during the war against the lakur, toward the end when we'd pretty much stalemated. The lakur couldn't mass enough forces far enough from the nest to take the City, and we couldn't put together enough strength to strike against the lakur queen."

"We knew where the queen lived?"

"Not for certain, but some of the magic users had a sensitivity to lakur communication and if not pinpointing the location, stated it lay within a small enough region a strike force might have been a deadly threat to the nest. They were the ones to develop a way of communicating with the lakur, though it remains a painful process."

"So I'm told. Commander Theodore doesn't talk about it much, continue."

"The wizards found a way to collect magic from more than one source. That gave them enough power to be a credible threat to the lakur, but instead of wiping out the nest, they took the stalemate and forced a truce. In exchange for giving the lakur a substantial section of forest they didn't need at that time, the lakur would not cross the boundaries of that section. The peace has stood since that time."

"Enforced by the lakur and the Crown. Any who cross the boundary forfeit their lives."

"The lakur have never stepped out of that boundary. However, several forces over the years have invaded the lakur attempting to regain the land. The last occurred some fifty years ago."

"I remember hearing stories about that," Karl stared up at the ceiling and forced his memories to surface. "The lakur chewed up the force, and the King captured the remaining men as they fled the forest. He then proceeded to hang them all within sight of the lakur."

"Since that time our population has continued to grow as we prospered. Land has been cleared to the north as far as the mountain range which runs Southwest from the ocean to at least the desert in the south. The mountains actually continue out into the ocean forming a series of islands."

"Right, and we've pushed as far as we're going to against the south, who have their own lakur nest. The rulers there have no interest in forming their own truce with the lakur. I was part of a force put together to support an incursion to strike at the lakur queen. We even had wizards with us. That's when we discovered the lakur can eat wizards without causing the deathburst which makes policing wizards next to impossible."

"There are no accounts of the deathburst until after the lakur truce."

"Something about using multiple sources created the bursts."

"That would be my guess too, but we digress." Sopha turned red again, but Karl smiled and waved for her to continue.

"I should say I got a lot of this information from a man in my quarter of the City who prides himself on being the Kingdom's historian. His family kept the records and histories until an ancestor was foolish enough to be part of that last incursion into lakur territory. The archivist work was given to a different family and his cast out from the inner circles around the King."

"Interesting, so does his background bias him in any way?"

"He is a little bitter and contemptuous of the modern nobility and even the Queen, but it doesn't change his essential conclusion."

"Which is?"

"We've run out of land. We can't push north, the mountains are in the way, attempts to find passes have so far failed. As you said, the south is also closed to us, and relations there are less than cordial. The lakur occupy a swath of forest running from the coast to the bend in the Queen's Road, then south to the Dragon River. There's enough land there to create a decent sized province, if the lakur weren't there."

"Are you suggesting someone is going to try to invade the lakur and kill their queen.?"

"They were going to try twenty years ago according to my historian friend. The wizards were pushing the Queen to allow research 'from a distance' on the lakur, in order to better understand them. Shortly after permission was given, the Reaper took children from the families I mentioned. With the riots, the Queen lost the support of most of the City and some of the nobility. The wizards moved inside the walls of their Guild. Recently they've been buying houses near their Guild."

"They're running out of space."

"And they may be running out of power. I expect they've been breeding sources to use. In the years since the lakur truce, the people have got used to wizards with power without thinking where they get the power from. Now, they need new blood, so the Reaper hunts the City again."

"Have there been any new disappearances?"

"No, and we're staying on high alert."

"I wonder if Apoxthenis was one of the leaders in their expansion. He had a house outside the Guild and he was the liaison with the Crown. His death may have set them back."

"I hope so, Sir." Sopha said.

CHAPTER THIRTY-NINE

"They haven't returned?" Staphoclest paced in the Council office.

"No, and there's no sign of them. Weszcals has a seeker spell looking for them, but I don't expect it will turn up anything." The server stood motionless and expressionless.

"Did they disappear before or after they recovered the conduit?"

"That's unclear. Weszcals has felt no trace of the conduit either."

"And the girl?"

"She is dead." The server turned slightly to look at the wizard. "The Guards sent her remains back to her family in the mountains.

"That's unfortunate."

"Yes."

"The sources?"

"The new training regime is working well. They don't know they are missing, thinking they are caught in a dream." The server's mouth turned down the slightest amount.

"Don't get soft on me. If the next part of the plan doesn't go well, we will need more of them."

"Of course, Great One."

"Make the arrangements needed to speak to the Queen. It is time she is briefed on the situation." The wizard stopped his pacing. "No more mistakes."

***

Tad woke coughing from the smoke in his face. The men around him laughed.

"You have a choice, slave." The speaker sat across from him, lit by low flames. "Join us and fight for freedom or die."

"Let me think on that." Tad crawled out of the smoke and rubbed his head. "Did you need to hit me that hard?"

"The seafarers might have tracked us from your bleating."

"The seafarers were only interested in what you left in the wagon."

"What is so important they wouldn't avenge the killing of their shield brothers?"

"The wulfkin. The sagaska snatched him from Beow, or whatever his name is in the village on the fjord. Wherever we were going, he expected a big reward. I was just along to die with my friend."

"Wulfkin? Are you sure?"

"He's my friend, a wizard messed him up. We were looking for the wizard so she could set it right, when these maniacs attacked our ship and burned it. They took us as slaves, mostly for him."

"Not good. Horald, the spellska has been looking for a wulfkin since the old lady told him one could give him the power to rule more than this pile of rocks." The new speaker inched into the light. A black cloth covered one eye, but the remaining one looked mean enough for two.

"Let the others know. We'll have to break camp and head for the high rocks. Get there before the spellska."

"I'm coming with you." Tad tried to stand and barely missed falling into the fire.

"We need warriors, not bleating slaves."

"You need a plan. How many did you lose to gain this one bleating slave? Huh? You going to jump out of the rocks, and surprise the spellska like you did the sagaska? You might be warriors, but you also need to be smart."

"And you're smart?" Horald looked doubtfully at Tad.

"You better believe it," Tad glared at the man. "Start by telling me everything you know about this spellska and the high rocks." He sat up and rubbed his head. "And bring me something to eat while he's doing it."

Someone handed him a bowl of stew and Tad scooped it into his mouth while Horald talked.

"The spellska is their name for a wizard here, but he can't work magic without the sagaska close by. The sagaska is not a young man. The spellska sends his sagaska out to find children who may be able to replace him, but he's yet to find an apprentice. Many have tried, but none of them survived the training. The spellska consulted an old woman reputed to be able to tell the future. She said he needed a wulfkin and that would give him the power he craved even with the sagaska getting old. According to our sources she gave him a ritual to use, it has to be done at the high rocks."

"What about those rocks? Tad finished the stew and held out the bowl, someone refilled it and he started into it.

"The rocks are the highest point of the island. They push out of the ground like teeth in a rough circle. Sacred ground to these people. They, the wulfkin and the sagaska, need to be inside the circle. You can bet his warriors are going to be outside."

"What kind of cover is there?" Tad wiped his mouth on his sleeve. "Any chance of a drink?" Someone took the bowl away and gave him a waterskin.

"You crossed the barrens getting here. That's it. The forests are in the valleys, there's a few farms around the fjords. This is a hard place to live."

"Direct attack isn't going to work." Tad coughed. Whatever was in that skin wasn't water. He took another drink. "All they need is to keep you away until the spellska's done his thing. We need someone on the inside."

"We have spies among the slaves."

"That's a start, but none of the slaves will be anywhere near the sacred grounds, and we need someone inside that circle." Tad set the skin aside. The drink burned in his gut, but he needed a clear head for this.

"Only the spellska, the sagaska and the wulfkin will be allowed in."

"Exactly. Which is why you need to get me to the spellska."

"Why?"

"So I can tell the spellska you plan to attack." Tad leaned toward the fire. "See, this is how I see it working."

CHAPTER FORTY

Slime choked Leedles, the monster tried to cough her out, but she'd jammed too tightly, arms pinned to her side. Shaking her head cleared the worst of the gunk and she gasped in air.

The monster dove under the surface. Leedles held her breath as ice cold water washed over her. The beast's attempts to swallow squeezed her painfully. The good news was the cold washed the confusion of the drug from her system. The liquid like magic of the ocean was happy to create gills so she could survive under water.

Now she needed to survive being swallowed.

Climbing out into the mouth even if she could; put her at the mercy of the rows of serrated teeth. In the stomach at least, she could shield herself from the acid and work on a plan.

Leedles wriggled and fought until she got one arm free, the second arm went easier. Taking in as much clean seawater as she could, she created a bubble around her, then used a spell to push herself down into the creature's gullet.

Between her screams of agony and the creature's roaring and writhing in the deep, she didn't know who hurt most. She dropped into a larger space. Her water shield would protect her from the acid for a while, but she didn't have time to waste. Urgency tugged at her painfully, more than the need to get her mission for the lakur queen finished. This came from a connection she'd created in ignorance to get a thief off her back.

Cordin called for her.

She'd deal with that when she'd survived this encounter.

Leedles put her hands against the stomach wall.

"We need to talk."

:Don't talk with food.:

You'll talk with me, or do you fancy having your throat blocked again? She didn't know if she could follow through on the threat, but it didn't know that.

:What does food want?:

"Peace, I have no argument with you."

:No peace. Will swallow the world.:

"Why?"

:Why not? It is what I am. The Swallower. You aren't the first wizard to end up in my stomach.:

"The first to stick in your craw, I'd bet."

The creature laughed.

:Might like you if you weren't food.:

"Must be lonely with nothing to talk to."

The creature laughed again. Leedles detected tendrils of magic coming from it. The thing was a wise one? It had to be old beyond imagining.

She gathered in magic and stored it. No telling when she'd need it next. Then she sat and considered her situation. The Swallower wouldn't be going far from the island where it had been eating all the fish and seals, unless somehow the witch in the village made a deal with it.

The Swallower did not feel evil. The creature cared nothing for good or evil, only its appetite.

"What will happen when you swallow the world?"

:The end.:

"What if it isn't? Something which can swallow the world isn't going to die easily."

:The end....: The swallower didn't sound as certain.

"Which is more important, the end, or the swallowing?"

:The swallowing.:

Leedles used some of her magic to strengthen the bubble, acid had started to burn her gills.

"I guess everything knows to stay out of your way."

:Hungry.:

"Of course. There will be a long time between swallowing the last creature in the ocean and when you will be big enough to swallow the world." Poor creature, it hadn't really thought out swallowing the world.

:Hungry, will hunt.:

"What if I could make it so you have much to swallow again?"

:?:

"You want to swallow. That is your being, but you got too big, and it is harder to find creatures to swallow. What if you were smaller again and could swim through schools of fish eating enough to fill you?"

:Smaller?:

"Yes."

:Will be the Swallower.:

"Does it matter what size the swallower is?"

:No, only Swallower.:

"I can help you, but only if you let me out."

:You will leave.:

"I won't abandon a friend."

:Not friend, food.:

Even with the water and the stronger magic, the acid ate at Leedles gills and burned her skin. She didn't want to hurt the Swallower, but there wasn't much time left.

:Friend.: The stomach contracted and Leedles followed the contents up the Swallower's throat, using her reserve of magic to keep from getting stuck again.

Cold water struck her like a balm, easing the pain. She swam around to where she could see the Swallower's eyes and put her hand on its head.

"You need to be where there are plenty of fish, Swallower. There is a place north of here I must go to. There will be shoals of fish, and seals to eat."

:North: The creature turned and Leedles caught hold of its horns and held on. The pull north was getting painful.

How had Cordin ended up there?

***

Karl got up and began pacing around his office. Sopha gave up turning in circles to face him and leaned against the wall.

"Information, we need more of it." He stopped in front of Sopha. "You're promoted. Sergeant should do for now. I'm putting you in charge of intelligence. Whatever you can find out, whomever you learn it from. Recruit the people you need. Let me know what budget you need; I'll push it past the Commander."

Sergeant Sopha had the same look on her face as the woman at the desk the night before.

"You'll be fine. I wouldn't give you the job if you hadn't already proved you could do it." Karl sat down at his desk and looked at the chart again. "We'll keep a close eye on these families."

Sopha saluted and headed out of his office.

"One last thing, there's a wizard, name of Widdershins, don't know where he lives, but it isn't in the Guild compound. Don't approach him, but if he happens to talk to you, pay very close attention and inform me immediately."

"Yes, Sir."

Karl needed more information about the lakur. He agreed with Sopha. They were the crux of the situation, but how was he going to learn more about them and their capabilities?

He could only think of one way, and he didn't like it much.

"Gather the sergeants and have them meet me in my office in ten minutes."

The Guard at the desk swallowed.

"Some of them live further away, they won't be able to get here in that time."

"Very good, ask the ones present to assemble."

"Yes, sir." The Guard rang a bell and a youth between the age of the runners and their new recruits came through a door.

"Orders?" The young man stood at attention. Not in uniform, but clean and in dark clothes.

"Vice-Commander wishes to speak to whatever sergeants are in the Compound. Have them gather as soon as possible in his office."

"Yes, Sir." The young man ran off back through the door. Excited conversation came back into the room.

"Whose idea was this?" Karl pointed to the door.

"I'm not sure, Sir, but with everyone out on the street we needed internal communication. Runners aren't reliable enough, so some of the Guards have brought in children or cousins to help out."

"How do they get paid?"

"I don't believe they are being paid, Sir, but they believe they will get credit for their work when they apply to be a Guard."

"Interesting. Don't tell them they're wrong. I'll need to speak to the commander. Make sure they get to eat in the mess, the least we can do is feed them. I want a report on their effectiveness, and if there is any trouble."

"Yes, Sir."

Karl climbed back up to his office. *Whose bright idea was it to put my office upstairs?*

Six of his ten sergeants assembled quickly and looked worried.

"At ease," Karl came around his desk and leaned against it. "I have some information for you to pass on to the Guards in your units. I will also have extra duties for you."

He handed one of them the rolled-up chart.

"There are three family names listed on that chart. Extra watches are to be concentrated on those families. That will allow the Guards to get more rest. We don't want to exhaust them."

The sergeants nodded, and some of them looked relieved. That was the easy part.

"I have to leave the City as part of my investigations. That's all you need to know and all you will tell anyone who asks, including Commander Theo. In my absence you, as a group will need to keep the Guard functioning and manage the day-to-day concerns. The City hasn't ceased to have problems because we are focusing on the missing children. Remind your people of their training."

The group looked at each other and began talking.

"We can handle it, Sir, as long as nothing major comes up." One of the older ones said.

"Very good, if something does happen you can't deal with, send a message to Commander Theo. Otherwise, send him reports, but he has his duties to the Crown, don't bother him with details.

"There are young people running messages within the Compound. I've provisionally approved the idea.

They will eat in the mess. Any issues with them are to be reported to the front desk to be noted. I want a clear chain of command, so we know who's in charge."

"One of my boys is here. I'll take on managing the squad."

"You will need to bring the sergeants who aren't here up to speed. Lastly, so you know. I've promoted Guard Sopha to Sergeant and put her in charge of Intelligence. Any snippets of information your people pick up are to be noted and sent to her."

"Question?"

"How long do you plan to be gone?" The one who'd volunteered to watch the youth asked.

"I'm not really sure. It could be a matter of days; it could mean Theo will need to recruit a new trainer. I'm hoping for the first option myself."

Karl dismissed the group who were already talking amongst themselves as they left the room. He packed a bag with what he thought might be useful, then signed out a horse and headed out.

"Reason for leaving the City, Sir?" The Guard on the gate looked a little nervous challenging his commander. Probably lost the coin toss.

"Investigation of a matter which must remain secret for the time being. Keep your vigilance up."

He headed south. Since he wasn't in much of a hurry, he wouldn't change mounts at the way station. It would take him a couple of days to reach the border of the lakur's forest. Then he'd have to figure out how to contact them without breaking the truce.

CHAPTER FORTY-ONE

The runaway slaves took far too much pleasure in beating up Tad. His tongue explored the gap in his teeth. Breathing pained him and he was reduced to a limp along the road.

The road lifted back up to cross another section of barrens and the wind sucked the heat from him. He couldn't take any of the furs the men wanted him to; someone who's been beaten and left for dead doesn't dress in fur.

He shivered to the point walking became difficult. Maybe he should have risked a fur. Too late to second guess himself now. Movement brought him out of a trance. Two men rode horses toward him.

He sat on a rock beside the road and waited.

"Kinsul," one said and pulled his sword.

"Kinsul, sagaska," Tad said and knelt. He said the phrase the men had drilled into him, which meant he belonged to the sagaska and had news.

The men talked to each other too quickly for Tad to pick out any words. One of them picked him up and slung him over the horse and rode back the way they'd come, the other continued along the path to wherever he was headed. If the runaways were right, all the villages would be gathered at the high rocks to witness the spellska's triumph.

Lying across the horse in front of the seafarer was uncomfortable, but warmer than walking across the barrens. They stopped at a circle of stones in a small depression.

Sheltered from the worst of the wind, the seafarer set up his camp. He peered suspiciously at Tad, but Tad sat close to the fire and nodded off. He ate the hunk of bread the man gave him then went back to sleeping.

The seafarer woke Tad with an ungentle nudge of his foot, but a blanket covered Tad and kept the worst of the cold off. The man made no move to reclaim the blanket, so Tad kept it wrapped around him as they once again rode across the barrens.

Today Tad sat on the horse in front of the seafarer. The barrens had to be the most boring landscape Tad had ever crossed. The grass and rocks were broken only by occasional patches of trees standing no more than ankle high.

They reached another stone circle, but the seafarer didn't stop. He rode onto a long switchback trail leading down to a sizeable community from the number of torches and fires below.

Night came and they had to slow to be sure not to ride off the edge of the trail. Tad nodded off in the saddle before they reached the bottom.

The horse broke into a gallop and the change of pace made him start. The seafarer kept him on the horse with one arm; said something and laughed. Probably at the weak slave who couldn't stay on a horse.

Men rode out from the settlement to meet them. The seafarer yelled something; the only word Tad heard was sagaska. They all turned and rode at a gallop, whooping and making enough noise to wake everyone in the village.

The sagaska came out in furs and carrying his staff with the skull on it.

"You're the wulfkin's friend, the one who ran off with the kinsulbok. Why should I not order you killed on the spot?" The sagaska glared at the seafarer as if Tad weren't the only one he considered slaying. The seafarer slid off his horse and spoke quickly to the sagaska. Without the man's support Tad fell off the horse and lay on the ground.

The fall made his ribs creak. He bit back a moan. The sagaska turned him over with a toe and peered down at him.

"I will hear your tale. If it doesn't please me, you will pray for death." He pointed to the seafarer kneeling on the ground. "This man's life is held in your mouth too."

The sagaska walked back into the longhouse, the men dragged Tad and the seafarer after them.

The longhouse odour washed over Tad after days of fresh air, the men dropped him in front of a huge fireplace with some animal roasting in the flames. The dogs crawled out from under the table to lick at Tad. He let them, their rough tongues the closest thing to a bath he'd had in weeks.

"So, kinsulbok." The sagaska sat himself in a chair with the fire behind him. This guy knew how to set a scene, but then so did Tad. "what news do you have worth your life?"

"I came with you to die with the wulfkin, my friend and blood brother. The kinsulbok attacked, tied to the wagon, I had no means to fight or flee. They grabbed me and fled into the woods to escape your men."

"All this I know." The sagaska's voice came out dramatically bored.

"We reached a camp where they licked their wounds. One told me to choose between joining them or dying. My only wish is to die beside my brother, so I refused. They beat me and threw me out into the forest."

"They are kinsulbok." The sagaska spoke as if that explained everything.

"They may be kinsulbok," Tad played his trump card. "but they are planning to attack the gathering at the high rocks."

"How do they know about the gathering?" The sagaska leaned forward his voice as cold as a knife left on the ice.

"They saw the wulfkin, but your warriors chased them off before they could capture him." Tad cringed waiting for a blow. "They know the story of the spellska's desires as well as anyone."

"You will live this night, kinsul." The sagaska spoke to the men around him, they picked him up and dragged him away. Part one achieved. They took him to a dark corner of the longhouse and tied him with his back against a post. His arms screamed at being forced into a position they'd never meant to assume.

Sleeping peacefully only a few feet away, Cordin curled in a nest of blankets. Tad smiled and breathed a sigh of relief.

CHAPTER FORTY-TWO

Riding the Swallower was a lot like riding Roc, only underwater, and it made little effort to see she stayed on. The ocean rushed past them so fast Leedles made a shield in front of her to allow her gills to work.

Once in while an unfortunate sea creature came too close to their path and the Swallower would gulp it down without slowing.

The call north didn't ease in its urgency, but it didn't get worse.

The Swallower lifted its head above the water. They faced a wall of mist. Leedles spent a panicked moment figuring out how to breathe again.

:Powerful magic keeps me out.: The Swallower did not sound pleased.

Roc?

:Child?: Roc's answer came back faintly.

If I do not return, take the egg to the lakur queen. She'll know what to do.

:The wise and the lakur do not get along well, but I will do as you ask. What do you wish me to do with the villagers?:

Nothing if they don't threaten you or the egg.

:Very well:

Leedles gathered in magic and split the mist ahead of them.

"Nothing like knocking on the door."

The Swallower swam between walls of mist, grey sky above them until a wall of rock lifted out of the ocean.

There will do. Leedles pointed to where a ledge hung far above the water. The Swallower lifted her as high as it could. Leedles jumped to the rocks and with the magic's help climbed to the ledge.

She sat with her legs dangling over the edge and contemplated the Swallower. Was she really doing the right thing? The Swallower was a wise one. He'd given his permission, was even eager. Time for her to keep her side of the bargain.

She pulled in magic from around her. It fought her as if it owed allegiance to another. The magic from the ocean mixed uneasily with the threads from the cold rocky land. Lastly, she took the threads from the Swallower. Since she'd broken the chain on the staff, she hadn't held so much power. It buzzed in her and the ants began to crawl within her.

Slowly, with more care than she'd yet used, Leedles wove the Swallower's desires with her will. It began to shrink, magic bled off and circled around them. She sent it against the mist. Making it writhe and fade into the ocean. Whoever made it used a more controlled version of the fog she'd made in Riverport.

The River Dragon made a good size for the Swallower, small enough to not run out of prey, large enough to be safe from creatures which might want to eat it.

:I am pleased, friend.: It dove under the water and vanished.

Leedles still buzzed with magic so she climbed the cliff, then clothed herself again. The garments weren't quite what she'd intended. The pants were some kind of leather; the shirt had scales on it and gleamed of gold. Her blanket came out as white fur, with the head of a bear forming the hat on her head.

When she looked carefully at her arms, the faint outline of scales showed on her skin. She'd deal with it later. First, she needed to find Cordin and resolve whatever made him call her from across the ocean.

The tug pulled her further north toward the island's interior. Leedles set out across the barren landscape, glad for the warmth of the fur cloak.

The wind roared past her ears. The magic whispered in a foreign language. The mountains hadn't made her so unwelcome. She'd had Karl for company. On the ocean she'd had Squirt and Roc. Even in the desert she'd had the Stick to talk to. None of those places had hated her. This island saw her as an enemy. The wind came to freeze her and slow her walk. The rocks and low brush clutched at her feet.

She fell and cursed, then walked a little way before falling again, this time she stayed on all fours and let the shape of the white bear take over. Nothing slowed the bear. It found small animals to eat, shelter in the rocks. She headed north to where Cordin called.

The land sloped upwards. In the distance rocks stood like teeth biting at the sky, people surrounded the rocks. A vast throng of them; but no matter how many there were, they'd be no match for the bear.

They ran in panic as she approached. Three figures occupied the centre of the circle, one of the hunched on his knees. One of the figures brought a staff down against the rock carved like an ancient altar.

Cordin lay on the rock.

The bear stood up to roar a challenge, when pain struck like a spear through her heart. Leedles lost control of the shape and fell to the ground in a heap as her magic hemorrhaged out of her and flowed through Cordin to the wizard who looked at her with greedy eyes.

***

Karl rode toward the border of the forest, using the approach known as the hanging tree. The tree itself loomed huge over the field next to the forest border. Its branches drooped with ropes, a reminder to all comers of the fate of anyone who broke the truce.

He left the horse at the tree. It began eating the grass around it. No one used this band of land from the road to the coast. A thin ribbon of safety between the Kingdom and the lakur. Karl walked toward the forest and stopped before he entered the shade of the trees.

"I need to speak to one of you. It concerns the truce." He yelled it as loud as he could, then sat on the ground and waited. When he grew still from sitting, he shouted it again. Alternating between sitting and shouting his message, Karl watched the sun move to the west with growing despair.

His throat hurt, his stomach twisted into knots, yet reminded him he'd yet to eat. As the shadows deepened a shape moved in the woods.

"Come closer, human." The voice sounded odd, spoken by a mouth not meant for language.

Karl stood and walked toward the forest. He really hoped he wasn't walking into a trap set by a hungry lakur. The war in the south didn't aid much in understanding them. Only in making him certain he did not wish to anger them.

"Stop," the voice said. No inflection or emotion coloured it to give Karl a clue to whether his scheme would work. "Speak what you wish to speak."

Karl opened his mouth and closed it. He knew what he needed to say, but it felt like treason, probably was treason. Yet no purpose would be served by coming this far and baulking at the finish.

"There are some in our City I fear plan to break the truce we've shared for generations of our people."

"Your Queen is changed?"

"We live short lives compared to you." Karl ached to see better, to read the face and body of the speaker.

"The pieces live but briefly, the nest is ancient."

"Right, sort of the same with us, only our rulers change with the generations. They forget, we forget, why the truce was made. Now we are divided, like a nest with two queens."

"This cannot be allowed, the queens must fight and one must carry the memory of the nest."

"And if the wrong queen wins and the truce breaks?"

"This one has fought humans for more hatches than you could count. This one will fight again."

"They will bring magic against you." Karl crossed the line, now he was a traitor to his own people, arming the enemy with information they could use against them.

"We have eaten your wizards before."

"They have grown stronger." He desperately needed them to understand.

"Even so."

"What would happen if they attacked your queen?"

The space before the lakur answer stretched on so long, Karl feared he'd lost them.

"Every piece would fight to its ending to protect the memory of the nest."

"The wizards can feel the way you communicate with your pieces. The lines of your thoughts betray your queen's location."

"The queen cannot move."

"The wizards do not know that."

The lakur went silent. The night had no noise, not the buzz of insects or the calls of night birds, nothing rustled in the leaves. Karl's head pounded in the silence.

"When queens fight, the pieces do not stand idly by." The voice came at last. "This one will think on what you said. Battle pieces once hatched are reluctant to rest. Fight for your queen." The brush rustled briefly, and the insects began to buzz again.

Karl walked back to the horse and mounted.

"Let's make it as far as the first way station."

As he rode, he turned the lakur's words over in his head. He'd faced battle lakur in the south, they were unbeatable in large numbers. If he'd made a mistake in coming here, he'd doomed his people. Even the walls of the city wouldn't hold for long against them. The only hope was they wouldn't be able to reach into the City.

Theo heard the call of the queen under the Inner Wall. Whatever held them back last time, wouldn't stop them now.

CHAPTER FORTY-THREE

Tad knelt in the circle of teeth; the wind tore through the rags which were all that remained of his clothes. The cold didn't burn as much as seeing Cordin lying on the rock, motionless as if he were already dead.

The spellska cared nothing for runaway slaves, the wulfkin would give him power enough to handle them. Oddly the spellska was a tiny mouse of a man. Tad had expected someone to dwarf the sagaska.

He spat on the ground in front of him, where his hands were tied in front of him. The sagaska told him he'd been granted his desire to die next to the wulfkin. Wind carried the spit away, but the tiny blade Tad had carried in his mouth for days fell in front of him. He bent over in agony that was all too real, and his frozen fingers picked up the knife and started sawing at the rope holding him.

The spellska motioned to his sagaska to lay the skull of his staff on Cordin. As soon as the skull made contact the wind stopped. Tad's ear's popped as if he'd descended a mountain road too quickly.

Off behind him a bear's roar shifted into a woman's scream. Cordin twitched and squealed on the stone, but the staff pinned him so he couldn't move. The spellska panted with his face distorted in ecstasy. He raised his hands and thunder rolled across the barrens.

The rope parted, Tad didn't try to stand, his knees wouldn't have cooperated. Instead he rolled toward the sagaska and slashed at the tendons behind his ankles. Hamstrung, the man fell on Tad and dropped his staff.

The spellska's face went dark with rage, he picked Tad up by the throat and pulled him from under the shouting sagaska. With strength far beyond what Tad expected of him, the spellska cut off Tad's air. Black spots formed in his vision.

It had always been a chancy plan. Might have worked if the blasted sagaska hadn't fallen on him. Just before the last of his vision faded, Cordin moved. He pulled the knife Tad hid on him after he'd stolen it and stabbed the spellska.

The man dropped Tad and stared at the knife sticking out of him. Cordin hadn't been able to drive it deep enough. As the spellska struck the wulfkin, Tad lunged forward and drove his hand with all his remaining strength into the hilt of the knife Henrik had given him to kill a wizard.

The spellska fell over to lie motionless on the ground as the sagaska twitched and lay still, burns appearing on his face and hands. The wind returned, but Tad forced his limbs to carry him back to the stone where he cradled Cordin in his arms.

"Sorry, buddy." Tad spoke quietly as if the surrounding warriors weren't engaged in a pitched battle with the kinsulbok hidden among them. Most of the warriors faced outward waiting attack, they had to push through their own fleeing people to reach the battle. "I wish we'd found that wizard. At least we're together. You were always a good one for coming through in the pinch."

Lighting arced around the tips of the teeth, knocking kinsulbok and seafarers both to the ground. The wind hissed and pinned them inches from their enemies, unable to fight.

Tad looked up to see a familiar figure walking through the motionless crowd.

"Cordin," Leedles said, "you called, and I am here."

Tad gauged the distance between him and Henrik's dagger. But Cordin put a paw on his arm.

Leedles came through the teeth and the wind died. She wore leather and fur instead of cotton and wool, her face hadn't changed, but her eyes were bottomless pools.

"I did warn you, magic was a chancy business." She spoke as if they'd only been apart for days and had met at a tavern. "But I have learned some since I made that bit of spell for you." She laid her hands on Cordin and closed her eyes. Light surrounded them and Tad as well since he refused to let go of his friend.

The light called to his true shape. Tad's body hadn't changed, but his spirit had bent and twisted under his anger against Leedles. He'd forgotten it had been Cordin who insisted on the magic, against Tad's warning and Leedles. Tears ran down Tad's face blurring Cordin's form as it shifted and stretched, fur receded, and his paws returned to human hands.

Cordin pulled away and light faded.

"You aren't completely restored," Leedles said.

"Perhaps I need something of the rat in me to keep me humble."

"Or the extra senses of the rat give you an edge."

"There is that." Cordin looked at Leedles, then dropped his eyes to the ground. "I almost despaired of you coming."

"I was half a world away," Leedles' face became strained. "I had to go aside from a mission. I hope the time does not mean it's lost."

"If there is anything we can do to help," Tad said, "only ask."

"I will need eyes to watch for trouble. There are those who won't be pleased with the nature of my task."

"Well, let's get going," Cordin spoke beside Tad. "I'm growing weary of this place."

"Indeed, but I think a little help is needed to keep them from killing each other." Leedles waved her fingers and clothes much like hers clothed Tad and Cordin.

"Nice," Tad ran his hands along the fur cloak.

"I always wanted a fur coat." Cordin laughed and pulled on his cloak. "Rat fur? You gave me a rat fur coat?"

"It looks good on you buddy." Tad's heart lifted to see Cordin back to his old self. "You'll look quite the knob when we get back to the City."

Cordin looked around. "That may take a while."

"Nah, we have Leedles here. She'll whip something up."

Leedles laughed as she went to speak the men still pinned to the ground.

"If I let you up," Leedles spoke quietly, but her voice carried and echoed as if she were speaking everywhere at once. "Will you refrain from fighting?"

One by one, the men opened their hands and let their weapons fall to the ground.

Leedles nodded and the men stood up. Looking askance at each other, but huddling away from Leedles.

"May I?" Tad asked. "If you can translate for me?"

"Speak, and they'll understand."

"The wulfkin struck down the spellska and his sagaska for overreaching themselves. They would sacrifice every one of you, kinsulbok or warrior to satisfy their greed. Now you have a choice. Do you follow in their footsteps?" He pointed to the twisted bodies in the circle. "Or do you make your own path? We aren't going to decide for you." He looked at Leedles. "Let's go, I think we have to leave it up to them now."

As they walked away, the buzz of argument sounded behind them, but no clash of battle.

CHAPTER FORTY-FOUR

Leedles walked with Tad and Cordin across the barrens. Now that Cordin was okay, her worry about the egg and Roc resurfaced. The magic of the island danced around her as if it too was glad to be free of the spellska's plans.

She looked at Cordin, any wizard might figure out his connection to her. Now she knew what to look for it stood out like flame on a dark night. Leedles whispered and moved a thread here and there.

Cordin looked at her and shrugged; then went back to talking with Tad about how they should rebuild the business they started in the Queen's City.

Leedles bent the space a little so the walk to the village on the fjord took only an hour or two instead of days.

"Nice trick," Tad said, "could have used it earlier."

Leedles grinned, these two were irrepressible. She walked straight through the village to the beach and looked at the boats hauled up on the sand. Tad had run over to speak to a little girl, then he ran back to join Leedles and Cordin.

"Had to say goodbye to my teacher, she was kind to me."

They climbed on board the ship and Leedles put her hand on the tiller. The ship moved off the sand into the water. It sped through the fjord and out into an ocean reflecting a bright blue sky.

The Swallower poked his head above the water and roared. Leedles waved back. The island already looked a more cheerful place with the mist gone. The Swallower would bring them luck.

"That sounded like the River Dragon," Tad said. Peering at where the Swallower had vanished.

"A cousin." Leedles grinned and let the wind play in her hair.

As the boat flew south across the water, Leedles called to Roc.

:I come.: Roc responded.

The sky darkened as the sun lowered, Roc appeared just before the light vanished. She perched on the mast for the night.

"The boat will take itself to the Queen's City. You can do what you want with it there." She handed Tad Henrik's knife. "Return it to the owner. It is helpful to know there is something which can kill wizards without destroying everything around."

"I will." Tad put the knife in his boot. "I'm sorry, Karl sent a letter with me. I hid it with the knife, but it must have got lost in the fight."

"No, it didn't," Cordin reached into his pocket and pulled it out. "I didn't know it was for you, or I'd have given it to you sooner." Leedles took the letter and created enough light to read by. The tears in her eyes made the process of reading slow. When she'd done, Leedles put the letter in a pocket in her shirt.

"Let Karl know I got the letter. If all goes well, I will see him again."

When the sun lifted above the ocean, Leedles jumped onto Roc and checked the egg. It didn't look or feel any different.

"Stay out of trouble," she yelled as Roc took off.

:You're changing, child.: Roc worked to gain height.

Yes.

:Your body is protecting itself against the burn of magic on flesh.:

I figured as much when I saw the scales on my arms. Leedles looked at her hands where her nails were shifting into claws. The scales were clearer too. *So every time I use magic I'll lose a bit of myself?*

:You won't lose yourself, but you will change.:

That's life, I guess.

They flew across the ocean. Leedles let her worries fall. Time enough for her to fret when she'd finished her work for the lakur.

Roc stopped at islands to rest for the nights. Tad and Cordin would get home before her at this rate, but flying with Roc felt right.

Leedles didn't wander far from Roc's side on those islands. She didn't need any more delays. The lesson that she could still be hurt by people was a good one, but it cost her precious time.

Four nights after they left the boat with Tad and Cordin, Leedles spotted land on the horizon.

:We'll be there by nightfall.: Roc soared faster through the air. She sounded as eager as Leedles to make landfall.

*****

Karl rode into the City a day after he left the lakur. Impatience caught up with him and he changed horses at the way stations and rode straight home.

He arrived stiff, sore and in a bad mood. The Guard at the desk, saluted and handed him a file. Karl crawled up the stairs to his office to read what had gone on in his absence.

One of the children taken in the night was found dead with no wound other than a burn at the base of her throat. The surgeon had checked and found nothing on her to indicate the manner of her death.

Sopha reported there were more wizards active in the City. They usually kept to themselves. Nothing untoward happened, but the citizens were either nervous or angry. Many had arrived at their own conclusions about who had taken the children.

Children were reported missing. then found not far away hours later; confused and afraid. None of them were hurt. None of them were from the families the Guard watched over.

Theo was not happy and wanted a report as soon as Karl returned.

The Sergeants had kept things running as if Karl had never left, the squad, as the young helpers were called, had caused no trouble yet.

Karl dropped the file on his desk and sat for a few minutes. Since the sergeants were running things so well, Karl felt no need to take back control. He could put his time into training the Guard in more advanced skills to work with the citizens. Time to get them running through the maze and learning more about the underbelly of the City.

He made a few notes then hobbled back down the stair and left his instructions with the Guard on duty at the desk. She read them over and called the squad out to send them running through the compound.

Within minutes the sergeants would know they weren't getting off the hook for the day-to-day running of the City Guard. Karl doubted they'd thank him.

A carriage waited for him and he climbed in, waiting until the door had closed and the driver started off toward Theo's to groan.

He had just long enough to stiffen up again before they arrived at Theo's residence. Karl hauled himself out without damaging his dignity too badly, then walked to the door. Theo opened the door before Karl could knock. From his black looks at Karl, he was less than pleased with his subordinate. Wasn't the first time.

"What do you think you're doing?" Theo barely had the door to his office closed before he rounded on Karl. "There's panic in the City over the children missing. I'm getting reports from sergeants and you have a woman spinning webs all over the City.

"I'm aware of all that," Karl sank into an armchair and sighed. "I left the sergeants in charge, and they'll stay in charge. Will give me more time to train the Guards, something I've not been doing since I took the position.

Sergeant Sopha reports the people are uneasy, but not yet in a state of panic. The children are being returned unharmed, so it has not been connected with the Reaper. She's spinning webs because I told her too. We desperately need intelligence separate from the Palace Guard. Our work is keeping the City safe, we need to know what is going on to do that."

"Our mandate is to keep the population under control." Theo made a face.

"If they are safe, they won't cause trouble."

"You hope."

Karl shrugged and groaned.

"What have you been doing?"

"I went to visit friends of yours. I was foolish enough to ride straight home instead of spending the night in a way station like any self-respecting old man would do."

Theo laughed and sat down in a chair.

"What did these friends have to say?"

"Not a whole lot useful. I have a hard time getting my head around how they think. I did leave them with the thought they could mislead certain people about where the queen lived."

Theo went serious. "I should charge you with treason."

"You should."

Theo got up and poured wine.

"We may have bigger problems." He handed Karl a glass, then drank his absently. "A wizard name of Staphoclest paid the Queen a visit to brief her on what they were doing in response to the missing children. The Queen has declared the situation resolved as no more children were taken."

"The ones who go missing for a brief time, none of them are related to the ones who went missing."

"I saw Sergeant Sopha's chart, all those children from three families."

"That's not the half of it." Karl sipped at his wine and filled Theo in on the rest of the conversation he'd had with Sopha.

"Now that explains a lot." Theo got up to pace. "I knew we were pressed for land; the Crown has a reward for anyone finding a pass through the mountains. But even if someone does, we'll probably meet people on the other side who won't be happy with the notion of us taking over. It will be the south all over again with worse supply lines."

"Can't argue with that."

"But taking on the lakur? That's insanity."

"The mess in the south was a test run after the riots set them back in their plans. What better way to find out if they could take on a next of riled up lakur, then to stir up someone else's nest?"

"The south still hasn't forgiven us for that. They lost some prime territory to the lakur, and their population crunch has to be worse than ours." Theo looked at his glass, surprised it was empty, and refilled it.

"If the wizards are going for the lakur, then they must have reasonable grounds for thinking they can destroy the queen."

"Sopha suggests they've been breeding those kidnapped children for twenty years and now are after even more power?" Theo leaned against the desk. "The wizards haven't shown off what they can do in the last twenty years. They make magic things and charge an arm and a leg for them, but nothing which shows their true capability."

"Maybe Apoxthenis jumped the gun. He had Leedles for a while and must have known exactly what kind of power she had. If he gave her one of those things." Karl pointed to the safe. "He may have tried to reconnect and tap into her power again."

"A window across the world?" Theo went pale. "Would explain the way he died. We never found his head. Make sense if it was somewhere else."

"Would take a lot of power to do something like that, maybe Sella ran out of power part way through."

"She was trained to absorb magic."

"Right." Karl rubbed his temples.

"We're back to having theories, but no proof. The names could be coincidence, the other things explained away as training for up and coming wizards. There's nothing we can take to the Queen."

"You're assuming she's still in a position to listen to our wild theories." Karl's head hurt worse. "We don't have any idea of what the wizards can do. Look how confused Sella was until we got that thing off her."

"How do we protect a Queen who may be under the control of the wizards? How would we even know?" Theo put his glass down.

"When she starts making decisions we know she'd never make."

"Only, if someone were to offer her a vast swath of undeveloped land in easy distance from the City, she could very well jump on the offer. She's got the same pragmatism as her mother..." Theo looked sick. "We have to be crazy. There's no other explanation."

"Maybe Henrik will let us join him on his goat farm."

CHAPTER FORTY-FIVE

As Roc flew toward land, Leedles' stomach tied itself in knots. She'd been lucky with the spellska; Cordin and Tad had saved her. A twinge of guilt made her wince. She hadn't thanked them properly, instead letting them think she'd rescued them.

Without their intervention, she'd be dead, or a slave of the spellska. Dead would have been the better outcome. Now she would be facing the wizards. The same ones who'd almost trapped her twice. She'd been away for, she didn't know how long, but did she really know if Karl still supported her? Moving from helping a helpless girl to supporting a wizard who blew up a tower and killed at least two other wizards - that was a stretch.

The land approached slowly. Night would come before they arrived. Better to arrive in the dark and cause less fuss. Leedles wanted to get the egg to the queen, let her manage whatever needed to happen, then leave with no one knowing she'd been there.

Whether she sensed Leedles' mood, or was tired from the long flight, Roc didn't have anything to say. It left Leedles in her bubble of depression. At some level she knew what was happening, but knowing didn't make it any easier to live through.

They landed outside the lakur forest as the moon rose.

:I'm not safe here: Roc said. :There is danger in the air, someone is building a lot of power. Enough to shake the world. Be careful, child. No matter how safe you feel, don't let your guard down.:

The wizard who used a portal to try to trap me wanted a wise one as a source. Go far from here.

Roc flew off into the night. Leedles huddled behind a shield of magic, half expecting a bolt to strike at any moment.

"Come," a lakur called from the forest, "This one has far to take you."

Leedles adjusted the sling on her shoulder and checked the egg. She walked into the forest letting her eyes see in the dark. The small use of magic lifted her mood, she'd need to watch she didn't go too far the other way. The claws and scales were reminders of the price magic exacted on her.

"You come from across the ocean," the lakur said, "tell this one about the lakur."

"The queen is poisoned with gold." Leedles painted a picture of the patches in her mind. "She fights to hold on to her pieces, but she's failing. I hope I'm not too late."

"Do they live at peace?"

"There is a chance for peace. If I get the queen egg back in time, if the King accepts the truce..."

"One came to warn this one, there are those who'd break the truce, attack the queen. Why would one do this?"

"Greed, power, fear." The sting of nerves hit Leedles again. The wizards plotted, there were many of them, one of her.

"This one understands, before your species spread across the world, lakur fought lakur for nesting grounds. Battle lakur, ones who spin the world's webs, and others lost to memory killed each other. Some grew tired of the slaughter, withdrew into far corners to hide. Uncounted hatchings later they emerged to find humans ruling where lakur had been. This one has memories of memories of that time."

"How old are you?"

"Old is not a concept this one understands well. Hatchings come and go, memories go on, bodies fail and become dust."

The trees spread out and let more of the moonlight in.

"How big is the boundary of the truce?" Leedles stopped to sit on a fallen log to rest a moment.

"This piece would take a day and a day to walk its length a day to cross its width."

"And your queen connects you all across that space?"

"Connects. Yes, this one can reach your Queen's truce piece in her nest."

"Can you hear the other lakur, I mean the other nests?"

"The queens touched memories when you bound them in your being, but this one is alone."

Leedles got up and followed the lakur again. They traverse open fields and picked their way through marsh. Small creatures rustled, once she saw deer before they bounded away.

"When I joined with the queen, I felt all the territory, does she connect the animals too?"

"They are not lakur, but this one cares for the balance of its nest. This may prune here, shelter there. A grove, not far from here, holds tiny white flowers. They grow nowhere else within this one's boundary. This one watches and preserves."

"Sounds beautiful."

"This one does not understand beauty."

"Something which gives you pleasure to look at or hear is beautiful." Leedles struggled to come up with an example the lakur might understand.

"This one has pieces who sing to the moon and sun. The song connects. Pieces shape the walls of the nest. They connect."

"I think beauty and connection must be very close."

Another lakur came out of the trees and handed her guide a fruit. It offered her one, the magic didn't say it would harm her, so she took it. The juice ran down her face as she ate and filled her mouth with sharp yet sweet flavour.

Leedles washed in the next bit of water they passed and drank her fill at the same time.

"I need to rest a while," Leedles said.

"This one will wait." The second lakur settled in beside her as the sun rose. The other had vanished.

When Leedles woke the sun shone straight down on them.

"Let's go," she stood up and checked the egg. Had the shell changed colour?

The lakur led her on until they arrived at a hole in the side of a hill.

"This one will take the egg and will do what is needed."

"How long will it take?"

"Three risings of the sun." The lakur accepted the egg and cradled it in one arm.

"This one asks you to wait. Water and food will come."

"Three days, I can do that." Leedles found a rock to shelter her from the sun and sat in its shade.

The forest lay peaceful and still around her, but the hairs on her neck stood on end. The storm was coming. Leedles drew in magic; if she must fight for her three days, better to be prepared.

CHAPTER FORTY-SIX

A runner pounded up the stairs into Karl's office.

"A magic ship docked in the harbour." She panted and leaned against the wall.

"Really?" Karl stood up. He poured the young girl a glass of water then sent her to the Guard desk for payment. He decided to ride a horse and headed to the stables. The crowd would be thick around the harbour.

By the time he arrived the boat had been tied up and much of the crowd dispersed. The two men standing beside the boat arguing with the harbourmaster looked familiar.

"It's ok, Harbourmaster," Karl tied the horse and joined in the discussion. "The Guard will cover your fee." He took a long look at Tad and Cordin, other than the strange clothes they wore, they didn't look much different than last time he'd seen them. "Hello, welcome back. Henrik told me you went looking for Leedles. You find her?"

"She found us, is more like it," Cordin said. "Got a bit dicey at times, but we managed. Seems we have a cargo of furs to unload. You got any ideas?"

"Henrik's more likely to say. I expect you'll want to see him anyway."

"Leedles got your letter, Karl. Didn't say much, but she kept it safe." Tad waved at a boy hanging around the docks. "Watch my boat for me, and I'll pay you when I get back."

"Sure." The boy sat on the dock and swung his legs. "Don't take long, I miss dinner, it costs you extra."

"Fair enough, one of us will be back or we'll send a runner."

"How'll I know he's your runner?"

"He'll tell you the wulfkin sent him."

Karl walked his horse along while Tad looked for a carriage for hire.

"You look well," Karl said.

"Got some things sorted." Tad shrugged and grinned. "Now we get back to business."

"Might have work you can do for me." Karl climbed up on his horse. "Contact you through Henrik?"

"Won't be sleeping on the boat." Cordin shuddered. "I'm looking for a real bed."

"Fair enough. Guard Sergeant name of Sopha may be around. Take it easy on her."

Karl rode back to the Compound to find Theo pacing in his office.

"Where were you?"

"Investigating a magic boat, couple of friends of mine."

"The thieves turned security?"

"That'd be them."

"Never mind that, we have bigger issues. Staphocest informed the Queen that Leedles flew in last night and disappeared into the lakur forest. She's probably welcome there, but the wizards are suggesting she's conspiring with the lakur queen. They're convinced she has a lakur queen egg and is going to plant another nest in the kingdom. The Queen is not happy, she's called up the Guards and sent for the regular army, they'll be marching before sunset. I'm to go with her and the rest of the Queen's Guard, you'll be here watching the city."

"How do the wizards know all this?" Karl leaned against the desk.

"I don't know, they're wizards, they probably can detect magic and your Leedles fair glows with it. It doesn't matter, they've convinced the Queen."

"Have you figured out how to check for..." Karl put his hands around his neck.

"Not yet, may have to knock her out and try what we did with Sella."

"Find a better plan, I have no interest in a promotion."

"Right, watch yourself, they're up to something, my gut is twisting tighter than a fiddle string."

"You too, it wouldn't take much to accidentally give you a hero's burial."

Theo winced and ran out the door. His yelling for his carriage faded quickly.

Karl sat down and ran through scenarios in his head. None of them good.

He rang for a squad member. The youth appeared in his office as if she'd flown up the stairs.

"All the sergeants are to meet me here as soon as possible. All members of the Guard are on active duty as of now. Organize runners to send with orders. They'll also carry orders to Guards on the streets. Hop to it."

She vanished as quickly as she arrived.

Sopha stepped in his door as he wrote orders for the runners to carry.

"I hear something's up. The army's marching, and the wizards are going with them. The citizens are unsure. I may be better out in the field."

"Go, send runners as often as you can."

The sergeants started arriving, when the last one arrived. Karl walked around to the front of his desk.

"Here's what I know. The Queen's taking the army, and the wizards, to pay a visit to the lakur. We're to keep order in the City while they're gone. No one wants to return to a burned-out home. My gut's telling me we're in for a bit of a wild time, so we're going to prepare ahead. If nothing happens, Theo will chew me out for wasting budget. You are going to go to your sectors and set up stations for Guards to report to. As soon as you're active, send a runner to me at the East Gate."

The sergeants left without any questions. Karl headed to the East Gate.

He hoped he was wrong about this, if he was wrong it would be a good test for the Guards. Even with new recruits they were understrength.

Karl found a quiet spot and watched the army gather. Men and women checked their weapons, tightened straps on the leather armour they were issued. Only the low murmur of conversation came to him. As he waited, the Palace Guard and Queen's Guard arrived in their heavier war armour with steel breastplates and helmets. He hoped they'd left a skeleton Guard at the Palace. No one gave him orders, so he put it out of his mind.

A boy stood and watched the preparations with wide eyes.

"Run to the Inner Gate with a message for the Guards at the gate and I'll give you a penny."

"Don't want to miss them forming up and marching out."

"If you do, I'll pay you extra."

The kid shrugged and put out his hand. Karl gave him a penny and the slip of paper with orders.

"Don't dawdle."

The kid looked insulted and headed out at a full run. The new ones always wanted to impress.

The boy made it back in time to watch as the army shifted from being people randomly scattered through the square to a column of marchers. The Palace and Queen's Guard led off on horseback, the army followed. The wizards rode in a bevy of black windowless carriages. After the last carriage passed the gate. Karl walked over to the Guards.

"Sorry, but you're stuck here for the time being. Spell each other off to get some rest. Keep the Gate closed, unless there is very good reason to open it. Use your judgement."

Karl sat near the Gate and waited. The army would take three days to reach the lakur. He didn't know what he expected, but the knot in his stomach said it was nothing good.

The runners started arriving at midnight, many with red eyes.

"The Reaper is taking children." They told him. From all areas of the City, from random families, not the three who may hold the secret to power. By the time the sun rose more than a hundred children were missing. Like the others, no one saw or heard anything.

Messages let him know the Guards were investigating. Some had deputized bystanders to keep order. They found footprints, dropped toys, one child who'd wet his pants sitting in the road crying. He told the Guards the Grey Man had taken him.

Karl passed the message back to the Guards. Wetting themselves, throwing up, whatever the children needed to do to be left behind, parents should encourage.

The day passed slowly with the City a little quieter, even a hundred children didn't touch everyone in the city. Guards spelled each other off and slept. As evening came volunteers patrolled the streets and alleys.

Near midnight the runners came.

Men in grey were spotted and chased then vanished into thin air. Children were left on the road, but still some vanished.

This was a coordinated attack on the people of the City. Karl didn't know why, but he'd find out, then whoever did this would wish they'd never been born.

***

Tad sat at a table in the corner of the Unkissed Toad. A prime spot, but no one questioned his right. Cordin sat beside him, Henrik on the other side.

"Sounds like you two did some good work out there." Henrik sipped at his beer. "Remember running a few operations almost as tough. Not easy waiting for the moment."

Tad tried to hand the knife back to Henrik, but it still sat in his boot.

"City doesn't smell right," Cordin said.

Henrik raised an eyebrow, but Tad nodded.

"Think you can track it down?"

"Can try." Cordin got up and headed for the door. Henrik gave a couple of men the eye. They sighed and followed Cordin out the door.

"With the folks on edge, don't want to take any chances."

"Good thinking."

Cordin returned as the sun lowered.

"Warehouses, near the dock, couldn't get any closer without setting off alarms. Our boat is still there, cargo's still there. Boys've been watching in shifts. They're chortling over the money their making. None saw anything, but caught plenty of fish."

The last light faded from the cobblestones outside as a woman walked through the door into the Toad. There was only one kind of woman came into this place. She didn't look the part. One of the men reached out to smack her butt. The women caught his arm and twisted, locking it painfully overextended.

"Orders are not to kill anyone," she said as if she were asking for bread at the bakers, "but making a eunuch of anyone who touches me probably won't kill them." She let go of man's arms and headed to the bar.

"Heard a fellow named Henrik, might be able to help me."

"Depends on what you're asking." Henrik spoke from where he sat beside Tad.

The woman came over and sat with them, turning a chair to keep an eye on the door.

"Name's Sopha, need some men for a rescue operation."

"Warehouse, down by the docks?" Tad poured a mug of beer and pushed it over to her.

"Thanks," she drank half of it, then put it down. "Only like the top half, never could figure why. Yeah, docks, don't know which building yet, but we'll spot it soon."

The door opened and a wizard staggered in. Tad reached for the knife in his boot, but Henrik put a hand on his arm.

The wizard stumbled over and sat, hunched as if he were in pain.

"Took away magic," he groaned. "Need it like a drunk needs wine." He looked up at Sopha. "You must find the children tonight, before midnight or there'll be blood on the streets."

"Can you help us, Widdershins?" Henrik leaned toward him.

"Not without magic." Widdershins put his head on the table.

"I can help with that." A soft voice came from the door to Henrik's office. The boy came over and put a hand on Widdershins. The wizard sat up and looked with wonder.

"You aren't supposed to be out here," Henrik said.

"He called me, can't explain it better than that." The boy, no Tad corrected himself, the girl set her chin stubbornly.

"With her, I can help you." Widdershins spoke softly, but without the slur making him sound drunk.

"You sure, kid?" Tad asked, "This isn't going to be fun."

The girl nodded once.

"Ok," Tad leaned forward to talk to his crew. "We need a plan..."

CHAPTER FORTY-SEVEN

For three days the feeling of impending attack grew like a storm on the horizon. Leedles sat on the rock ignoring everything but what she felt from the magic around her. The whisper of magic sounded mischievous, little children plotting trouble. Once or twice, in the wizard's tower it had cried with pain. Her heart went cold as the voices of the magic sounded more and more afraid.

She didn't want to meet what made magic fearful.

"Whatever protections you have, put them in place." Leedles said, "Then clear your pieces from this area."

"This one asks how big is 'area'." The lakur stood and cocked its head at her. Over the days, Leedles learned to spot the subtle differences between the pieces. They weren't ants, each one identical. The pieces were themselves, connected into one mind through the queen. Their conversation had kept Leedles from insanity as she waited.

"The size of the place I burned." Leedles' stomach twinged with guilt. How many pieces had she killed? Bits of the lakur lost?

"Where are you in relation to this spot?"

"This one is within the boundaries of the nest."

"I mean where is the queen in relation to this spot?"

"The queen is the distance a piece can walk between morning and noon."

"Good, the queen should be safe."

The sun set and Leedles sat in the dark, nerves on a hair trigger. She'd taken in all the magic she could hold.

Ants marched in her gut. Holding the shield burned her, but she didn't want to risk the time needed to build it when the attack came.

The moon rose and turned the forest white and black. Leedles started to tire, the nerves, the burn, started taking their toll. Maybe there would be no attack. It could be all a figment of her imagination. Maybe –

A bolt of light streaked across the sky and as quick as Leedles saw it, the bolt hammered into her shield and splashed across the forest. The force of the blow drove Leedles to her knees. She whispered to her shield and changed its shape to shed more of the power of the attacks.

Another one hit, she still knelt on the forest floor. Where there had been trees and brush and birds, now only was ash. The destruction more intense than the circle of fire she'd blasted at the other end of the nest.

Bolt after bolt slammed into her shields. She used up her reserve and drew from around her, but the bolt didn't only burn the forest.

They were burning the magic itself. Each one left her less to pull in. Pain spiked through her body as the magic burned her. She didn't have much more times before a bolt blew through her shield and incinerated her.

Leedles lay on the ground now, choking on ash and desperately holding her hands between her and the attacks. She had nothing left. The wizards only needed to keep sending their bolts of magic destroying energy and she'd die.

The lakur would die, the egg would be destroyed, war in Chen's country would continue.

Leedles reached out as far as she could, her mind barely holding together. On the edges of her consciousness, the Swallower hunted, the River Dragon lay in the mud beneath the bridge. Roc flew over the mountains. Even the wolf touched her briefly.

She had a second to say goodbye, then she opened herself up and let the vacuum within her absorb the next blow.

Pain exploded as the bolt reduced all that was left of Leedles' body to ash.

***

Theo stood in the Queen's tent with her Guard and the wizards who advised her. He didn't know if he shook with rage or fear. Probably both. She'd ordered the army to be ready to advance, when the bolts of light flashed through the sky, she told the generals to sound the attack. Under the light of moon and magic the army marched into the forest looking for lakur to kill.

After the attack had started, the crowded tent emptied leaving only Theo, the Queen's personal guard, and the wizards. The hair on Theo's head stood and the tent held the same atmosphere as when he'd been caught on a mountain side in a storm of lightning.

He lost count of how many magic bolts the wizards sent over the forest to pound on Leedles and the lakur. Each one lit the tent as it went over, then again from the forest side as it struck.

The Queen didn't flinch. She panted as each bolt struck, mesmerized by the light over the forest.

"The army will be at risk of fire soon," Theo stood and approached her, but the bodyguard stepped between them.

"Just the army," the Queen said as if she weren't really there, "they are paid to die."

Then a bolt hit and didn't light up the tent. A cry of pain rang in Theo's head. The wizards winced and one staggered. One of the bodyguards fell, his eyes and ears leaking blood. Only the Queen stood unaffected. Her eyes avid on the destruction. She stroked her neck and Theo's worst fears rose.

The guard on the floor moaned and Theo turned to look at him. One wizard held a ball of flame in his hands while the other watched the forest burn.

Theo didn't wait for the ball to move. He shot the wizard with the bolt from his right arm. The wizard fell without a sound, but the flames lit the tent. The oiled canvas burst into flame like it was tinder.

"Kill them both." The second wizard screamed and pointed his hands at the bodyguards. Their necks gleamed briefly. The standing guard drew his sword and advanced on Theo. He drew his own blade, but the guard's stroke dashed the sword from Theo's hand leaving his arm numb and useless. The wizard laughed and ran from the tent.

Theo ducked under the bodyguard's next swing. The fleeing wizard was lit by the burning tent. Theo fired his second bolt and rolled away. The bodyguard thrust his sword through the leather back plate of Theo's armour. Theo couldn't move, couldn't draw his dagger with his numb hand.

The Queen stood still fascinated by the forest, ignoring the fight behind her. The fallen guard pushed himself to his feet as his partner drew a dagger to finish Theo.

***

Tad crept through the sewer with Cordin, Widdershins, and Sella. The men from the Unkissed Toad supported Sopha and a handful of Guards up above.

"There are two wizards in the room with the children. Another one outside by the door." Widdershins had his hand on Sella's shoulder.

"We need to draw that outside wizard away," Tad rubbed his eyes the reek of the sewer made them water.

"I can do that," Cordin said.

"You just want out of the sewer." Tad punched his partner's arm.

"That too." Cordin grinned briefly and ferociously.

"The magic in your body will make the wizard think you have magic to use, but it won't protect you. If he can see you, he can kill you." Widdershins' face showed lines around his eyes. His skin looked grey in the lantern light.

"I'll be careful." Cordin ran back to a ladder they'd just passed. "Give me a minute or two." He scampered up the ladder and out onto the street.

"Let's get into position." Tad forced his voice to stay business like. Sella gave him a concerned look. *Great, the kid is worried about me.*

Like many of the warehouses, this one had a grate through which water could run into the sewers. The grates were charmed to keep the smell on the sewer side. Widdershins assured them it would also confuse the wizard's magic.

"The outside wizard has moved onto the street, one of the inside wizards has taken his place." Widdershins looked at Tad and waited.

"We go, you take the outside wizard, I'll deal with the one inside. We don't want stray magic hurting the children." Tad drew the knife from his boot. "Move the grate quietly, let me get up there before you make your move."

Widdershins put his hand on Sella and the grate floated up and out of the way. Tad jumped caught the edge and rolled out onto the floor of the warehouse. Children lay on the floor everywhere he looked. He didn't have time to check if they were breathing. The wizard happened to be looking straight at Tad as he entered the warehouse. He threw a bolt of energy and it splashed against a shield.

The warehouse rocked with the blast and children woke to run screaming away from Tad. The wizard waved his arms, not wasting anytime attacking again. No way Tad could reach him. Not with children running in his way, and in the way of the next bolt.

"Down!" Tad flipped the knife as an older boy tackled two smaller children and rolled away. As the wizard threw his spell, Tad flung the knife. They crossed in the middle, Tad rolling away as soon as he'd thrown the knife. The wizard stood still, watching to match sure his attack worked.

The knife hit him in the throat, dropping him to the warehouse floor. The spell had brushed up against Tad, burning his arm and sending fire along his nerves. The other wizard burst through the door throwing fire, but Widdershins was there with Sella standing beside him.

Widdershins blocked the other wizard's flame and sent a spear of ice back at him. It shattered on a shield. The children huddled against the wall, staring with wide eyes.

Tad rolled to his feet and staggered toward where his knife stuck out of the first wizard. The one by the door flung a bolt at him which Widdershins blocked, but it gave the wizard an opening. His next bolt hit close enough to burn Sella. She screamed and fell to the floor, breaking the contact between her and Widdershins. He threw his hands as if he were throwing another ice spear. The wizard threw his hands up to block only to have nothing come at him. He smiled and drew a ball of fire up between his hands.

"I don't know how you found a source, traitor. But now you both die, and all these with you."

A boy by the wall ran over to pull the knife from the dead wizard. He charged the one with the fireball and plunged the knife into his leg. The wizard screamed and lost control of the fireball sending it up and through the roof of the warehouse. The wizard backhanded the boy away and pulled the knife out of his leg.

Tad ran at him as fast as his pain wracked body would let him. He wasn't going to get there in time.

The wizard's hand flew up and plunged the knife into his own heart. He crumpled to the floor. Sella and her crew ran into the warehouse and organized the children to run into the night as Tad limped over to retrieve his knife from the wizard. He then went to check the boy who'd attacked with the knife. He still breathed.

"Over here." Tad waved one of the guards to him. "He's injured. Get him out of here."

"You don't look so good yourself." The guard took the unconscious boy.

"There's still one out there." Tad wiped the knife on his leg.

Widdershins came over carrying Sella.

"She'll be okay, but needs rest."

"I didn't think magic could affect the knife." Tad looked at the blade in his hand.

"It didn't." Widdershins grinned crookedly. "But magic will work on a wizard's hand if he's not paying attention."

"Nice work." Tad waved him to the door. "Get her somewhere safe."

Out in the night, Tad listened. Cordin would have led the wizard away from the guards. Tad limped toward the end of the docks, hoping he got there before Cordin ran out of room to hide.

CHAPTER FORTY-EIGHT

Leedles wasted a second wondering how she still lived. Another bolt flung through the night to crash into her scales and vanish. It didn't hurt.

Nothing hurt. She'd never felt so free of pain. The wizards had been attacking too long without an answer. Time to deal with them.

She spread her wings and launched into the sky roaring loud enough to set the trees on the edge of the ash trembling. Soldiers creeping through the forest with swords drawn clapped hands over their ears.

Leedles caught the next bolt and absorbed it, and burned with a fierce gold flame. The carriages were drawn into a circle. *Wizards.* She landed in the middle of the circle and blew the wagons apart with the force of her landing.

She ravaged the wizards, snatching their magic from them and leaving empty husks on the ground. A bolt from the city flew by and disappeared into the night, no longer directed by the wizards in the carriages. Leedles leaped into the sky and streaked toward the City.

As she flew, Leedles sought ahead of her, as invincible as she felt in this new form, she didn't trust it. Too many times she thought she couldn't be hurt only to be proved wrong.

No more flashes of light traveled the sky. They knew she was coming. Leedles roared again as she flew over the City wall. A massive hand swatted her to the ground.

She rolled through the rubble of abandoned buildings coming to a stop with bricks and wood covering her.

She hated being right. Leedles shook the wreckage from her and flew toward the guild. The magic flowed around her, more real now than the air. A disturbance warned her, and she rolled out of the way. The invisible hand flattened buildings beneath her.

Get the fight away from the City. Leedles banked toward the harbour and the ocean. Below her adults herded a group of children, she increased her speed to get away from them.

She almost missed the wizard on the wharf. He drew in magic, oblivious to everything but the figure standing on the end of the pier. Cordin. Tad limped toward them but was too far away. Leedles dove low to the ground blasting through an empty warehouse and snatching the wizard in her jaws. He didn't have time to scream before she crunched down and swallowed his magic.

The wizard had distracted her, and the magic hand swatted her into the ocean. Instead of returning to the sky, Leedles folded her wings and swam toward the twisted tower and the Wizard's Guild. At the last second, she lifted above the waves and streaked under the broken bridge before slamming into the wall.

She'd gone through the City Wall like it was paper, but she bounced off the Guild wall and fell back into the ocean. The hand gripped her and squeezed. It stole magic from her and turned it back against her. The rigid magic of the wizards eluded her grasp. Her enemies held her motionless in the sky and drained the gold from her skin. They stole her glorious shape until she hung naked and cold in the air, threads of magic around her and through her.

All the threads came from the same hall deep under the Guild buildings. Sources slept, sending their power to the wizards. As she watched one, then another flickered and vanished.

People were dying because of her.

Leedles couldn't save herself, but she might be able to save them.

"Wake up!" she screamed back along the threads. A thousand sleepers opened their eyes and screamed back. The wizard's power vanished, letting Leedles fall into the water.

It closed cold and dark around her. She couldn't breathe, but didn't have strength to swim.

At least the sleepers are free.

***

Theo raised his left arm to block the dagger strike. The knife jammed in his armbow. As the bodyguard struggled to pull it free, Theo rammed his knee into the side of the man's head. The guard's eyes rolled up into his head and he fell to the ground. The other guard had his sword drawn and approached the Queen, who stood as if frozen while the tent burned around them.

Feeling returned to Theo's right arm, he forced it to work and wrenched the knife out of the wreckage of his armbow. He flung it as hard as he could at the bodyguard. It didn't turn properly and struck hilt first, doing little more than annoy the man. He turned to lumber toward Theo.

A golden streak came from the forest and landed off where the wizards had pulled up their carriages. Dust and wind from the landing blew through the camp, lifting Queen and bodyguard to fling them out of Theo's sight.

He wrestled with the sword and freed himself. The wizards were crumpled among the shards of carriages. Theo staggered toward where the Queen lay. The second wizard had fallen with the black bolt sticking out of his back. Theo pulled it loose and kept moving.

She was slumped in a heap, but breathing. Theo slid the bolt up her neck, it caught on something he couldn't see. Carefully he worked it over her head. Palace guards ran toward him. He slid the bolt and necklace out of sight inside his armour.

"How's the Queen?" The general fell to his knees and put his hand by her mouth to check for breathing.

"Pull back the troops." Theo said. "I'll stay with her."

"What?" The general glared at Theo.

"You saw that thing destroy the wizards. Do you really think our men can stand against that? We could lose our entire army, and we haven't seen the lakur yet."

"Call the men back!" The General ran toward the signalers who blew recall on their trumpets. Orders came faintly from the dark woods. Maybe they'd get them all out before the lakur found them.

Over the next hour the men straggled in, exhausted, terrified, but all present. Not one had seen any sign of lakur. The Queen woke confused, wondering why she lay in a dark field instead of home in bed. Theo briefed her quickly, showing her the necklace.

She struggled to her feet with Theo's help, calling her staff to report.

"Get the men out of here." She pointed to the fallen bodyguards. "Take them with you, but be careful, they may be compromised by the wizards."

Slowly the army led by the palace guards marched away. The Queen stood looking into the forest surrounded by what remained of her Queen's Guard.

"So, Theo, will it be war after all this time?"

He fetched an overturned chair and set it down for her.

"The lakur withdrew from the border, I don't think it wants war any more than we do."

"Something comes." One of the guards stepped in front of the Queen.

"Let it come," she said. "It deserves to meet with me face to face."

"This one would speak with the Queen of the humans." The lakur walked into the circle of light without hesitation.

"I am she." The Queen stood and bowed.

"Do you intend to keep the truce?" The lakur stood still in front of them. Theo saw movement in the forest. The lakur was present in force.

"If you will allow us." The Queen sat and slumped in the chair. "We have been the aggressors, and we wouldn't blame you for refusing our word."

"There is a way for this one to know your mind."

"My Queen," Theo knelt beside her. "It is painful, but may be the only way to peace."

The Queen put her hand out to the lakur.

"Let us meet mind to mind, Queen to Queen."

The lakur plunged its antennae into the Queen's hand. The two froze for a long moment, then the lakur withdrew.

"This one is content." The lakur turned and vanished into the forest.

"Gentlemen," the Queen said, "let us return to our City. We still have treachery to avenge."

CHAPTER FORTY-NINE

Tad surfaced, holding Leedles' head above the water. Cordin threw a rope down from the boat and pulled them in. In minutes they'd wrapped Leedles in furs and set the boat to return to the dock.

"Useful thing this," Cordin said. "We should keep it."

"I don't know, mate." Tad wrapped himself in a fur and leaned against the side of the boat. "What are we going to do with it?"

"That island is going to want trade. They're a new market, fresh for the plucking."

"It might be nice to see Terteky again."

Leedles moaned as they tied the boat up and lifted her to the dock.

"We aren't done yet." She tried to stand up and Tad caught her as she fell.

"I'm not sure you're going anywhere."

Leedles closed her eyes and clothes formed around her, then she started to glow with a soft light.

"That should be enough for now." She rolled to her feet. "You want to come with me? There should be witnesses."

Tad checked the knife in his boot. "Let's go."

Leedles led them along the wharf then around the shore to where guards in red stood watching them uncertainly.

"Your masters must answer for their crimes."

"They ain't our masters, lady. They just pay us." The guards dropped their weapons and walked away. "Not enough for this."

Leedles walked to the door and put her hand on it. Nothing happened for a long moment, then it crumbled into dust.

"Nice," Cordin said.

Tad caught the faintest hint of a smile on Leedles.

She walked through the complex without hesitation. Men in women in grey stood and watched them, they didn't look happy, but none made any move to attack.

"They are the servers, Tad. Those born without power to either wield or store magic."

They walked through another doorway into a large chamber. Leedles lifted her hand and light filled it.

Wizards lay on the floor twisted and still. There weren't as many as Tad expected from the size of the complex. A dozen perhaps. They walked through the hall and started down a long ramp.

"How far down does this thing go?" Cordin stayed away from the edge.

"To the bottom." Leedles giggled. "I'm not very good at being an inscrutable wise one."

Tad's legs ached by the time they reached the floor. People stretched out in all directions. Some old with white hair, others, children who looked barely past being able to walk. They came to Leedles and circled her.

"Wise one," An old woman stepped out of the crowd. "What would you have us do? All we know is the serving of magic."

"The power is yours." Leedles voice echoed off invisible walls and Tad shivered. "From now on, don't let anyone take your power unwisely. The world needs magic, it needs wizards, but it needs them to work for the good of the world, not their own good."

The woman bowed her head. "We will not sleep again." She pulled a necklace off and dropped it on the floor. All around necklaces fell like rain.

"The servers are above," Leedles spoke more quietly. "Be gentle with them. Teach the children of the wizards to love service instead of power."

"We will."

"Can we go home now?" A child stepped out of the crowd, she held two younger children by the hand. Four others stood behind them.

"Yes, you may." Leedles nodded to the sleepers. They raised their hands and pointed at her.

Tad's feet left the floor. He might have panicked if Cordin hadn't grabbed him wide eyed. The children didn't take their eyes off Leedles. At the top of the ramp, the servers waited.

"The sleepers will need your help." Leedles stepped off the air onto the floor. "The next generation of wizards will need you to teach them. You have a choice of what you will teach. Obedience is no longer enough."

The servers knelt as Leedles walked past, then they flowed in all directions, some heading down the ramp, others following them outside. Tad wished they would make some noise.

When they got to the street, Leedles looked at Tad.

"Thank you. That's twice you have saved my life. I will not forget. Take the children home. Let the City proclaim you as heroes. You deserve it."

Tad watched her walk into the darkness.

"You heard the lady, time to get you back to your families."

***

Leedles walked through the City to where Karl stood surrounded by his Guards, taking reports and giving orders.

"Take whatever volunteers you can scrounge and check the rubble. I don't want anyone getting missed." The guards saluted then walked past Leedles to find whoever might lie under the destruction where she'd fallen from the sky. She almost went with them to move the debris with magic.

"Leedles," Karl stood looking at her as if she might disappear.

"Hello, father." She let herself be surrounded by his arms. Even more than the whisper of magic, his hug made her feel safe.

"The wizards?" Karl stepped back and became a guard commander again.

"They will not be a problem." Leedles sighed, aching to stay in her father's arms a while longer.

"The dragon?" Karl stood with that stillness she'd always loved.

"I took away their power." Leedles let tears run down her cheeks. "All who conspired against the people are dead. A new generation will learn new rules."

"If they don't?"

"I will be watching." Leedles reached out and caressed her father's face. She leaped into the sky and circled over the City, roaring until people came out of their homes to point upwards at the golden dragon flying above them. The guards and volunteers paused to look up. Leedles sent a thread of magic down to lead them to survivors.

Then she streaked away toward the forest.

From above the circle of ash was a small dot in a vast green sea. Leedles landed in the centre and met the lakur there.

"Here is the egg, the queen will be healthy and carry the memories long."

"Thank you."

"This one thanks you. For one of us to pass out of memory is a loss to the world."

Leedles cradled the egg and set off across the ocean.

***

Karl sat in the corner of the Unkissed Toad. Theo had given him the day off after the Queen had returned to address her people. Already, pictures of a golden dragon decorated houses and walls. Where the dragon had fallen, people were clearing away derelict buildings. There would be a straight road from the Guard Compound into the City

Widdershins came through the door, followed by Sella. Her burns were healing well. The servers were teaching the wizard how to heal. The walls around the Guild were coming down. The sleepers came and went.

"I never thought I'd say this." Widdershins sat across from Karl, Sella beside him. "I'm enjoying teaching the young wizards. We've gone back to the old ways, one wizard, one source. We'll keep the knowledge of how to blend the sources, but there will never be sleeping sources again as long as I live.

"You okay?" Karl looked at Sella.

"Not quite what I expected, coming to the City, but I'm good. Never got to wear my dress." She shrugged.

"Took the liberty of sending for it. It'll be here in time for you to meet the Queen." Karl grinned at her stunned face. She finally looked like the Sella he remembered.

"The Queen?" She elbowed Widdershins. "That blue suit of yours would go well with it, just wait until you see it."

"My dear," Widdershins looked at Sella with a face Karl knew well from his time with Leedles. "I will wear whatever you want, you've saved my life, in more ways than you know."

Karl caught his eye and nodded. Widdershins and Sella had been instrumental in clearing the rubble from the hole in the City Wall. The Queen had decided not to repair it for the moment, so the cleared area got called "Dragon's Court" and already merchants were setting up stands to sell goods.

The children were back with their families, the City was at peace, the wizards defeated. Maybe, finally, he'd get to the advanced training he had in mind.

***

"Goats?" Tad looked at Henrik in disbelief.

"What's wrong with goats?" Henrik stuffed a last bottle into his pack and carried it out back to put on the wagon.

"But... goats?" Cordin was no help, he leaned against the wall laughing at them both. "Who's going to run the Toad?"

Henrik dug in his pouch and pulled out a ring of keys. He tossed them to Tad then climbed up on the wagon and clicked his tongue. The horse pulled the wagon down the alley and around the corner.

"We'd better go in before they drink up all our stock." Cordin plucked the keys from Tad's hands.

"But what about our business? Our boat?"

"I'm sure we'll find people to help." Cordin held the door for Tad. "I wonder if he left any of his good stuff behind."

"You are not drinking all the good stuff," Tad turned and pointed a finger at him. "Not without my help."

***

Leedles watched the tiny queen settle into a cave her pieces dug. She'd touched feelers with the golden queen and Leedles felt her presence already filling the area the King had set aside for the lakur between his kingdom and Lovaris. She'd do fine.

Chen had been sent to talk treaty with the Lovaris people. He'd been relieved he wasn't required to hunt with the King.

Leedles looked east. Chen hadn't been sure what lay past Lovaris.

The golden dragon jumped into the air.

I'm going to go find out.

OTHER BOOKS BY ALEX

Series:

Calliope Books
Calliope and the Sea Serpent
Calliope and the Royal Engineers
The Third Prince and the Enemy's Daughter
Calliope and the Khishan Empire

Spruce Bay Books
Wendigo Whispers
Cry of the White Moose
Disputed Rock

The Belandria Tarot
The Devil Reversed
The Regent's Reign
The Empire Unbalanced
The World Widens
The Fury Unleashed

Stand alone books:

Generation Gap
The Gods Above
Tales of Light and Dark
Like Mushrooms (poetry and photography)
The Heronmaster
Blood and Sparkles, and other stories
Princess of Boring
By the Book
Sarcasm is My Superpower
Playing on Yggdrasil
The Unenchanted Princess

Read short stories and excerpts from his novels at alexmcgilvery.com

Alex lives with his dog in Kamloops on the banks of the North Thompson River.